THE WHITE DRAGONS

CHARLES RAY

North Potomac, MD

An Original Publication of UHURU PRESS.

For information about this book, or other works by this author, contact charlesray.author@yahoo.com or check the author's website at: http://charlesaray.blogspot.com/.

Printed in the United States of America.

ISBN: 0615780490
ISBN-13: 978-061578-498 (Uhuru Press)

This book is dedicated to the gallant men and women of the U.S. Foreign Service, who serve unheralded around the world, often in places and under conditions more dangerous than those faced by our uniformed services. They come from all walks of life, and truly represent what is best about America.

CHARLES RAY

Prologue

Sunday, May 4, 1975, Dagastan

The black ZIL threw up a rooster tail of dust as it sped along the winding dirt track that passed for a road.

The sun was a semi-circle of dull orange, handing in a dead gray sky behind the jagged peaks of the mountains to the west, casting elongated purple shadows over the bleak and desolate landscape.

There were few trees; a few stunted saplings, gnarled and twisted by the wind, hunched over the parched earth like ancient gnomes, their roots penetrating deep into the earth in search of the rare underground pool of water. Here and there, small flocks of sheep that had spent the day grazing on the rough grass that was scattered about the dry ground were being driven back to the cabins made of blackened logs, to be lodged in pens attached to them, pens made of the same misshapen logs. The rest of the livestock, one or two skinny cows, maybe a pig or two, and some chickens, ducks, and rabbits, would already be in the back room of the little four-room hut which they shared with the farmer's family. The family, except for the farmer and perhaps his oldest sons, would already be huddled in the central room, around the clay oven for warmth, for even in early May, the night air was cold.

The three men in the ZIL, though, paid no attention to any of this. The driver kept his eyes on the road ahead, ready to brake should a flock of sheep suddenly appear. Seated in the back were two men, each on his own side of the scuffed leather seat, back against the door, speaking quietly.

"Are you sure this is a wise thing to do, Vasily?" the younger of the two, a clean-shaven man in his mid-twenties, wearing a gray suit and a white shirt that was open at the collar.

His companion was in his late forties. He had a high forehead, with his hairline somewhere near to crown of his skull, jet black hair combed straight back and down. Piercing brown eyes sat on either side of a thin nose that hung like a hawk's beak over thin lips set in a neatly trimmed moustache and pointed goatee. Vasily Shermov looked like Vladimir Ilyich Lenin, and was proud of the resemblance, even taking to wearing dark suits like the Russian Communist leader. He laughed, harsh and guttural, spraying spittle across the seat.

"There is nothing to worry about, Pyotr," he said. "My cousin, Dmitri, will certainly approve of what I'm doing."

"And, if he does not approve?"

The question hung in the air like a threat. Shermov didn't need to answer; both he and his young assistant, Pyotr Ksolvi, knew the answer to that question; they would simply be made to disappear, to vanish from the face of the earth as if they'd never existed. Shermov's cousin, Dmitri Kovasc, was the First Secretary and head of the Central Committee of the Dagastan Soviet, and concurrently, head of the dreaded Dagastani Secret Service. He'd been merely the chief intelligence officer for ten years until he'd engineered the overthrow and murder of the former First Secretary and assumed that position as well.

Dmitri, Shermov knew, did not tolerate opposition or failure, and he had only one response to either; a response that was final and fatal.

Dagastan, a small landlocked country straddling the Arctic Circle in the near west of the USSR, surrounded by Russia, with the Cherskiy Range to the east and the Indigirka River to the far west, it was little more than a dot on the Russian map, about the size of the American state of New Hampshire, with a population of slightly over one million. Its people were mainly nomadic herdsmen and hunters, scratching out a living from undernourished flocks of sheep or from trapping animals for fur in the remaining forests at the foot of the mountains.

The main ethnic group, the Kazbektuni, for whom the country's capital, Kazbektun, was named, was a result of intermarriage of Rus, the light-skinned invaders from Scandinavia, and Khan, the descendants of the Mongol invaders from the east. Although they accounted for sixty percent of the population, they were among the poorest of the poor, mostly subsistence farmers, herdsmen, or trappers. In the entire governing structure of Dagastan, a bloated bureaucracy of over one thousand officials, there were only two Kazbektuni, both low level functionaries. The country's ruling Central Committee had one Kazbektuni, an elderly man who spent most meetings with his head back, sound asleep. Among the menials; drivers, janitors, and other laborers, the Kazbektuni were vastly in the majority. The ZIL's driver was Kazbektuni. While he understood the Russian his two passengers were speaking, his preference was to speak his native Dagastani.

The Khan ethnic group made up ten percent of Dagastan, and remained mostly on the vast desolate steppe, herding sheep and living in conical tents made of sheepskin, after the manner of their Mongol ancestors. Aggressive and militaristic, they held ten positions in the Central Committee's membership of one hundred. Short of leg, and barrel chested, they had the broad foreheads, slanted eyes, and flat noses of the Mongols. They were excellent horsemen, and it was said that one Khan soldier was worth fifty other Dagastani. Over time, the Khan had come to speak Russian, but with a thick accent.

The remaining thirty percent of the population was Rus, the descendants of Norse invaders who hadn't stopped in Russia, but had pushed on toward the west. They tended to light skins, brown or blond hair, high foreheads, and superior airs. Rus held all leadership positions that counted, including control of the intelligence, army, and police. The country's central bank was in the hands of a Rus, and most of its preferred customers were Rus.

Vasily Shermov and Pyotr Ksolvi were Rus, and had grown up speaking only Russian. Shermov knew a few words, but his young companion knew not one. Vasily was an official of the economic planning committee, and he'd come across information that would, he felt certain, change the future of Dagastan.

He hadn't taken news of his discovery to his superior or to his cousin, wanting to verify it first, and then ensure that things were arranged in a way that ensured the future prosperity of all of Dagastan's people. If he could get everything lined up properly, he felt sure his cousin would forgive his breech of protocol.

The sudden deceleration of the ZIL, and a muttered curse in Dagastani from the front seat, startled both men.

"What is it, Leonid?" Shermov demanded.

"Flock of sheep in the road," the driver said in horribly-accented Russian.

"Well, drive around them, fool. We must make our schedule."

"Sorry, sir; is not good idea. The ground off the road can be tricky. We might get stuck. The flock will pass soon."

"Well, it better," Shermov said, and settled back, turning his attention to his companion.

He didn't see, therefore, the driver, Leonid, reach over and flick the light switch quickly, blinking the headlights. Nor did he see the four shadowy figures dressed entirely in black that emerged from behind the flock, menacing looking AK-47s held across their chests. They wore balaclava masks pulled down over their faces.

Two moved to the left and two to the right, stopping at the passenger windows. Pyotr Ksolvi was the first to see them, and his eyes opened with fright. Noticing his young companion's expression, Vasily looked up, and his mouth dropped open. "What the bloody hell?" he said, and turned toward the front.

Before he could complete the turn, the four men, aiming downward to avoid hitting their companions, released a deadly stream of bullets shattered the windows of the ZIL and tore into the soft flesh of the two men, tossing them around the seat like limp puppets. Blood spattered the car interior.

It happened so quickly, neither man had had time for more than the beginning of a scream of terror before silent darkness descended. The two corpses lay entwined like two lovers, their facial features unrecognizable after being ripped and shredded by the force of the projectiles.

A pale of gray smoke hung over the car and the smell of cordite was thick. The driver reached for the door handle. One of the men on his side put his hand on the door, jamming it shut.

"I'm sorry, Leonid," he said, his voice muffled by the mask. "But, we must make this look like it was an act of terror, and there must be no way of it being linked to us." He spoke in Dagastani.

Leonid's mouth dropped open. "But, I was promised – -"

His words were cut off by the staccato drum

beat of the man's AK-47, which tore through the driver's window, showering him with shards of grass milliseconds before his chest was torn apart by the projectiles. He was thrown back against the far door, his face frozen in an expression of disbelief.

The taller of the black-clad men took a dirty, oil-stained gray bricklike shape from his pocket and, walking around to the rear of the ZIL, stuffed it into the space between the exhaust pipe and the gas tank. He then inserted a short fuse, and using a battered lighter, lit.

"Let us get out of here," he said. "The fuse is good for two minutes."

The others ran toward the front of the car, shooting and yelling at the sheep to move them. Some of the animals ignored the noise and continued to graze on the rough grass. The four men ran flat out until they were about two hundred meters from the hulking shape of the ZIL. The sky had darkened considerably, but was suddenly lightened by the orange fireball of the ZIL being tossed into the air as the block of C-4 explosive detonated and the fumes from the gas tank ignited. The noise of the initial explosion was loud, but the explosion of the gas tank was deafening. The car was quickly engulfed in flames, spreading an orange glow in a circle expanding out several yards. Black smoke billowed upwards. Along with the smell of burning petrol, there was the sweet smell of roasting flesh.

The sheep that had not been killed by the concussion, or roasted in the ensuing fire, fled across the dusty ground, bleating in panic and kicking up a cloud of dust as they stampeded toward the safety of the hills. The four men stood in silence, gazing at their handiwork. After a few minutes, the tall man spun on his heels and started walking toward the hills. The others followed.

The incident wasn't known of or reported in Dagastan's capital city of Kazbektun for a full day, and only after two Khan tribesmen had come upon the still smoldering wreckage. Outside Dagastan, it didn't even rate a small space in any international media.

But, in a short span of time, it would have impact far beyond Dagastan's borders.

CHARLES RAY

Chapter One

Lesley Carter was worried.

First, she'd been held up by her boss, and feared she'd miss her bus. The L1 Metro bus arrived at the stop at Twenty-third and I Streets at 6:40 pm, and was seldom late, nor did it wait long. If she'd missed it, she would have been looking at more than an hour wait for the next bus. She could take a cab for the 20-minute ride to her neighborhood, on Calvert Street, near the National Zoo, but didn't feel like paying the ten dollar fare.

She was breathing hard as she arrived at the already crowded corner, near Washington Circle, just north of George Washington University Hospital. She'd nearly run from the Department of State building's E Street side, fearing that her short legs wouldn't enable her to move fast enough. She found a clear spot near the front of the crowd and proceeded to pay her fellow commuters no mind; a small group that included several elderly black ladies in gray-green scrubs who worked at the hospital, a portly white businessman in a suit that was rumpled from his own walk in the humidity of mid-May in Washington, DC, three young men who looked like students from the university, and two girls in the plaid skirts and white blouses of a nearby private Catholic high school. She didn't notice the slender, narrow faced man with close set eyes and dark brown hair combed straight back from a high forehead, dressed in dark blue shirt and pants who had been behind her from the moment she crossed F Street, and who now took up a position at the rear of the crowd.

She was breathing hard from her walk, but a glance at the cheap Timex watch on her left wrist showed her that she'd made it with ten minutes to spare.

Despite not missing her bus, she still felt antsy. It had been a surreal day.

She was just settling into her first month on the job as desk officer for the tiny Central Asian country of Dagastan in the European Bureau of the Department of State. A grade 3 Foreign Service Officer, she was on her fourth tour, the first domestic assignment since finishing the orientation course and French language training seven years earlier. Getting the desk officer slot had been a surprise; she was a consular officer, and would normally been assigned to the Bureau of Consular Affairs upon return to the U.S., but, in her last posting, at the U.S. Embassy in Dakar, Senegal, she'd been assigned to the political section's most junior position with responsibility of reporting on activities among the country's ethnic minorities. She had so impressed the embassy's deputy chief of mission, he'd run interference to get her a coveted desk officer job, which would prepare her for more senior assignments outside the consular area; and, this was her dream.

A conscientious person; typical of her Wisconsin Protestant upbringing; she threw herself fully into the job, often working late into the evening, surpassing even some of the workaholics who routinely stayed in the office until past six to show how 'hard' they were working. In her case, she actually worked.

A detail oriented person, she often noticed the small things that others missed; thus, when she noticed a small item, only a few sentences really, in the intelligence digest prepared by the department's Bureau of Intelligence and Research, or INR, about the killing of two Dagastani government officials with the suggestion that foreign elements might have been involved, and then, after crosschecking, discovered that the embassy hadn't reported anything on it, she sprang into action. First, she drafted a cable to the embassy, for the political counselor, asking for any information the embassy had on the incident, and its assessment of the impact it would have on Dagastani politics. Not wanting to bother the office secretary, a sour faced civil servant who liked to remind the young desk officers that she worked for the country director, not them, she'd prepared the cable herself, requiring the typing on a cumbersome multi-copy form of ten green sheets with carbons interlaced, requiring that each sheet be dealt with to make corrections. For that reason, she kept the message short; tactful, but brief. It was when she'd taken it to James Whitman, the country director for that region that sat on the border between Europe and Asia, that her troubles began.

As soon as Whitman had finished reading, he put the paper on his desk, pushing it away as if it was a dangerous animal; and frowning up at her.

"Just what is the meaning of this, Lesley?" he asked. His New England accent, not quite British, but close, was cold, as was his expression.

"Uh, well, sir," she said. "I saw a report about this in the intel traffic. I noticed that the embassy hadn't reported it, but, because of the implication that there might be foreign involvement, I thought they should look into it."

Whitman's expression got even colder. "You thought they should look into it? And, just what makes you think you have any business telling the embassy what they should be doing? Ambassador Ellingsworth is a capable Foreign Service Officer, and if he hasn't reported what is no doubt a minor incident, I'm sure he has his reason, and it's not for a mere desk officer to question him. Do I make myself clear?"

Lesley felt like crying, but held back the tears. She knew he'd expect her to do that. Whitman was one of the people who'd objected to her assignment, stating that a woman, and a consular officer at that, didn't have the necessary qualifications to perform well in the high stress environment of the country directorate. That had been, Lesley find out early on, total bullshit. While they worked often insane hours due to the time difference between Washington and most of the embassies with which they worked, the stress level was less than having to deal with a plane crash or a missing American whose relatives in the U.S. were constantly on the phone insisting that the U.S. Government find their kin, things that even the most junior consular officers had to learn to deal with very early in their careers. The desk officers read cables, wrote bullshit instruction cables, and wrote or cleared on even more bullshit memos for the various senior officials on the sixth and seventh floor of the

State Department's C Street headquarters.

This, she thought, should have been just another routine request for additional information. The frosty look on Whitman's face, though, told her it was anything but. She'd done enough time behind visa interview windows, querying foreigners seeking visas to the United States, that she could spot deception with her eyes closed. Whitman was concealing worry; no, she thought; fear; behind his expression of frosty superiority. As he tore the green sheets, carbons included, into pieces and dumped them into the brown paper bag at the corner of his desk, the 'burn' bag into which classified trash was placed for incineration; she noticed that his hands trembled ever so slightly.

Something about the incident bothered him. Lesley Carter was determined to find out what, but decided not to press the issue with him.

"Yes, sir," she said, trying to put a tone of meek submission into her voice. "I just thought it might be useful, but, I see your point."

He nodded, looking at her from beneath his bushy brows. "Very well then; you have more important things to do, so I suggest you get to them. Where, for instance is that analysis of the crop production reports I asked for this morning."

"Uh, it's almost completed. I'll have it for you first thing in the morning."

This meant, she knew, that she'd have to take the files home and would be up all night drafting and redrafting. She'd been working on it intermittently for most of the day, taking the occasional break to read items in the thick read file that circulated through the warren of tiny boxes that passed for office space for the half dozen desk officers she worked with. When she'd come across the intelligence report, it had piqued her interest; here at last was something besides boring columns of figures enumerating the hectares of wheat and other grains produced by the large state farms of Dagastan, outputs that were barely enough to feed its small population, requiring large shipments of grain and other foodstuffs from the country's Russian neighbors.

Dejected and disappointed by Whitman's reaction to her initiative to do something interesting, and to work on something that might actually have some political impact on U.S. relations with the tiny, insignificant country, she turned and with shoulders slumped, headed back to her tiny space; little more than a broom closet in comparison to the large corner office Whitman occupied.

She would have been even more dismayed had she seen Whitman reach for the phone as she left; his narrowed eyes on her retreating back.

Back in her little cubbyhole, Lesley took the

carbon copy of the cable Whitman had so casually dismissed and started to crumple it up to put in the burn bag. Then, she hesitated, looking at the purplish type on the green paper.

"No, dammit," she said quietly. "There's something here, and I'm getting to the bottom of it, one way or another."

She carefully smoothed out the single sheet and folded it in thirds. She put the folded paper in a legal size envelope, folded it in half and stuck it in her purse. Technically, she was about to commit a serious security violation, because, as was practice, she'd classified the cable CONFIDENTIAL, but she was so angry at the way she'd been rebuffed, she decided, to hell with it. No one checked employee purses on the way in or out of the State Department, and she could always burn it later.

She then took a sheet of plain paper and in her precise handwriting, wrote a short note. She folded the paper in half taped it, then put it in one of the brown interoffice envelopes used to ferry documents around the warren of hallways of the Department. Addressing the envelope to Alison Chambers, Central Asia Analyst, INR/EUR, she got up and went outside. The secretary was bent over her desk, reading the *Washington Post*, and paid her no attention as she slipped the envelope into the stack of outgoing interoffice mail.

Back in her office, she spent the rest of the day making notations on the report Whitman had demanded. She was almost cheered up by the fact that she might actually be able to get most of it down before leaving for the day, alleviating the need to spend all night working on the damn thing.

When the hands of the circular clock mounted on the corkboard wall of her office were at six-fifteen, she removed the ribbon from her typewriter and locked it in the single drawer safe behind her chair, cleared her inbox of all papers, grabbed her purse, and, without looking around to see if anyone was noticing, left for the day. She had no doubt that some, if not all, the desk officers, all male, were sitting hunched over their desks watching the clock, waiting for a suitable 'late' hour to depart. She figured one or more of them would be making a mental note of her 'early' departure. The eight-to-five announced workday was a joke throughout the building. Only the civil servants who had permanent tenure could afford to actually work an eight-hour day.

To hell with it, she thought. The annual performance evaluations, the EERs, had already been done for the year, and she hadn't been in the section long enough to warrant a rating; she'd gotten a glowing evaluation from her last post, which would stand her in good stead when the summer promotion boards met beginning in June.

She was thinking about her prospect for promotion when the big red, white, and blue Metro bus pulled into the stop with a loud hiss of its air brakes, and the group on the sidewalk surged forward even before passengers getting off at that stop could exit the bus.

In the middle of the mass of people, Lesley managed to get on without being pushed around too much, and, luckily, snagged an inward facing seat near the front.

Sitting with her back against the wall, jammed in between a sweaty businessman who smelled of too many martinis with his lunch and an elderly black woman who was reading a dog-eared Bible, she kept her gaze fixed on the scuffed floor of the bus. She didn't notice, therefore, the quick glance she got from the man in black as he made his way past her to the back of the bus, where he stood, holding one of the overhead straps.

The L1 bus made its way up Twenty-third Street, around Washington Circle and onto New Hampshire Avenue, and then northwest on Connecticut toward Woodley Park and the National Zoo. By the mid-way point of the journey, and several stops where people got on, but few got off, the bus was crowded to capacity.

The twenty minute journey to Connecticut Avenue and Calvert Street, Lesley's stop, seemed like an eternity on the crowded vehicle with the smell of sweaty bodies and sweaty clothing assaulting her nostrils. The evening air, even with the mixture of gas fumes from all the cars roaring past on Connecticut, was a relief when she stepped down from the bus and headed up the hill toward the little town house she'd been able to rent a week after arriving in Washington for her assignment. Her air freight had arrived, but she was still waiting for her sea freight shipment, so the place was empty except for a card table and folding chair that did duty as dining surface and work space, and a futon upon which she slept. The few books she'd included in her limited air freight shipment were stacked neatly on the floor next to the futon, beside a gooseneck lamp she'd bought at a little shop in Bethesda. She hadn't bought a TV, so when she didn't spend the time before bed reading, she listened to a little transistor radio that her cousin had given her for her thirtieth birthday the previous year.

She was looking forward to getting inside her empty house; empty though it was, it was her territory, and she felt comfortable there, away from the pretense and coldness of official Washington.

She was completely unaware of the man in black, who had exited via the center door when she went out through the front, and was now trailing her, about twenty feet back. The sidewalk was deserted but for the two of them, and even at seven, the sky was still too light for the street lights to be turned on. Towering trees cast islands of deep shadow across the sidewalk. The man stayed as much in the shadows as possible, but it wasn't necessary, Lesley's attention was focused in front of her, and her destination, about half a mile farther along.

The dark stranger used the pools of shadow to close the gap between them, and it was only when he was no more than six feet behind her that Lesley Carter became aware of someone near; it was a feeling of sorts, the kind of itching tingle at the base of your neck that tells you that you're no longer alone. At first, she merely increased her pace. Only another hundred yards or so to go, and she would be inside her house; not, she thought, that she should really have anything to worry about. After all, Woodley Park was a nice area, populated by middle class families and professionals; not at all like some of the other DC neighborhoods where it was unsafe to wander out alone at night. It was probably just a neighbor, like her, coming home from a day of toil in some government office downtown.

It was after she'd made the turn up the side street on which her house stood that she began to have second thoughts about the sound of the footfalls behind her. They'd turned into the tree-lined narrow street that ended in a cul de sac three houses beyond hers moments after she had. She didn't know any of her neighbors, but couldn't recall any of them who would be coming from downtown at this time of day. Most were elderly retired couples who spent all day sitting on their porches or working in their tiny gardens.

She walked faster. Her house was now in sight, but the sidewalk, a dark gray blur in the shadows of the overhanging trees, seemed to stretch on forever. Her heart began to race, pounding in her chest like the native drums she'd heard during her visits to villages in Senegal. She clutched her purse against her small breasts and lowered her head. Could it be, she asked herself, a mugger? One of the lowlifes that infested the downtown areas, including the National Mall, preying on unwary tourists? If so, why was he so far out from town? She thought of the document in the folded envelope in her purse. What if he wanted her purse? Could she perhaps remove the money and placate him, thus not risking the incriminating document accidentally falling into the wrong hands?

The sound of the footsteps behind her was getting closer. Lesley wanted to run, but knew that her short, stocky legs weren't up to it. Suddenly, she felt the heat of anger and stopped in her tracks. The sound of footsteps stopped as well.

She turned slowly, glaring at the surprised

man who had followed her from the bus stop. Her heart was pounding. She took a deep breath to try and keep her fear from showing in her voice. "Why are you following me?" she demanded.

The dark figure smiled; a slight upturn of the corners of the slit that was his mouth. The close set eyes bored through her, sending chills coursing throughout her body. She clutched the purse closer to her body.

Slowly, ever so slowly, as if he had all the time in the world, the figure advanced. He had his right hand in his pocket, the left hanging loosely at his side.

"If it's money you want," Lesley said. A bit of panic was creeping into her trembling voice. "You can have it; just leave me alone."

The man, who stood less than an inch taller than her five-eight, but who had broader shoulders and a narrow waist, was now less than arms' length away. She could smell the musky cologne he wore. His smile broadened, showing gleaming white teeth.

Something deep in her lizard brain told Lesley that this was no ordinary mugging. She began to take a step backwards, still holding the purse against her chest.

The stranger's hand came out of the pocket and darted forward. Lesley got only a glimpse of the glittering length of steel before she felt the hot piercing in her chest just above her hands clasping the purse.

At first, it was as if someone had touched her flesh with a hot ember, a burning sensation that seemed to spread from the dark man's hand which seemed to be resting between her small breasts. She tried to will her legs to move, to back away from his too familiar touch, but they wouldn't respond. Then, the heat was replaced with an intense feeling of cold that seemed to radiate outward from his hand to all parts of her body.

Slowly, she was immersed in a mixed web of feeling, fire lanced through her chest, and she could feel warmth flowing down over her abdomen; at the same time, she felt cold, oh, so cold. Her vision began to blur, and it was as if she was floating in the air some feet above herself, looking down at her body as it began to slowly crumple toward the sidewalk.

As she lay on the rough concrete, a pool of her blood spreading out around her, the light slowly fading from her eyes, the stranger knelt and removed the purse from her clutching fingers. Smiling, he stood, looking down at her with no other emotion.

He stood there until the erratic rise and fall of her chest had stopped and the life had completely gone from her eyes. Then, he turned and walked back the way he'd come. After turning onto Calvert, he stopped and opened the purse, removing the folded envelope and stuffing it in his left pants' pocket. He then tossed the purse into the foliage and continued walking toward Connecticut Avenue, whistling softly to himself.

Chapter 2

Alison Chambers arrived at her office, a windowless space on the State Department's seventh floor at the end of the building opposite the office of the Secretary of State himself, and unlike his sumptuous office, one without fancy carpets, or expensive pottery and artwork; a utilitarian space with institutional green walls covered with soundproofing and behind layers of steel doors requiring special codes for entry, and restricted to all but a few of the building's inhabitants.

Not that the lack of windows made much difference; it was five thirty in the morning, and the sky outside was still dark. She knew it would be dark before she again emerged from the warren that was the department's Bureau of Intelligence and Research, known to everyone simply as INR; home to the small number of intelligence analysts who tried to make sense of the reams of data and information flowing in from all over the planet, and then communicating the meaning of that flow to those who had to make decisions that affected the fate of the free world – or so Alison and her colleagues told themselves.

At least, she thought, it was Friday, and she could look forward to two days of relaxation; maybe a trip to Ocean City to sit on the beach; provided some little hot spot of simmering revolution didn't erupt.

She put her thermos on her desk and turned to open the gray, three-drawer safe that sat next to it. From the top drawer, she pulled a thick brown folder; the project she'd been wrestling with for several days, and opened it on her desk. Quickly, her mind began to drift as she stared down at the rows of meaningless figures. The Friday blues were kicking in before her day even started.

Closing the folder, she opened the thermos and poured some of the still warm coffee into the top and took a sip. She had a strong feeling that she'd have to make at least one trip, maybe more, to the cafeteria in the basement of the building to refill the thermos if she was to make it to the end of the day without falling asleep at her desk.

Just as she was wiping out the thermos cap with a tissue from a box she kept on her desk, the section secretary, a tall black woman with iron gray hair, stepped in and handed her a brown messenger envelope.

"Is this all you have for me this morning, Earline?" she asked.

"Hey, girl, it's Friday; be glad you only gettin' one," the woman said, laughing. "Some of the other folk gettin' theirs delivered on a cart."

Alison laughed. "Thank God for small favors."

"Now, you just keep your fingers crossed something don't come in just before you gettin' ready to leave for the day."

Alison smiled up at the older woman, who beamed back at her in return. The secretaries, almost all women, and many black or other minorities, liked Alison, one of the few female senior analysts in the bureau. Unlike most of the men, who mostly ignored them, or treated them like domestics, she took the time to talk to them, and more importantly, listen.

"Let's hope nothing pops before you get out of here for the weekend either," Alison said. "How's that new granddaughter of yours?"

"Growin' like a weed, and already talking even though she's just fourteen months old. She's gonna be a smart one; like you."

"By the time she's in first grade she'll

probably be able to do what I do," Alison said, laughing derisively. She'd not been given anything more challenging than analyzing the impact of reduced rainfall on the wheat crops of Central Asia since being assigned to the office two years earlier, despite being one of the more senior people in grade, all of the sexy assignments seemed to go to one of the male analysts.

"Don't sell yourself short, honey," Earline said. "Your time will come."

The woman smiled again, warmth in her light brown face, and left quietly.

Alison's face screwed up in frustration. She'd been waiting for two years for her 'time to come,' and it wasn't yet in sight as far as she could see. She toyed with the idea, as she so often did, of approaching her supervisor, Dudley Lakeworth, the recently assigned Senior Foreign Service Officer who was chief of the office, and demanding she be given something more interesting or important to work on. But, she knew what his response would be. She'd only met him once, but, when she'd complained that the projects she worked on were boring and uninteresting, he'd informed her that in the intelligence game, every fact and incident was important; even the most seemingly insignificant fact could be of critical importance under the right circumstances. In other words, 'get back to your desk and quit complaining.'

The day after their meeting, he'd passed her in the hallway without even a nod of recognition, his expression that of a person looking at a stranger.

She looked at the messenger envelope, noting that it was from Lesley Carter, the new Dagastan desk officer. She'd met Carter a few days back, and had developed an instant liking for her. She was one of those uncomplicated, straight forward Midwesterners, so different from the kind of people she'd grown up around in her native Atlanta, Georgia. A bit old for a junior desk officer, but she'd informed Alison that it had taken her four tries to pass the Foreign Service examination, so she was a few years older than most of the other officers in her Foreign Service orientation class, and one of only two women. Like Alison, Lesley Carter had been assigned backwater duties; Dagastan, as Alison recalled from her study of the region, was a small, insignificant state, surrounded by Russia, with no strategic importance, and an economy about the size of Washington's Georgetown area.

She unwound the string used to keep the messenger envelope opened and extracted the single sheet of paper, tossing the empty envelope into her out tray. She laid the paper on her desk and glanced down at it. At first, it made no impression; given the lack of importance of Dagastan, she'd been expecting some personal note; but, as she read, her interest perked up.

The message, in neat handwriting, was short: "ALISON: I READ AN INTEL REPORT SAYING THAT TWO DAGASTANI OFFICIALS WERE ASSASSINATED IN AN ISOLATED AREA OUTSIDE KAZBEKTUN A FEW DAYS AGO, AND THERE WAS SUSPICION OF FOREIGN INVOLVEMENT. EMBASSY HASN'T REPORTED THE INCIDENT. DOES INR HAVE ANYTHING? LESLIE"

She looked down at the note. There was nothing strange about desk officers sending notes to analysts in INR, but it was usually to double check embassy reporting. She wondered why the political section of the embassy in Kazbektun hadn't reported such an incident, which would be a bit more interesting than the usual rehash of local newspaper reports they usually sent in. At a minimum, she thought, there should have been a short report from the station. The agency folks in the embassies usually kept an eye on the political happenings in country, and tried scooping the political officers with their reports.

It wasn't in her usual portfolio, but it looked like it would be more interesting than what she was currently working on, so Alison got up and went outside to the main area where Earline, the section secretary worked.

"What can I do for you, hon?" Earline asked

as Alison approached her desk.

"I need to check on intel reports for a few days ago regarding Dagastan," she said.

The secretary pointed at a row of six four-drawer gray metal cabinets that lined the wall behind her desk.

"Dagastan; that'll be second cabinet from the left, probably third drawer. You want to tell me what you looking for; I can get it for you."

Alison waved her hand in a polite dismissal. "No need, I can do it."

Earline smiled broadly. Another thing she liked about this middle height, bordering on skinny white girl with the slight southern accent and the dark brown hair pulled back severely; unlike the other analysts, who would have expected her to drop everything and fetch things for them, she didn't mind getting her hands dirty.

"Okay, go ahead; but, if you need help, just yell."

Alison went to the second cabinet, which was unlocked as they all were during normal work hours, and, bending, opened the third drawer. She flipped folders, scanning the labels, and, as the secretary had said, the Dagastan Intelligence Digest for the current month was there, third folder from the front. She pulled the buff-colored folder from the drawer. It wasn't half as thick as the folders for other countries, indicating that little ever happened in this backwater. This made the note from Lesley Carter even more puzzling. In a country where little happened, she would have thought the embassy would have been all over an assassination for no other reason than it was a break in an otherwise boring routing.

She pushed the drawer shut and took the folder back to her office.

There weren't too many pages in the folder, and she found what she was looking for about halfway down. It was a report from the Central Intelligence Agency, less than a page long; basically a summary of an article in the Dagastan Daily, the state news organ. Following a string of cryptic acronyms and numbers that identified this as an agency report, without specifically identifying the reporting officer, it accorded with what had been in Carter's note:

SUMMARY OF DAGASTAN DAILY, MAY 6, 1975 – THE HEAD OF THE NATIONAL POLICE, GENERAL LIEUTENANT COMRADE MIKILAI GVORIC, REPORTED THAT THE REMAINS OF THREE INDIVIDUALS, BELIEVED TO BE COMRADE VASILY SHERMOV, AN OFFICIAL OF THE STATE ECONOMIC PLANNING COMMITTEE, PYOTR VKSOLVI, ASSISTANT TO COMRADE SHERMOV, AND LEONID KAZONIK, A DRIVER FOR THE COMMITTEE, WERE FOUND IN THE BURNED WRECKAGE OF AN

AUTOMOBILE ON THE HIGHWAY OUTSIDE THE CAPITAL KAZBEKTUN YESTERDAY. COMRADE GVORIC TOLD THIS NEWSPAPER THAT IT APPEARS THE VICTIMS WERE SHOT BEFORE THE CAR WAS DESTROYED BY EXPLOSIVE, AND THAT EXTERNAL ENEMIES OF THE STATE ARE THOUGHT TO HAVE COMMITTED THIS HEINOUS ACT. ALL RESOURCES OF THE STATE WILL BE EMPLOYED TO BRING THE KILLERS TO JUSTICE, COMRADE GVORIC SAID. (ANALYST NOTE: THERE IS NO INDEPENDENT VERIFICATION OF THIS REPORT, AND THERE HAS BEEN NO FURTHER REPORTING. VASILY {SHERMOV} IS REPORTEDLY THE FIRST COUSIN OF FIRST SECRETARY OF THE DAGASTAN COMMUNIST PARTY DMITRI KOVASC).

That was it; she flipped through the entire folder, and there were no other reports of the incident. Strange that the embassy wouldn't have reported the death, no the possible assassination, of a relative of the country's leader, she thought. She could understand the desk officer's puzzlement, but wondered why she hadn't just queried the embassy about it.

She pulled the department phone book from the shelf over her desk and looked up the number of the Dagastan country desk, then dialed the five digit extension. The phone rang ten times, but no one answered. Alison looked at her watch. It was already a quarter past seven; well past the time when all the desk officers in every bureau and office throughout the building would already be slaving away at their desks, the purported 8 am start of the work day be damned. *Maybe she's in a meeting with the country director,* Allison thought. Other than generating reams of useless memoranda, that floated from desk to desk collecting initials, the other product of the building was hour after hour of meeting, where everyone sat around reading from their prepared talking points, each speaker attempting to outdo the previous speaker by proving that he, and, in some rare cases, she, knew more about whatever unimportant topic that was being discussed than anyone else around the table. *I'll try her later.*

She closed the folder and pushed it aside; and to pass the time until lunch, decided to go ahead and work on the boring rows and columns of figures.

Chapter 3

Tuesday, May 6, 1975, American Embassy,
Kazbektun, Dagastan

David Morgan, deputy chief of mission at the
American Embassy, a two story cinder block
building located on Kazbektun's main
thoroughfare, sat in his office. It was half past
six, and the sky outside was still a dirty blue,
with a hint of pink from the sun that had not
yet risen.

It had been dark when he'd arrived at the
embassy at five, as had been his practice for the
sixteen months he'd been in Dagastan. For the
first twelve months, he'd been deputy to
Ambassador Eloise Tarkington, a heavyset
blonde from Minnesota. When her tour of duty
had ended, she'd been replaced by Robert
Ellingsworth, a tiny, ascetic looking man with a
nearly bald bullet-shaped head, from Boston.
Like Tarkington, Ellingsworth was a member of

the Senior Foreign Service with rank of Minister-Counselor, the second highest rank of that class of career Foreign Service Officers, and, like her, this was his first assignment as ambassador. But, unlike Tarkington, who had been a cheerful woman who seemed to genuinely care for those on her staff, and who got along with every member of her Country Team, Ellingsworth was an aloof, imperious sort, who seldom even acknowledged the greetings from junior staff when he entered the building; instead, he tended to seclude himself in the large, well-appointed corner office in the west corner of the second floor, requiring that anyone wanting to see him first get make an appointment with his secretary, a horse-faced redhead who had accompanied him to post. Even Morgan, who had had free access to Tarkington, had to make an appointment. It was unheard of, but, as ambassador, Ellingsworth's word was law, and those under him had no choice but to comply.

Morgan had quickly run through the day's message traffic, marking those dispatches he felt should get the ambassador's attention, and routing others to members of the staff for revision, answers to questions he'd penned neatly in the margins, or with instructions that he knew would be carried out as he directed.

His own secretary, Mary Sung, a tiny Chinese-American woman who'd been assigned by the central personnel system, arrived at about the same time he did every day, and in addition to placing the reading file on his desk, had brewed a fresh pot of coffee. He was on his second cup, and preparing to do his daily walk around the embassy as soon as he finished it, when the door to his office opened.

He looked up; an expression of query on his broad brown face, when he saw that it was Carlton Raine, the chief of station. Raine was a tall, broad shouldered man with reddish brown skin and lightly curled brown hair that was beginning to gray at the temples. Like Morgan, he was the only black assigned to the embassy, and the two men got along well, despite the gap in their ages; Raine was in his mid-fifties, serving for the first time as a chief of station, one of the first minorities to be assigned to what was the agency's prime field positions. Morgan, now in his tenth year of service, was forty-one, having served ten years in the army as a signal officer after graduation from Howard University with a degree in electrical engineering. When he passed the Foreign Service examination after his third attempt, he'd resigned his commission to enter the diplomatic service. He'd done the obligatory tour of duty as a consular officer, doing visa interviews in Manila for eighteen months, followed by tours as a political officer in Nairobi, economic reporting officer in Milan, and a tour as a desk officer for southern Africa in the department's Africa Bureau.

When Tarkington's deputy had to be

curtailed for medical reasons, his assignment counselor had recommended he try for the job, and, to his surprise, had been accepted to be her deputy chief of mission for the final year of her tour. Ellingsworth had inherited him when he'd been confirmed to the post, and would have to deal with him for the remaining sixteen months of his three-year tour before he could select his own deputy.

Raine, on the other hand, was more or less on an indefinite tour. He'd already been in Dagastan for a year when Morgan arrived, and whenever they talked, he was always cagey about when his tour might end. Morgan suspected that the agency left him in place to avoid having to assign him to one of the more prestigious stations, or to a director's position at Langley, but Raine didn't seem to mind.

"Morning, Blood," Morgan said, using Raine's nickname, which the man steadfastly refused to explain despite Morgan's repeated inquiries. "What brings you out of the cave so early in the morning?"

Raine spun the chair next to Morgan's desk around and plopped down in it, his muscular brown arms, with golden brown hairs bristling along his forearms, across the back. "I wanted to show you this report I'm about to send to Langley," he said.

He handed a single sheet across the desk.

Morgan took it and read it quickly.

As he read, his brown brow furrowed. When he'd finished reading, he passed it back. "Yeah, I know about this," he said. "Dennis Larson briefed me on it yesterday." Larson was chief of the political section; a grade one FSO like Morgan, but his subordinate in the embassy chain of command.

"If it's true that the top guy's cousin was assassinated, that could mean trouble on the horizon. What kind of report are you guys doing on it?"

Morgan's frown deepened. He'd had a contentious discussion with the ambassador on this very topic late the previous day. "We're not reporting it."

Now, it was Raine's turn to frown. "You're kidding, right? I mean, Shermov is Kovasc's cousin. Dmitri's not gonna take this well; in fact, I imagine that if he didn't have it done himself – and, I wouldn't put it past him – he'll be treating it as a personal attack. That son of a bitch didn't get the nickname *The Butcher* for nothing, you know. I can't believe you guys aren't reporting on it."

Morgan wrestled with what for him was a moral dilemma; he fundamentally disagreed with Ellingsworth's decision not to report on the incident, but as the man's deputy, he felt he owed him loyalty. He wasn't sure that discussing it with the chief of station was appropriate. The whole mess was upsetting his stomach. In the end, he decided that he could trust Raine's discretion.

"Dennis had one of his junior political officers do a report," he said. "But, the ambassador wouldn't approve its release. Said it wasn't important enough to bother Washington with it."

"You disagree with that, of course?"

"Sure, and I pushed back on it. I think this could signal some critical fractures in Kovasc's government; even a threat to his continued hold on power; but the ambassador disagrees. He basically handed me my head on a platter when I told him I thought not reporting on it was a bad idea."

Raine shrugged. "For the record, I agree with you, which is why I'm sending this intel. There's something going on, but I can't get a finger on it. Our usual sources are being shut out of a lot of what's going on, and that's troubling; especially with the rumor of foreign involvement."

Morgan frowned. "You think the ambassador's not gonna try to spike your report as well?"

Raine laughed; a harsh, guttural sound. "Sure, he won't like it, but he can't stop it. Best he can do is add a comment; which I fully expect him to do. I'll be sending a separate signal, though, to put his non-concurrence in context."

Morgan didn't ask about this 'separate' signal. He'd been in the business long enough to know that all of the other agencies at the embassy, from the CIA to the Defense Attaché, had channels of communication to their headquarters that bypassed the ambassador; the agency most of all.

"Why are you telling me this, Carlton?"

"I got me a feeling about things, David. Maybe it's just him being new on the job, and being a first-time ambassador, but Ellingsworth hasn't really impressed me since he arrived. I don't know what it is; just a gut feeling really, but I have a sense he's not really value added."

"I shouldn't be hearing this. He's the ambassador, for Pete's sake; the President's representative, and for good or bad, he's the man in charge."

"Dammit, man, I know that." Raine's voice was hard. "But, we also took an oath to support the Constitution, and far as I'm concerned, that trumps loyalty to any individual. I have a sense that deep down, you feel the same way. Anyway, I didn't want you blindsided by this."

Just then, came a soft knock on the door.

"Yes?" Morgan called.

Mary Sung stuck her head around the edge of the door. "The RSO would like to speak to you, David," she said.

"Can it wait? I'm in a meeting with Carlton right now."

She pulled away, and then her head popped back. "He says it's urgent, and he'd like to speak to Mr. Raine as well."

Morgan knew that Pete Jeffers, his Regional Security Officer was an experienced Diplomatic Security agent, a former army military policeman who'd served in Vietnam before his discharge and recruitment by DS. If he said it was urgent, it was. He waved for his secretary to let him in.

Jeffers wasn't the picture of what one might expect a tough federal agent to be. He tended to a bit of flesh around his middle, although, Morgan knew that the man could still prevail physically over men half his age, which was forty, and his cherubic face topped by unruly brown hair that he kept cropped short, in almost military regulation style, made him look like a fast food chain manager. More than one obstinate visa applicant who'd expressed displeasure at being denied a visa had discovered that appearances were deceiving, when Jeffers had him in a headlock being crab walked to the embassy's front door.

"What is it, Pete?" Morgan asked as the agent, dressed in his usual khaki pants, plaid shirt, and hunting vest, walked into the office. His usual boyish grin was missing. He looked serious.

"Sorry to bother you, Dave," he said. "Mornin', Blood. I got something that's been bugging me, and I need to run it past the two of you."

Morgan motioned him to the other empty chair next to Raine.

"What is it?" he asked.

"Well, you know I have two of my local guards assigned as a personal security detail for the ambassador when he travels outside the chancery."

Morgan nodded. He'd often thought it unnecessary, but under the present circumstances it was probably wise. If rumors of any kind of foreign involvement in local affairs started floating around, there was the potential for incidents.

"I never had any problem with Ambassador Tarkington," Jeffers said. "Other than bitching now and then about not having any privacy. For a while it was the same with Ambassador Ellingsworth, but yesterday, it changed."

"You mean, he finally decided to quite bugging you about it?"

Jeffers shook his head, running a large hand through his short hair. "No, not at all," he said. "He just fired them. Said he didn't want, need, and wouldn't accept, any more security detail."

Chapter 4

Friday, May 9, 1975, Washington, DC

DS Special Agent Lee Kennedy sat at his desk on the sixth floor, at the corner of a long corridor on the D Street side of the State Department building, staring at the clock on the wall above his desk, and wishing the day would end soon so he could get home to spend time with his thirteen year-old daughter, Rachel.

A 16-year veteran of the Diplomatic Security Service, Kennedy was just starting the second year of a two-year stint in DS headquarters, and was angling for a second two-year stint in Washington so that Rachel could at least get a most of her high school studies completed in the U.S. before he was posted overseas again. He'd come to Washington the previous hear from an assignment as one of many assistant Regional Security Officers, or ARSOs, assigned to the embassy in Saigon, leaving that posting just a year before North Vietnamese tanks rolled into the South Vietnamese capital, forcing closure of the embassy and the hasty withdrawal of Americans from that defeated country. Prior to joining DSS, Kennedy had worked four years as a patrolman for the Baltimore Police Department.

He'd been assigned duty as DS liaison to the Washington Metropolitan Police Department, a position that had few responsibilities, but fit perfectly with his desire to get to know his daughter better. His wife of 14 years had walked out on them midway through his Saigon tour, leaving Rachel with Kennedy's elderly parents in Baltimore, and run off with a real estate broker from Delaware. He'd spent the bulk of his free time helping Rachel overcome the feeling of devastation caused from being abandoned by one parent while the other was half a world away.

Resilient, though, as only a teenager who'd spent her entire life packing and moving every two years can be, she was coming back remarkably well. Kennedy resolved that she would never be made to feel abandoned again. For that reason, he was pushing his career development officer to get his extension in his current job approved. If that failed, he'd given serious consideration to resigning and applying for a job with the DC police. It wouldn't come close to matching the life he'd come to know and love, but it would enable him to make a stable home for his daughter.

He was contemplating whether to go down to the cafeteria in the basement, or leave the building and try one of the nicer places to eat up around George Washington University when the phone rang.

"Special Agent Kennedy," he said into the receiver. "How can I help you?"

"Lee, Al Murphy here, I have an incident that I think you'll be interested in."

Al Murphy was a detective lieutenant with the DC police, and was Kennedy's main contact at the department. At 46, he was only a year older, and a native of DC. A native Baltimorean, Kennedy developed a liking for the gruff redhead third generation Irish-American at their first meeting.

"What is it, Al?"

"We had a homicide last night in Woodley Park; Caucasian female, mid-thirties; looks like a mugging that went bad. She didn't have any ID, but when we ran her prints through the system, we identified her as Lesley Carter, a State Department employee. Thought you might be able to help us track down her next of kin so we can notify them."

Shit, Kennedy thought, that's all I need; having to hassle with central personnel to get a contact card. Then, of course, there'd be the reams of paperwork the system would require. At least, he thought, he wouldn't have to worry about having to investigate the incident, as he would if it had taken place overseas.

"Okay, Al," he said. "It might take a while, but I'll run it down and get back to you."

Chapter 5

In a different part of the building, Alison Chambers was securing the documents in her office in preparation for going out to lunch.

After spending the first half of the day cooped up in a tiny box with no windows, the last thing she wanted to do was descend into the basement and eat in a place where she couldn't look out and see the sky. She let the secretary know she'd be out of the building, and then walked the fifty feet down the corridor to the elevator.

As the cage started to descend, she pushed the button for the third floor. The Dagastan desk officer's office was on that floor, and Alison figured she might as well touch base with her to see if she'd heard anything sense sending her cryptic note. She couldn't believe the embassy hadn't reported on something as significant as the killing of the head of state's relative;

probably just took them time to get it polished and approved for transmission. She knew that many of the officers who did political reporting treated reports on the most mundane subjects as if they were the great American novel. In a sense, though, she knew they were in a way; this was often the only thing their performance was judged by, so naturally they'd fret over them.

When the elevator stopped at the third floor, and after what seemed an extra-long time, the doors whispered open, Alison exited, and for a moment was disoriented as she stood and tried to remember in which direction she should turn. She knew her away around on her own floor, and could find the cafeteria and the employee exit, but on any other floor in the long rectangular building with even numbered corridors from the C Street side to the D Street side, and odd numbers between 21st and 23d Streets, she often found herself having to retrace her steps in order to get to her destination. She hadn't been on the third floor in months, but quickly remembered that the Dagastan desk was near the center of corridor 2, which put it on the front, or C Street side of the building.

Having puzzled out the direction, she found herself at the door to the European Bureau's smallest office in no time. She entered a small space containing one desk, behind which sat a bored looking woman with mousy brown hair, who looked up idly at her. The walls behind and in front of the desk were decorated with photos of rugged mountains, poor villages, and herds of sheep. A hallway directly in front of the entrance stretched right and left. She could see two doors, which she knew to be the tiny offices; even tinier than her own; of the various desk officers.

"Can I help you?" the woman asked.

"I'm here to see Lesley Carter," Alison said.

"I don't think she's in today, but you can go on back and take a look. Her office is the last one down to your right," the woman said, pointing.

There were three offices in that part of the hallway, and, as the receptionist has said, she found Lesley Carter's name on the little placard next to the last door. The door was closed. Alison rapped lightly. There was no answer. She tried the handle; the door opened onto a small rectangular cubicle containing a gray metal desk, a government-issue gray chair, a small two-drawer safe, and a three-drawer filing cabinet. The lights were off, but the window, looking out over the buildings across C Street in front of the State Department, and the top of the Lincoln Memorial beyond that, gave enough illumination. Unlike the other offices, from which she could hear the clatter of typewriters as she passed, this office was as quiet as a library under the control of a stern librarian, without even the rustle of pages being turned. The desk was bare.

Even though she had top clearance, far beyond that possessed by mere desk officers, she was reluctant to enter someone else's office without an invitation.

Retracing her steps, she returned to the entrance area.

"She's not in her office," she said to the woman. "Do you know if she's in the building somewhere?"

With an expression of someone who has been interrupted in the middle of doing something important, despite the fact that she was just sitting staring at the clock on the wall opposite, the woman looked up at Alison. "I have no idea. She left around five-thirty or six yesterday; that's the last I time I saw her."

"She didn't call in or anything?"

"She didn't call me. You might check with her boss, Mr. Whitman; his office is the last one on the left." The woman went back to staring at the clock as if Alison wasn't there.

Back in the narrow, gray-carpet-lined hallway, Alison turned left. The country director's office was at the end of the hallway, facing down it. Unlike the desk officer name plates, which were regulation issue brackets with hastily done stenciled signs, the sign beside his door was a brass rectangle with his name, JAMES LATIMORE WHITMAN, COUNTRY DIRECTOR, in ornate script.

Alison knocked.

"Come in," a deep male voice said from behind the door.

Whitman's office was four times the size of the office she'd just seen, and instead of the regulation gray metal desk, he had a large wooden desk of some polished brown wood. A large wooden bookcase sat behind the desk. It was filled with expensive looking books, certificates and figurines. More certificates and pictures, mostly of Whitman with various distinguished looking men, lined the walls.

Whitman was medium weight, and even sitting, Alison could tell, medium height, wearing a three-piece dark blue suit with white shirt and red tie. His medium brown hair was combed back on his round head. He wore wire rimmed glasses that perched on a patrician nose. Cold blue eyes looked up at Alison through the round glass of the spectacles.

"What can I do for you?" he asked. His voice was as disinterested as the receptionist's had been. His mouth curled up in a slight smile that had all the warmth of a block of ice.

"I'm Alison Chambers from INR," Alison said.

"I'm looking for Lesley Carter, but she doesn't seem to be in her office."

"I haven't spoken to Lesley today. Did you ask the secretary out front?"

Alison assured him she had. There was a slight note of petulance in her voice as she did; did this pompous fool think she'd just fallen off the turnip truck, she thought. Of course I would have asked the secretary first. One would think, though, that as her supervisor, you would know as well.

"The secretary said she hasn't called."

"Well, she hasn't called me either. What was it you wanted to talk to her about?"

"That's just it; I had the feeling she wanted to talk to me. Something about the recent assassination in Dagastan."

There was the slightest flicker in the cold eyes. Anyone less observant than Alison Chambers might have missed it, because his face otherwise remained still. "Assassination in Dagastan? Oh yes, you mean the First Secretary's cousin. She spoke to me about that, but there was nothing there. She wasn't working on that issue."

"Who was? I haven't seen any embassy reporting on it."

Now, there was an expression; mild anger or

annoyance. "I'm sure that if the embassy thought it important they would have reported it." There was ice in his voice. "In any case, it wasn't Lesley's to determine. She had other, far more important things to do."

Sure, Alison thought, like crop or weather reports, or any of the other dozen or so meaningless reports demanded by Congress or someone somewhere in the labyrinth of offices and agencies that was official Washington. It was obvious, though, that the man didn't want to discuss the issue. *At least, the agency reported it. Maybe this is one they're handling, and keeping State out of the loop.* Even as she thought it, though, she discarded it. There was nothing in Dagastan important enough for the CIA to expend more than the minimum of resources on. Far better to let the State Department do most of the scut work of gathering the routine information.

Something was amiss, but Alison was at a complete loss as to what that something might be. She wasn't, however, planning to waste too many minutes of her lunch hour worrying about it. She smiled at Whitman and backed out the door, determining to purge the whole matter from her mind.

CHARLES RAY

Chapter 6

Saturday, May 10, 1975, Dagastan

David Morgan's Saturday had started quietly
enough. Having never married, he had a
Saturday bachelor routine that had only varied
when he was serving in war zones that made it
impractical.

He got up around five-thirty, as he did every
day of the week, went out for a morning jog of
three or four miles, then came back and
showered, dressed in a Dallas Cowboys' jersey
and faded jeans, and cooked himself a large
breakfast of sausage, scrambled eggs, pan-fried
toast, and hashed brown potatoes. He then
piled the food on a large plate and put the plate
on a large wooden tray with a pot of freshly-
brewed Jamaican coffee, a glass of grapefruit
juice, and one of buttermilk. He'd had to talk
the defense attaché into getting a couple of
gallons of the thick milk brought in on the
monthly support flights out of Frankfurt,

Germany. Fortunately, the colonel was from North Carolina, and understood the love for the stuff, which no one else in the embassy drank. He took the heavily laden tray out to the cobblestone patio at the rear of the two-story house that was assigned to him. It was too large for a single man, but it was his by position, not family size, so he made the most of it. He only used the kitchen, bedroom, bath, and a small room off the main living room, which he'd converted into a home office.

As he ate, he reminded himself that he needed to eat a bit less, and run a mile or two more. He was no longer the trim and fit army captain he'd been when he left the military after eight years and joined the Foreign Service. He'd entered the army right out of college, having been the honor graduate of his Reserve Officer Training Corps class. As the top ROTC graduate, he had his pick of assignments, and he'd selected the infantry. He'd put on the uniform just in time for the increased involvement in Vietnam in 1966, and after his advanced training had been assigned as a second lieutenant platoon leader in the 173d Airborne Brigade at Fort Benning, Georgia. The unit was preparing for deployment to Vietnam as part of the increased American involvement in the war there. Morgan had served his year in country with distinction, earning a Bronze Star with V Device for pulling one of his men out of the line of fire during a Viet Cong attack on their night position.

Back in the U.S., and a first lieutenant, Morgan had heard of the famous Green Berets, and had applied. To his surprise, he'd passed all the entrance requirements, and soon found himself at Fort Bragg, North Carolina, at the JFK Center for Special Warfare, the school named for President John Fitzgerald Kennedy, the commander in chief who had first authorized the green beret as the distinctive headgear for the elite Special Forces soldiers. Upon completion of the sixteen weeks of training, and graduating in the top ten percent of his class, Morgan had been sent to a nondescript red brick building in Washington, DC's Georgetown area where he spent ten months learning to speak the horrifically difficult Vietnamese language. Again, he'd distinguished himself.

Before being sent back to Vietnam, he'd spent three weeks in Panama at the army's jungle warfare school, learning to survive in a hostile jungle environment with the minimum of equipment, and depending almost entirely on your individual skill and determination. It was the hardest three weeks of his life, but he emerged from the school with the red, white, and blue Jungle Expert patch which he wore proudly below the right breast pocket of his jungle fatigues. His orders to Vietnam had him assigned to the 5th Special Forces Group, based in Nha Trang, on the coast north of Saigon, but as soon as he arrived, he was informed that he was being reassigned to an outfit called the Studies and Observation Group, which had its headquarters in a modest looking villa on Pasteur Street in Saigon, not far from the Presidential Palace and the American embassy. He'd been interviewed by a gruff talking, cigar smoking army colonel, who told him little about the organization, but seemed more interested in whether or not Morgan was the adventurous type. He didn't remember how he'd answered the colonel's questions, but it must have worked; the day after the interview, a sergeant driving a black jeep with yellow plates instead of the normal military markings, picked him up at the in-processing station where he'd been staying and took him to Tan Son Nhut Airport, where he was put on a Huey helicopter which flew him to the highland town of Ban Me Thuot. He spent the next twelve months there, either leading or directing ten-man reconnaissance teams of Americans and Montagnards, ethnic minority hill tribe people of Vietnam, on clandestine patrols across the border into neighboring Cambodia, their mission to locate and identify infiltrating North Vietnamese units, locate and mark weapon and supply cache sites, and on occasion, try to capture an enemy prisoner who could be exploited for intelligence purposes. The skills he'd learned during his three weeks in Panama had come in handy on more than one occasion.

After SOG, the army hadn't been able to find an assignment for Morgan with the same level of excitement. He'd hung on for four more years, finally resigning his commission after passing the Foreign Service examination and being offered a job by the Department of State. He was at the time one of few military veterans in the diplomatic service.

The memories of his time in the military, with the boring parts edited out, often flooded back into his mind when he was sitting alone on the patio. Something about Dagastan reminded him very much of Vietnam, but he couldn't pinpoint just what.

The sky overhead was a grayish color at that time of morning, with the sun just rising over the distant mountains to the east, a pale orange disk that looked fuzzy around the edges. The mountains, partially obscured by the early morning haze, looked like some hulking beast with a serrated back, crouching in wait for prey, with nothing on or around them to soften the image. It wasn't the best of views, but it beat what he could see from the front of the house; the row upon row of flat-roofed adobe dwellings clinging to the gently sloping hill upon which his house stood; lining each side of the potholed, poorly paved lane that was Gorsky Street.

He'd finished off the food, and was sipping his second cup of coffee, when the short, elderly, bow-legged houseman, an ethnic Kazbektuni named Karislov, who kept the place clean and did his laundry; on occasion even preparing a supper of local dishes, mainly grain-based bread and stringy beef, came through the glass double doors onto the patio.

"Meester Morgan," Karislov said in horribly accented English. "You got visitor."

"Who is it, Karislov?"

"Is Meester Cheffers. He say he must speak wiz you on metter of urgent."

"Send him out, and bring another cup."

The old man bowed, smiling, showing uneven rows of brown-stained teeth, and withdrew. A few minutes later, he came back, holding a coffee cup. Pete Jeffers, dressed in jeans and a red and black plaid shirt, followed him.

"Morning, boss," he said. "Sorry to bother you at home on a weekend, but something's come up that I think you need to know."

Because of his boyish face, Jeffers usually tried to have a stern look, on the theory that people expected a cop; which is what in essence he was; to be a serious person. His expression now, though, was seriously serious.

Morgan waved him to the empty chair. "No problem, Pete. I'm on duty around the clock anyway; at least, that's what they told me when I took the DCM Course. Have some coffee. Now, what's got your knickers in a knot this fine Saturday morning?"

Jeffers poured coffee into the empty cup that the houseman had placed in front of him, and took a sip. After putting the cup down, he looked across the table at Morgan, a sad smile on his round face.

"David, I've done something wrong, really wrong; but, for all the right reasons; and, now I've come across something that puts me in one hell of a corner."

Morgan smiled, his brown face showing concern. He knew Jeffers to be a straight shooter, and couldn't think of anything really drastic that he would have done.

"Unless you hotwired the First Secretary's car, I doubt if whatever you might have done could be so serious."

Jeffers, like him, was single, and Morgan thought it might have to do with the sidelong glances one of the local female employees in the embassy's consular section gave the security officer whenever he passed. While it wasn't exactly illegal, romantic relationships with other members of the staff were never a good idea.

"Oh, it's serious all right," Jeffers said. "You remember me telling you the ambassador fired his security detail?"

Morgan nodded. He felt an itch at the base of his neck. He didn't like where the conversation seemed to be going. Ellingsworth struck him as the vindictive type.

"Well," Jeffers went on. "I didn't feel comfortable about him going about with no security; so, I put two of my best locals on him."

Damn, Morgan thought, I really didn't need to hear that. "Don't tell me you were guarding him, despite him saying he didn't want guards?"

Jeffers face reddened. "I know, I know. If he ever found out, he'd have my ass, and he'd probably go after you just out of spite. But, I don't intend to let something happen to him that I could have prevented."

"Yeah, but if he knows you're doing it, he won't go after our asses until he's taken our balls."

"Not a problem; he hasn't tumbled. The man's so preoccupied with himself, a tail could be three feet away and he probably wouldn't notice, and the guys I have on him are experts. If they don't want to be seen, they won't be seen."

"Well then, what's the problem?"

"Last night, they followed him from the

residence around half past eight, thinking he was going to one of the local ptomaine palaces for dinner. Only, he didn't. He dismissed his driver in one of the seedier parts of town, and went on foot to a house."

"Please don't tell me our ambassador is visiting hookers."

"I wish it was as simple as that. When he knocked on the door, my guys got a glimpse of the person who opened it. It was just a glimpse, but they both swear to what they saw, and it wasn't a prostitute."

"Who in hell would he be meeting that late at night?"

"My guys said the guy that opened the door was Milosevic Dragov, the deputy head of the security services."

CHARLES RAY

Chapter 7

Sunday, May 11, 1975, Washington, DC

Sunday started off bright and cheerful for Lee Kennedy. He'd risen early and prepared a light breakfast for Rachel, just eating a piece of lightly buttered toast, washed down with black coffee himself. He preferred to save his big Sunday meal for midday. His plan was to surprise Rachel with a trip to the steak house on Columbia Pike, not far from the little two-bedroom red brick townhouse they shared.

There was nothing worth watching on the little black and white TV, so after breakfast, Rachel had kissed him on the top of his head and gone to her bedroom to read. Pouring a second cup of coffee, he went to the tiny back yard and sat on the bench he and Rachel had built the previous month when he'd had a fit of do-it-yourselfness. It swayed a bit when he lowered his bulk onto it, but Rachel was so proud of the project she and daddy had built, he didn't have the heart not to use it.

He spread the Sunday *Post* out on the picnic table he'd wisely bought from a local hardware store and started reading the comics. He'd just finished the comics and was about to turn to the sports page when Rachel stuck her head out of the glass doors.

"Dad, there's a guy here says he wants to talk to you," she said. "He looks like a cop to me."

Al Murphy, dressed in tan slacks, a white shirt, open at the neck, over which he word a medium brown sports coat, pushed past Rachel, tousling her medium length brown hair as he did so. "This is one smart kid you have here, Lee," he said. "She's only seen me a hundred times, and she remembers every time that I'm a cop."

Rachel laughed. "I'd know you were the fuzz even if I'd never seen you before. You look, talk, and act just like my dad."

"More like a smart ass kid," Kennedy said. "What brings you across the river on Sunday, Al? Hey, would you like a cup of joe? Rachel, bring your Uncle Al a cup of coffee."

"Would you like a doughnut with the coffee, Uncle Al?" she said, poking Murphy in his ample gut.

"Nah, just coffee, princess," he said, tweaking her button nose. "You know how I like it."

She laughed again and headed toward the kitchen.

"I picked up something on that homicide, Lee," Murphy said. "And, I wanted to run it past you."

"You got any suspects?"

"Nope, and no witnesses either. That time of day, in that neighborhood, not too many people on the streets. But, we did find the victim's purse. It was in a trash bin a few blocks away, back toward Connecticut Avenue. We know it's hers because her work ID was in it along with her driver's license."

"I guess the mugger just took the money and decided to ditch the purse, eh?"

"That's just it," Murphy said. "I'm not sure it was a mugger. Her credit cards and fifty bucks cash were still in the damn thing."

Alarm bells went off in Kennedy's head. No mugger would have left the money and credit cards, and, if . . . he had to struggle to remember the victim's name; yes, Lesley Carter . . . if Carter wasn't robbed, that left a big question mark as to why she was killed. "Shit, you're right; it doesn't sound like a robbery. But, she was just a low level State Department employee. I don't think she'd even been in Washington all that long."

"That's what we heard from her neighbors when we canvassed the neighborhood. So, if she wasn't here long enough to piss somebody off in the area where she lived; and everyone we talked to said she was a quiet person who kept mostly to herself; that could mean it was someone connected with where she works."

Kennedy didn't like what he was hearing. A murderer inside the State Department; could that even be possible? The bureaucrats who inhabited the wandering, labyrinth of corridors that was the eight-story utilitarian looking building killed lots of trees with their meaningless memos, and killed lots of time with their endless meetings. But, he found it hard to believe that there could be anyone there who would actually kill another person.

"She hasn't been in Washington long enough to really make any enemies where she works either," he said.

Murphy took a sip of coffee. "I know it's hard to take. I'd feel the same if you told me we had a rogue cop in our midst; but, I been working homicide for ten years, and I've found that in most cases, the killer is someone well known to the victim."

"I know; I'm just having a hard time picturing anybody in that building as a murderer. I mean, man, this is the biggest bunch of pacifists and do-gooders you've ever seen in your life."

"Yeah, but I have to track down every lead." Kennedy nodded his understanding. "Problem is," Murphy continued. "That building, being a federal building and all, has all kinds of entry requirements, and I guess a big part of it is classified. I'm gonna need your help identifying people who had contact with the victim, and arranging interviews."

Kennedy knew that he was right. While most of the building was unclassified; they even conducted public tours several times a day, taking people to the eighth floor to see the collection of colonial-era antiques there; it had enough sensitive and classified areas to make allowing the public to wander the halls wasn't possible. He didn't relish the idea of having to get clearance for Murphy to come in and interview people either. The paperwork alone would take him days.

"Okay, Al; I'll get started first thing tomorrow. You know, there's likely to be some pretty senior people who had contact with her, so we'll have to handle this with kid gloves."

"Hey, buddy," Murphy said, laughing. "I've been a cop in this town a long time. I know the drill; the politicians think they're untouchable, and the senior bureaucrats *know* they are. I'll be as gentle with them as a mother rocking her baby to sleep at night – until I find the guilty one. Then, the son of a bitch gets the cuffs slapped on just like any other perp."

Kennedy laughed so hard he sputtered coffee across the table.

"And now," Murphy said. "Where's that doughnut Rachel promised me?"

Chapter 8

Alison was, by her usual standards, late arriving for work on Monday. It was nearly seven when she walked through the employee entrance on D Street, flashing her building pass at the security guard in front of the bank of glass doors.

Inside the building, she turned left and took the stairs down to the first floor, which on this side of the building was actually below ground, to the cafeteria, where she bought a large Styrofoam cup of coffee. She then went to the C Street side of the building's first floor to take the elevator up to her office.

Just as the elevator doors were about to close, a broad shouldered man with fairly close-cropped brown hair, and the bluest eyes Alison had ever seen on a man, slipped through. He nodded at her, his lips curling up slightly in a smile. Alison acknowledged his nod, but avoided too much direct eye contact. She watched him, though, out of the corner of her eye. His jacket was tight across the shoulder, but tapered toward the hips. A fine specimen, she thought, especially in a building of people that tended toward pear-shaped bodies.

The man reached up to the rows of buttons and pushed the one for the third floor. That reminded Alison of the note from Lesley Carter. She'd pushed the button for the seventh floor, but decided to get off on three and make another run at talking to Lesley.

The elevator stopped on the second floor, and several people got on, blocking Alison's view of the man. What she couldn't see was that he'd been looking at her out of the corner of his eye as well, and when the crowd came between them, blocking his view, his pleasant, noncommittal expression turned into a frown.

He was pleased, therefore, when the doors whispered open at the third floor, the good looking woman from the first floor got off as well. Lee Kennedy thought she was beautiful; not fashion model beautiful, or Playboy centerfold beautiful; just a simple, well-proportioned face, with a smooth flawless complexion, dark eyes that seemed to look right through you, and a figure that, while not exactly voluptuous, had the right amount of curves in all the right places.

Even better, when he turned and headed toward the Central Asia office, she went the same way. As they walked, they kept several feet of space between them, and looked straight ahead, walking in silence.

As they arrived at the office, Kennedy looked up, a bemused smile. He'd looked up the office location, and had found it funny that the Office of Central Asian Affairs, under which the Dagastan desk officer worked, was in the Bureau of European Affairs. Even after sixteen years, he didn't understand the rationale for the State Department's demarcation of the world's geographic and political regions.

Next to him, Alison Chambers noticed the smile, and looking up, saw that he'd been looking at the sign.

"Strange, isn't it?" she said, by way of breaking the silence.

"Yeah," he responded. "You'd think it would be part of Asian Affairs."

Alison shrugged. "Ours not to reason why. For the longest time, relations with the African countries were managed through the Bureau of European Affairs as well. I guess it's just a holdover from when the Europeans had most of the world colonized."

Kennedy laughed. Of course; and the blue bloods who dominated policy in the State

Department were, everyone knew, the most Eurocentric bunch in the world, so no surprise they'd think that way. He pushed the door open and waited for her to enter. The chair behind the reception desk was empty. The two of them stood there, waiting for the secretary to return.

"I'm Alison Chambers," she said. "I work in INR."

Kennedy stuck out his hand. "Lee Chambers, DSS. I'm the liaison with local law enforcement."

Alison liked the way he smiled when he introduced himself. She could feel her pulse quicken as his hand engulfed hers. "I haven't seen you in the building before."

"When I'm here, I don't get out of my office that much," he said. "The paperwork keeps me pretty much chained to my desk."

"Do you take your lunch in the cafeteria?"

"Not if I can help it. When the weather's good, I walk up to one of the places near the university."

She caught herself before she could do something stupid like inviting him to lunch. *Whoa, girl,* she thought, *you just met this guy, and he's probably married anyway.* She gently extricated her hand from his grip. "I know; the food downstairs could gag a maggot. I usually eat outside as well."

He cocked his head to one side, the smile on his face widening. She found herself hoping. But, her hopes were dashed by the return of the secretary; the same woman who'd been there on her previous visit. The woman gave her a blank look, but when she caught sight of Kennedy, her face brightened.

"Can I help you?" she said to Kennedy, completely ignoring Alison.

"This lady was here before me," he said. "You can help her first."

My, my, Alison thought; handsome, and a gentleman too; he must be married. The secretary frowned slightly, but turned to Alison, a half smile pasted on her face. "Yes, ma'am," she said. "How can I help you?"

"Is Lesley Carter in today?"

Kennedy stiffened at the sound of the desk officer's name.

"No, she didn't come in yet," the secretary said.

"You're looking for Lesley Carter?" Kennedy asked.

"Yes; she sent me a note last week, and I've been trying to follow up with her about it."

Alison could sense tension in Kennedy; his face had gone still, and he stood more erect.

"Uh, I think you and I need to talk," he said. "I was here to see her supervisor, but I think I should talk to you before I do."

Something about his voice raised alarms in Alison's mind. She opened her mouth to ask a question, but his stern expression caused her to immediately close it.

"We could go up to my office," she said.

"No; let's go outside the building," he said. He took her by the arm and guided her back out to the hallway.

The secretary watched them leave, a look of query on her thin face.

Kennedy walked close beside her to the elevator, and remained silent for the ride down to the first floor. He led her to the C Street doors and outside to the sidewalk. They walked in silence to Twenty-Third Street and he motioned left, south toward the Lincoln Memorial.

No words were spoken as they crossed Constitution Avenue and walked along the azalea lined street that led up to the high marble sides of the memorial to the sixteenth president. Kennedy led her around the front of the building to the base of the steps. Alison remembered this spot, twelve years earlier, shortly after she'd come to Washington, when Martin Luther King, Jr. had stood on those steps and told over 200,000 people about his 'dream.' Kennedy stopped, and looked around them.

"What's going on?" she asked.

He frowned as a noisy group of teenagers rushed past, jostling and shoving each other, and ignoring their adult guide who was trying to explain the history of the monument, which they were also ignoring.

"How well did you know Lesley Carter?" Kennedy asked her when the group was out of earshot.

"Not too well. I met her a couple of times; once at a meeting for female employees of the department, and once in the cafeteria, she was eating alone and I joined her. Why do you ask?"

He ignored her question, his eyes boring into her like two orbs of ice. "So, you don't know anyone in the building she might have had issues with?"

"No; like I told you, I only met her twice. I thought she was okay. She seemed to be a nice enough person; a bit driven; but, what Foreign Service Officer, especially a woman, isn't? She hasn't been here long enough to make any real enemies, and at her grade, she probably won't."

"Why did you go to see her?"

"I told you; she sent me a note. It was about

an incident in Dagastan, she . . . hey, wait; this is beginning to sound like an interrogation. What's this all about?"

Alison was familiar with the way DSS agents had acted during the McCarthy era, when the pugnacious senator had gone on a witch hunt to rout co-called Communists from the government, including the State Department. Her cheeks felt warm.

His expression softened somewhat. "Sorry if it comes off that way. I just need some answers. I promise you, I'll tell you what I can. Now, what was this note she sent you?"

"It was about some relative of the Dagastani leader being assassinated. Lesley said the embassy hadn't reported it, and she wanted to know if we had anything in INR."

"Funny that the embassy wouldn't do a report on something like that." He'd been in enough embassy assignments to know that embassy political officers would be all over an incident like this like flies on stinky cheese. "Did you ever find anything?"

"Yeah; the station did a report, but it was just a summary of local news; no real analysis. One of the guys who was killed was the cousin of the Dagastani First Secretary, a real tyrant. I can imagine this will have an impact on our relations with them in one way or another, so it's strange the embassy seems to be ignoring it.

I spoke with Whitman, the country director, but he just gave me the brush-off."

Kennedy cupped his chin in his hand and looked down at her. "What's your assessment of this Whitman?"

That one was easy. "A time-serving, careerist jerk; who is concerned only with what benefits him personally. When I asked him about it last week, he said Lesley had more important things to do. Funny, though; this is the second day in a row she hasn't been at work, and no one there seems the least bit concerned."

"You said Carter was a bit driven; do you think she was driven enough to keep digging in something her boss wasn't interested in?

"Just a guess, but probably. Say, you keep referring to her in the past tense . . . ," Then a thought hit her. "Oh my God, please don't tell me . . . she's not –"

"Afraid so. She was attacked near her house in Woodley Park last week. The cops thought it was a mugging at first, but they found her purse nearby Saturday, and it still had all her cash and credit cards. No mugger would have left stuff like that."

"You're saying . . . you . . . think . . . someone in the Department . . . killed her?"

"At this point, I'm not saying anything. The police are checking her neighborhood, but she hasn't lived there long. I'm helping them out by getting a list of people in the Department who knew her. You'll probably get a call from the cops to make a statement." She frowned. He held his hands up. "But, don't worry; you're not a suspect. They'll just want to ask you what you know about her."

The warmth was back in his voice now. She felt relieved that she'd passed muster, but a bit peeved that he'd suspected her in the first place.

"Why am I not a suspect? If she was killed by someone she works with, it could be me as much as anyone else."

"No," he said, laying a hand on her shoulder. "I have a sense for these things, and while you might be many things, Ms. Chambers, you're not a murderer."

"You seem pretty sure of your abilities. I bet you drive your wife crazy."

His face creased in a slight frown, but it only lasted for a heartbeat. He smiled down at her. "Actually, it drove her right out of the marriage. It's just me and my daughter, Rachel, now." He grinned, and his eyes twinkled. "What about you, you married?"

Alison's face colored. She could feel heat in her cheeks. "Uh, uh, well . . . no, as a matter of fact, I'm not."

"Good; then that means you're free to have dinner with me tonight."

"Is that ethical, I mean, can't you get in trouble becoming involved with the subject of an investigation?"

Kennedy laughed; a deep, throaty laugh that caused a tingling feeling in Alison's midsection. "Lady, the only investigation you're the subject of is how I managed to miss you in the building for the past year, and, the only trouble will be how I feel if you say no."

"Are you always this direct with women?"

In truth, he wasn't. In fact, he'd not dated for more than a year, and the last time had been a blind date arranged by a friend of his in his office and had been a disaster. There was, though, something about Alison Chambers that gave him the courage to venture into the uncharted territory of male-female relations. He just hoped it wouldn't be a disaster.

"I'll tell you the truth if you promise not to laugh."

She crossed her right index finger over her left breast, and then raised her hand to shoulder level. "Cross my heart and hope to die, stick a finger in my eye."

Kennedy laughed at her childish verse. He was feeling more drawn to her. "Okay, this is it; I haven't asked a woman out on a date since I asked my ex-wife out about fourteen years ago."

Alison started to laugh, and then caught herself, coughing to cover it. "You're kidding right? A good looking guy like you hasn't had a date in fourteen years?"

"Come on; I was married for a large part of the time. You promised you wouldn't laugh." He feigned a hurt expression. "Do you really think I'm good looking?"

"I didn't laugh. Well, I almost did, and I apologize; but, I just find it hard to believe, and, yes, I do think you're good looking."

He puffed out his chest and took her arm gently. "Well then, it was worth waiting for, I'd say."

Alison wasn't given to public displays of affection, but she allowed him to take her arm. She found herself beaming inside at the looks of envy she got from the women they passed.

She would have felt less comfortable had she noticed the thin man in black, standing in the grove of trees adjacent to Constitution Avenue, across the street from the Federal Reserve Building, who watched them cross the street with narrowed, cold, snakelike eyes.

Chapter 9

Monday, May 12, 1975, Dagastan

Morgan and Jeffers met in Morgan's office at 9:30. They sat in the corner, at the teak coffee table that was the only fancy furniture in Morgan's otherwise sparsely decorated office. His secretary had made a fresh pot of coffee and placed it, along with several cups, on the table. Their faces were serious as they sat across from each other sipping at the strong brew.

"Okay, boss," Jeffers said. "It looks like we got ourselves a situation here. What are we gonna do about it?"

What indeed, Morgan thought wryly. They hadn't mentioned what to do with rogue ambassadors in the short course the Foreign Service Institute in Rosslyn, Virginia, just across the Potomac River from Foggy Bottom, had taught to newly assigned deputy chiefs of mission. The course for new ambassadors, Morgan assumed, taught them the need for teamwork and keeping their subordinates informed, but Ellingsworth had apparently been sleeping through that lesson, for his clandestine meeting with the deputy head of the Dagastani Security Service was something that he definitely should have informed at least the RSO about, or even better the chief of station. Morgan had sent word to Raine that he needed to speak to him urgently, and was expecting him to join them at any minute.

"I frankly don't know, Pete," he said. "Until we know more, I don't think there's much we can do."

"I briefed Carlton yesterday like you told me to. He said he'd put feelers out among his sources, but not to expect much on such short notice."

"How did he react when you told him?"

"You'd think I'd just spit in his coffee. He was surprised, and not a little bit pissed."

That was reassuring and worrying at the same time. Morgan had been concerned that maybe the ambassador and the chief of station were conducting some kind of operation for which he hadn't been cleared. Problem was, if it went awry, his neck would still be on the block, and he was upset at the thought that Raine might blindside him. So, it was reassuring to know that his friend hadn't betrayed him.

But, if the ambassador was freelancing, it could be really troubling. Morgan had seen a number of senior officers like that during his career. So obsessed with establishing a personal reputation and getting promoted, they ignored basic rules of common sense. They were, too, lousy leaders; leaving their subordinates in the lurch, and not caring about the negative impact their behavior had on them. Ellingsworth was an arrogant ass; that had been established within days of his arrival at post, even before he'd presented his letter of credence to Dmitri Kovasc; but, Morgan hadn't reckoned he would be irresponsible as well.

"It's good to know he's not involved in whatever the ambassador's up to. I hope he can come up with something from his bag of intelligence tricks to help us avoid a catastrophe."

"I've had some troublesome senior officers over the years," Jeffers said, shaking his head. "I know having security guards hovering around can be a pain in the ass; but, I just wish people would understand we're doing it for their own good. This is just my second tour as RSO, and if something happens to the ambassador on my watch, my career's in the toilet. I'll be lucky they don't send me to some shithole to supervise the guards on the motor pool."

Morgan could sympathize with him. If Ellingsworth came to harm; despite it being of his own making; his own career would probably take a downward spiral as well. Deputy Chiefs of Mission were ostensibly in charge of internal management of the embassy, while the ambassador served as the external face of the U.S. Government, but, the DCM was also there to keep the ambassador out of trouble. It didn't matter that he had zero authority, if things went wrong, the system would come down on him like a bag of wet shit. He'd find himself suddenly unable to get the good assignments; consigned to taking a job in some back office somewhere in Washington, out of sight and out of mind when the plum jobs were given out. It wasn't for nothing that the number two job in the embassies had the highest failure rate of any job in the diplomatic service.

"Whatever happens," he said. "I'll do what I can to protect you."

"I appreciate that boss, but, I have a feeling if the shit hits the fan, you and me both are gonna be busy ducking flying turds."

They both laughed, but it was laughter without mirth; gallows humor.

Mary Sung stuck her head around the door frame, making a discrete coughing sound. "Dave, Carlton's here," she said. "Can I send him in?"

Morgan nodded. "Sure, Mary; and, hold all calls until you hear from me."

Carlton Raine eased past the tiny secretary, his wide shouldered frame filling the door. He had a scowl on his light brown face.

"Dave, Pete; sorry I'm late. I had some last minute traffic to deal with."

"Come on in, Blood," Morgan said. "We were just sitting here moaning over our situation. What can you tell us about what's going on?"

Raine walked over and sat in the empty chair next to Jeffers. He poured himself a cup of coffee and drained half the cup. After refilling it with the nearly black liquid, he leaned back in the chair and sighed.

"One of my sources in the Security Service got to me around midnight, and what he told me is not going to make your day," he said in his cultured southern accent. "Something's going on, and for the life of me, I can't make any sense of it."

"Well, don't keep it from us," Morgan said.

"For starters, the meeting Pete's guys saw wasn't the first time the ambassador's met with Dragov. The two of them have been meeting in various locations around town two or three times a week for the past two months."

"Shit," Morgan said. "Why in hell would he be doing that and not sharing it with me; or, with you for that matter. Aren't the security service guys part of your portfolio?"

"Yeah, I'm declared to them, but I don't have

much dealing with Dragov. My main contact is the director-general. I've only met Dragov once. A real snake, that one is. He turned me over to Karlov, the director-general, and I've not seen him since. Something strange is going on in the service. I called Karlov this morning; just to chat; and, I sort of dropped the news that I'd heard his boss was meeting with the ambassador. He might have been screwing me, but I don't think so; he knew nothing of it."

"You mean our ambassador's meeting with the deputy head of security, and his own people don't know what's going on?" Jeffers asked. His face had an expression of skeptical amazement. "I thought you spooks were supposed to know everything."

Raine's brow furrowed. "If I didn't know you better, Pete, I'd say you just used a racial slur."

Realizing his mistake, Jeffers' face reddened. "I, uh, you know . . . I mean –"

"Just pulling your leg, son," Raine said, laughing. "Had you going, though, didn't I?"

Morgan raised his hand. "Okay, guys; enough of the horsing around. We have a serious situation here. Come on, Blood, what *do* you know?"

"Not a hell of a lot, Dave, and some of what I know doesn't make a lot of sense." Raine took a sip of coffee, and made a face. "Damn! What does Mary put in this coffee; tastes like a mixture of battery acid and cleaning fluid." He put the cup down. "Look, my source tells me Dragov meets with Ellingsworth two, maybe three times a week. Each time in a different place; and it's just the two of them. Dragov has the place swept for bugs and then sends everyone away. They meet for about an hour each time."

"It'd be useful to know what they discuss," Jeffers said.

"Tell me about it. My guy did overhear scraps of conversation from the last meeting. He hung around just outside the door. But, it was only scraps, and it doesn't make a lot of sense."

David Morgan looked from one man to the other. "If scraps are all we have, we'll have to make do with that. What did your source hear?"

"He heard Dragov saying the pieces were all in place and the game would begin. The ambassador said something; he couldn't hear it all, but he heard the words 'white dragons.' Then, Dragov said something like 'it will be as I promised, you have that from the top.' That's it; my source got his ass away from the door when he heard footsteps approaching. Dragov's the kind to shoot anyone pissing him off on the spot."

Morgan's face was a study in concentration as he looked across the table. "Game pieces, white dragons; what the hell does it all mean? I'm assuming 'from the top' means from Kovasc himself, but what has he promised and to whom?"

"You got me. I have my analyst working on it, but it's got to compete with our top priority collection requirements. I sent a squib to Langley and asked them to see if they could make any sense of it."

"Do you think the White Dragons refer to the Chinese? Since the Communists finally won in Vietnam last year, relations between China and the Soviets have become a bit frosty. Looks like the North Vietnamese are leaning more toward Moscow than Beijing, and I imagine that's not making out Chinese friends happy."

"We're looking into that," Raine said. "The Kazbektuni and Khan here are closer to Chinese ethnically than they are to Russians, and everyone knows there's no love lost between them and the Rus. Could be the Chinese are stirring up trouble, but this doesn't seem like their style. I don't see what they have to gain."

"Well, if not the Chinese, who?"

"You can't ignore the Russians, Dave. Dagastan might be a part of the greater Soviet empire, but not everyone here is enamored of Ivan. Hell, even a lot of the ethnic Rus resent the way they get treated by Moscow."

"Chinese, Soviets; it could be either; but, why is our ambassador mixed up in it?"

"Yeah, that worries me. Oh, by the way, my guys back at Langley are telling me you guys in State have our own little drama going on. Your desk officer, Lesley Carter's her name, right? Well, she got herself killed a while back."

Morgan's brows lifted in surprise. "Lesley, killed? How?" There'd been no notification from the Bureau as he would have expected. "Was it an accident?"

"Hardly; a sharp object was thrust into her heart. Happened right near her house."

"A mugging?" Jeffers asked.

"That's what the cops thought at first," Raine said. "But, they found her purse later, and nothing of value had been removed. Looks like someone had it in for her."

"You're saying she was murdered in cold blood?" Morgan said.

"Looks that way. The DC cops are looking at the possibility that it was related to her work in the Department. What that means, I don't know." He turned to Jeffers. "You know a guy named Lee Kennedy?"

Jeffers nodded. "Not all that well, but I've run across him from time to time. He's an old DSS vet; why?"

"He's liaison with the cops on the case. Anyway, just telling you guys this so you're not surprised when you can't get anyone in Washington to give a rat's ass about our little problem out here."

Chapter 10

Tuesday, May 13, 1975, Washington, DC

Alison hadn't turned down Kennedy's invitation to dinner, but she hadn't been prepared to go anywhere with him on short notice, so she'd agreed to meet him the following day.

This had given her time to get her hair done and agonize over her wardrobe.

After work, she'd walked home to her little two-bedroom brick house located on a narrow side street between Twenty-Third and Whitehurst Freeway, near the George Washington University's sprawling campus. Built in the late 30s, the house had been owned by an elderly lady, the daughter of the original builder. Alison had bought it shortly after coming to work at the State Department; at a reasonable price because the old woman had decided she'd had enough of Washington's frigid winters and torrid summers, and planned to relocate to Florida, where the only thing she had to worry about was hurricane season.

The house was small, with a combination kitchen-dining nook, and the two bedrooms together were barely larger than her bedroom at her parent's home in Georgia, but it suited her. She often took her meals on a tray in the living room, a room at the front of the house with large plate glass doors looking out onto the brick-wall enclosed flagstone patio with little earthen circles cut out in which azaleas and other brilliantly flowering plants poked up through the black earth. A little pond, complete with lily pads, sat in the center of the patio, and when the weather was really nice, she'd eat sitting on one of the black wrought iron chairs that she kept on the patio.

Her bedroom was crowded with a double bed she'd bought to replace the rickety canopied bed the owner had left, a large dresser and a table with a large wood-framed mirror, that had been left as well, but she kept it as neat and organized as she did her files in the office.

The closet, opposite the room's only window, that had a view of her back yard, a square of hard packed earth where she kept her garbage bin, was small and jammed with her clothes. She kept both winter and summer clothing hanging because, except for the attic crawl space, which she avoided because of a dread of spiders and other insects, there was little space for storage.

Pawing through her things, she realized that

she had little that was suitable for socializing; because, since coming to Washington, DC, she'd done little socializing, so hadn't bought any of the type clothing her mother would call 'frillies.'

She finally settled on a tan blouse with a pixie collar and a dark brown skirt that stopped just below her knees. Standing in front of the mirror affixed to the closet door, she decided that the outfit set off her complexion, already tanning from walking to and from work every day, and showed off her legs, which she considered her best asset.

Kennedy had said he'd pick her up at seven. She was dressed and ready at six, and sat on the sofa in the living room for an hour, idly flipping through the *Washington Post*, and feeling like an adolescent about to go on her first date. In a way, she thought wryly, it was; she hadn't been out with a man for over a year. The last time had been a blind date arranged by one of the younger secretaries in INR; with a cousin of hers who was in town for the weekend. She laughed as she recalled it. The young man, only a few years older than her, was as clumsy as she knew she had been, and was in Washington for the first time from some small town in Iowa. At the end of a boring evening, he'd brought her home in a taxi, and walked her to her door. A clumsy effort to kiss her had caused them to bump noses, and after an even clumsier goodnight, interspersed with apologies for his forwardness, he'd left.

She was wondering if Kennedy would try to kiss her goodnight, when the doorbell rang.

As she reached the door, realizing that she'd rushed, Alison paused. *I don't want to look anxious,* she thought; *can't have him think I'm desperate or something.* She waited until her breathing was completely under control, and then opened the door.

Kennedy stood there, a goofy looking grin on his face. He was wearing dark brown slacks, a white shirt without tie, and a medium brown sports jacket. His hair had the spiky look of having just been wet and brushed down. "Wow!" he said. "You look great."

"You don't look too bad yourself," Alison said. "We almost have matching outfits."

His grin widened. "Yeah, ain't that something."

He stood there in the door, shuffling from one foot to the other.

"Oh, where are my manners," Alison said. "Would you like to come in for a minute?"

"Uh, sure, but only for a minute; I made reservations at Carlisle's, and they don't like to hold tables."

He walked in, looking around approvingly.

He noticed that her place was as big as the house he and Rachel shared. *Probably cost twice as much too; here in the District,* he thought. "You probably ought to get a light sweater, too," he said. "It can bet a little nippy at night this time of year."

"Yes, why don't you make yourself comfortable?" Alison indicated the small upholstered couch that sat facing the patio doors.

She then rushed off to the bedroom, coming back a few moments later with a pearl gray cashmere sweater over her arm. Kennedy was standing at the big glass double doors, looking out on the patio. "Nice view you have here," he said. "I wish I had a back yard like that."

"It's actually the front," she said. "My back's just packed dirt; I use it for storage space. You noticed how the steps up from the street curved around?"

The steep steps up from the sidewalk had made a dog leg left, he recalled. The place, with its high brick wall, made him think of some of the small houses he'd seen during his tour of duty as an ARSO in Amsterdam at the Consulate General there, but her house, as small as it was, was nearly twice the size of the dwellings he'd seen there.

"Ready?" he asked.

Alison nodded, and opened the door. She held it for him to exit, and then followed him out, pulling it shut firmly to engage the lock. When she turned, he'd already made the turn right, and was out of view behind the wall. She followed him down. He was standing next to a white Mustang with Virginia plates. He held the passenger side door for her.

"Nice car," she said, as she slid into the seat, holding the hem of her skirt to keep it from riding up.

Kennedy didn't miss the glimpse of tanned thigh as she'd grabbed the hem a fraction of a second too late. "Uh, yeah, thanks," he murmured, and it wasn't just her compliment on his car he was thanking her for.

Carlisle's was in Georgetown, south of M Street, in an area that was dominated by large buildings that looked like warehouses, which is in fact what most of them had been at one time, but the area was undergoing renovation, and most of them were now converted into condominiums or office space. Kennedy pulled into the underground parking garage in the building next door to the restaurant, and luckily, found a slot on the first level not too far from the entrance.

The restaurant was crowded, but they arrived five minutes before the time Kennedy had reserved, and only had to wait ten to be seated by a pimply faced boy with blonde hair that hung over his ears, both of which contained little gold rings. The large dining area was broken up by trellises at intervals with plastic ivy leaves and paper orchids, and was dimly lighted by faux torches set in sconces along the wall, and fake candles in chandeliers suspended from the dark wood ceiling. The waiter was dressed in a dark green two-piece outfit with a little pointed cap, like one of Robin Hood's merry men. Most of the men in the place were dressed in dark suits with ties, and the women wore a ton of jewelry and makeup. Alison felt conspicuous, but Kennedy didn't seem to notice as they followed the waiter to their table.

The boy took their drink orders; Kennedy ordered Brown Derby beer, while Alison asked for a glass of *Chenin Blanc*. She wasn't much of a wine drinker, and had no idea what it was, but had read about it in a magazine, and thought it sounded sophisticated. That Kennedy was unaffected by the tony atmosphere of the place impressed her. When the waiter brought their drinks and then took their food order, Kennedy deferred to her.

"I can eat just about anything," he said. "So, you decide."

He took a long swallow of the amber liquid that had been served in a large crystal mug.

In the dim light, Alison had to strain to read the Old English script on the menu, but finally managed to order fish and chips and fresh garden salad, which were the only dishes she recognized.

"Hope you don't mind," she said. "Some of the other dishes sounded a bit too exotic for my taste."

"It just so happens that fish and chips is one of my favorites," he said.

They sipped their drinks silently until the food was brought.

The fish had been breaded and fried until it was golden brown, and flaked easily when pierced by a fork, and the chips, the British word for French fries, were irregular pieces about two inches long each, and also fried to a crisp golden brown. The waiter also brought a bowl containing hot chunks of bread on the side.

As soon as the food was placed in front of them, they fell to eating. It was only when they were nearly half finished that Kennedy put his fork down and looked across the table at Alison.

His cheeks were flushed.

"Gosh, Alison," he said. "I'm acting like a real klutz, eating like there's no tomorrow. Not what you expected, I imagine, huh?"

Alison put her own fork down.

"Who am I to complain? I've been wolfing down my own food as well."

They laughed. Kennedy thought that he liked the sound of her laughter.

"Aren't we a pair? I don't know about you, but I feel like a kid on his first real date."

Alison's cheeks felt warm. "Funny you should mention that; so did I."

"Dang, we're both too old for that."

"Speak for yourself, buster. I'm not old."

"N-no, I didn't mean . . . I mean; you're a neat looking woman . . . aw, hell, you know what I mean."

Alison laughed again, and Kennedy felt his heart pounding. "Sorry, Lee. Yes, I know what you mean. And, like I said at the house, you're not too bad looking yourself; for an old man, that is."

The ice was broken. Suddenly, they both felt as comfortable with each other as if they'd been friends and companions for years. Kennedy found himself wondering if Rachel would like her.

The rest of the meal went slowly as conversation was interspersed between mouthfuls of food.

"Oh," Kennedy said. "There was something I meant to tell you earlier, and forgot. You know that girl who got herself killed, Lesley Carter? Well, I got a call from the RSO out in Kazbektun, and, I'm wondering if it might be related."

"How could something in Dagastan have anything to do with a crime here in Washington?"

"I don't know, just my cop instinct. Seems that the reason the embassy hasn't reported on that assassination is because the ambassador won't let them."

"That's odd."

"Even odder; the RSO, a guy named Pete Jeffers, told me in strictest confidence that the ambassador's been acting real strange."

Alison's eyebrows raised in a querying expression.

"He ditched his security detail," Kennedy continued. "And, they found out he's been having secret meetings with some high muckamuck in the local security service."

"Isn't that breaking some regulation?"

"Not really, at least, none that I know of. But, it's dangerous and pretty stupid. If the fool gets himself in trouble, or hurt, the RSO will take the fall for it. Jeffers is in a bind out there."

"Can't he appeal to the DCM? Or, maybe get someone here in Washington to do something?"

"The number two out there; he's also a pretty straight shooter, I served with him in Korea; hell, he's as much in the dark as Pete. Even the station chief's been kept out of the loop. No, the damned ambassador's freelancing, and none of them know what the hell he's up to. As far as getting someone back here to intervene, good luck with that. Ambassadors are pretty much sacred cows; representing the president like they do; and if you mess with one, you'd better have an ironclad case. Not too many bureaucrats in that building where we work have the balls to even try."

Alison shook her head. "I guess the old saying's right; before you complain, walk a mile in someone else's shoes. I still don't see how that relates to Lesley's death."

"Me neither," he said. "Pete mentioned one other thing; have you ever heard of the White Dragons?"

"No," she said, shaking her head. "What are they, some kind of gang?"

"Damned if I know, but somehow these White Dragons are involved in what the ambassador's doing. It does sound kind of like a gang, and I guess that's why my gut tells me the incident here and what's happening there might be related."

"A bit far-fetched if you ask me."

"You're probably right. Maybe my gut's reacting to being out with a beautiful woman, and it's not working right."

Now, Alison was blushing deeply. "I'll bet you say that to all the girls."

The rest of the evening proceeded along the same lines; little flirtations and unspoken promises between them as they finished off the food and ordered a second round of drinks.

It was after ten when they finally, by mutual consent, decided that the evening had reached its conclusion; not necessarily satisfactory, but not totally unsatisfying, and walked, shoulders brushing against each other lightly, back to the garage to retrieve Kennedy's car.

They didn't talk during the short drive from Georgetown back to Alison's house. The traffic was light, with only a few cars weaving drunkenly from lane to lane, or shooting through red lights; students on their way home after a mid-week night of carousing, or late workers who'd stopped for drinks before going home to their cozy homes in the suburbs.

Kennedy's mind was whirling. One part of him kept thinking about Lesley Carter's murder, and what could be behind it; another focused on the woman sitting in the seat beside him, wondering if the evening was the start of a more meaningful relationship; but, more importantly, and in some ways, more troubling; was he ready for it.

CHARLES RAY

Chapter 11

The street on which Alison's house sat was deserted when Kennedy turned onto it. The houses, some sitting right on the street like the buildings in many parts of Europe, were dark this time of night.

Kennedy pulled to a stop in front of the house, letting the engine run.

"Alison, I just want you to know, I had a great time tonight."

"So did I, Lee. I hope –"

"Can we do it again sometime?"

"I was just about to say the same thing myself," she said. In the glow from the dash panel lights, he could see the shy smile on her face.

He wanted nothing more than to lean over and kiss her, but something held him back. Don't rush things, he thought to himself.

"How about lunch tomorrow?"

"Great, as long as it's not in the cafeteria."

"Deal. I'll stop by your office around noon."

"Maybe we should meet downstairs by the employee entrance. No need for you to have to go through the hassle of our entrance procedures."

Kennedy nodded. He knew that Alison would be put through the same rigmarole if she came to his office. Despite both of them having the highest clearances, each office treated outsiders, who happened to work for the State Department, like potential criminals or spies. Foreign visitors and family members visiting employees found it easier to get into the building.

"Good point," he said. "See you at noon on the second floor. Any special kind of place you'd like to eat at?"

Alison didn't really care; she was only interested in seeing him again. "No, I'm pretty much okay with anything."

"Well, I guess I should say goodnight." He got out and walked around to the curb and opened the door for her. "I'll walk you to your door."

She laid a hand on his arm. "That's not necessary. You go on home; your daughter's probably up waiting for you."

Kennedy laughed gruffly. "She'd better not be; she has school in the morning. Okay, goodnight."

When she removed her hand from his arm and turned toward the steps, he could still feel the warmth. He stood at the car watching her mount the steps, noticing how nice her legs looked in the reflected glow of the street lamps, and hoping she wouldn't look back and see him ogling her.

Just before she reached the point where the steps turned, Kennedy noticed out of the corner of his eye, a slight movement in the dark foliage to the right of the steps. At first, he thought his eyes might be playing tricks on him, but as he looked, a darker shape began to form against the background of the large bushes fronting the wall around the house. Warning bells began going off in his brain, and he felt a tingling sensation at the base of his neck, as the dark shape began moving toward Alison.

The shadow began to take the shape of a slightly built man, a dark figure only just visible against the dark background. Then, Kennedy saw a glint midway down the length of the shape, the street light reflecting off something metal, and he instinctively knew what he was seeing.

"Alison," he yelled. "Look out behind you!"

Time seemed to slow as Kennedy yanked the door open and reached in to open the glove compartment. He removed the .38 caliber revolver, which was his service weapon, pulled it from the leather holster in which it was kept, and whirled around, raising it toward the dark shape. At his shout, Alison had turned around, looking in his direction. When she saw the dark shape at the bottom of the steps, she felt a stab of fear in the pit of her stomach. She could see the sharp glint of the knife in the figure's right hand. The man in black, stopped when he heard Kennedy's shout. His head swiveled slowly, taking in Kennedy crouched in a shooting position beside the Mustang, then he turned back to look up at Alison, who, having gotten over her initial shock, had removed her shoes and was now cocking her right hand back.

"Damn you; get away from me," she shouted, and let fly with the shoe.

Alison had played baseball with her cousins growing up, and didn't throw like a girl. Nor was her aim bad. The shoe caught the man in dark squarely in the chest, heel first, and while Alison didn't wear extremely high heels, the one-inch wooden heel of her shoe made an impact when it hit. The figure grunted in pain, and staggered backwards.

Kennedy meanwhile was moving to get a clear shot at the dark figure without risking a stray shot hitting Alison.

As Alison transferred her other shoe from

her left hand to her right, the man in black made a grunting noise and darted quickly into the dark foliage to his right. Kennedy rushed forward. The rustling sound of the fleeing man, and both of them had come to the conclusion that the figure was male, was fading.

Alison stood at the turn in the steps, holding her shoe, a wide-eyed look on her face. Kennedy ran up to her, grasping her gently by the shoulders.

"Are you okay?" he asked. There was no mistaking the concern in his voice.

Alison leaned her head into his shoulder. "I'm fine. I . . . what . . . the . . . hell . . . was . . . that –"

"I think that guy was planning to kill you."

"What . . . me . . . why?"

"I don't know. There's something going on that I don't understand. Look, it's not safe for you to be here alone tonight. He might come back."

"You can't leave your daughter alone tonight either," Alison said, although she would have welcomed him staying.

"You're right. So, let's go inside and you can get some things. You're coming home with me. I'm not letting you out of my sight until I figure out what the hell's going on."

Alison had been on her own since leaving home to attend college, but for once, she didn't feel all that independent. No one had ever tried to kill her before. Quietly, she accepted. After packing toiletries and a few changes of clothing into an overnight bag, she locked the front door and joined Kennedy in the Mustang.

Neither of them spoke during the drive to Kennedy's house in Arlington, lost in their own private thoughts.

Alison was wondering who would want to kill her, and why. Kennedy, too, was wondering the same thing, but a major part of his mind was wondering how he was going to explain Alison to Rachel.

Chapter 12

The man in black hadn't stopped running until he was four blocks away from Alison's street, and sure he wasn't being chased. He was winded, and felt a stitch in his side from the unaccustomed exertion, and a dull ache in the chest where the damned woman had hit him with a shoe.

Leaning against the corner of a building near Twenty-Third Street, catching his breath, the man cursed himself.

"A total fucking cock up," he murmured to himself. "Moved too fast; should have waited to make sure that fucker was in his car."

Nothing about the operation had gone right. The man not getting into the car right away, and then having a gun; the woman, standing her ground and attacking him by throwing a shoe instead of freezing in panic. Not like the other one, who had, in the last moment before he slipped the blade into her heart, had a resigned look on her face. That's the way it's supposed to be, he thought; the prey knows its time has come, and it accepts death meekly.

They're not supposed to fight back, dammit!

This, he knew, would be news that the man who had hired him would be unhappy to receive. As unhappy as he was to be delivering it. He'd never failed before. *Dammit*, he thought, *I haven't failed yet. The woman will die, and I think I'll throw that fucker with the gun in for free.*

Pushing away from the building, he walked until he spotted an empty phone booth. He entered the booth and lifting the receiver, fed coins into the slot. He then dialed the number he'd committed to memory.

"Yes, I take it the job is done?" a cultured voice answered after three rings.

"No," the man in black said. "She got away."

There was a long pause. "We're disappointed in you. How could this happen?"

"She had someone with her, and he was well-equipped."

He wanted to be specific, but there was no way of knowing that the phone at the other end wasn't being tapped. The verbal circumlocutions were an established part of his communications with the shadowy figure with the New England accent; a man he'd never seen; who called him from time to time to 'clean up a few messes.' He knew the man would understand that 'well-equipped' meant armed;

the man had established the code after all. The man in black thought it all childish, but they paid him well, fifty thousand for each 'job' wired to his Swiss bank account. So what if he had to play their little cloak and dagger game.

"It is imperative that this piece be removed from the board," the voice said. "We trust that you will rectify this mistake?"

The man in black hated the way this supercilious mother fucker always referred to himself as 'we,' but again, made no comment. The Golden Rule, he thought; the one with the gold makes the rules.

"Don't worry," he said. "It'll be done. I'll throw in the guy for free."

"No messes, you understand. We wouldn't like that."

"I said, don't worry. I'll get it done."

The man in black broke the connection and exited the phone booth. He patted his pocked. His weapon of choice, a switchblade knife with a five-inch blade, nestled against his thigh, was comforting. But, he knew, he'd need more than a knife to deal with the guy with the gun. *Never take a knife to a gunfight*, he thought.

As he walked, the man in black whistled, a doleful melody like a funeral march.

CHARLES RAY

Chapter 13

Wednesday, May 14, 1975, Dagastan

David Morgan glanced around the big oak conference table. The members of the embassy country team were assembled, all but its leader, the ambassador.

Ellingsworth did that at every one of the Wednesday morning country teams meetings; insisted that everyone be in place by half past seven, and then didn't appear himself until after eight, sometimes as late as eight-thirty. Morgan fumed inwardly each time, but had held his counsel. He kept reminding himself that Robert Ellingsworth was the Ambassador Plenipotentiary and Extraordinary, possessing a letter and certificate signed by the President of the United States attesting to said status, and had the authority to do just about anything he damn well pleased. It wasn't *right*, but it wasn't illegal, and with promotions riding on the all-important annual appraisals, none of the senior staff were about to make a fuss.

Morgan knew that the man just did it to show everyone who was in charge; not that he needed to do it; but he seemed to like doing it.

Morgan sat in the first chair on the right at the head of the long table; his rightful place as the embassy's number two. Arrayed around the table, more or less in order of their perceived importance in the embassy, were the chiefs of section and heads of agencies who made up what was known as the ambassador's country team; those people to whom he was supposed to turn for expert advice on the best way to carry out his mission of advancing American foreign policy and national interests in Dagastan.

Dennis Larson, a grade one officer who had actually been promoted before Morgan, was the political officer, and he sat next to Morgan. The slightly built man with dark wavy hair, and dark brown eyes, had a swarthy complexion courtesy of his maternal ancestors from southern Italy. He was an ambitious career-ladder-climber who, when someone in a superior position ordered, jump, usually asked 'how high?' as he left the ground. But, he was, Morgan had to concede, a loyal individual and a damn fine writer.

Next to Larson was Lieutenant Colonel Patrick Duggan, an army officer who served as the Defense Attaché. With twenty-two years of service, Duggan was in line for promotion to full bird colonel, and had taken the assignment to Dagastan in an effort to ensure that the promotion came through. A phlegmatic forty-eight year old, with bad knees from fifteen years as a paratrooper, he seldom smiled, and had never been known to tell a joke, or laugh at anyone else's efforts to be funny.

Cory Lane, the embassy public affairs officer, worked for the U.S. Information Agency, which overseas was known as the U.S. Information Service, the theory being that the agency's initials, USIA, was too associated with the dreaded CIA in people's minds. Although only in his early thirties, he was already a grade one officer, reflecting the more rapid promotions in his agency, and making him the target of envy of many of the State Department officers. He sat at the end of the table, next to Duggan, and made a deliberate show of ignoring the military man.

At the end of the table, directly under the gaze of the ambassador when he was present, sat Montgomery Cornelius, the embassy's administrative officer. A grade three specialist with twenty years of service, he was the only section chief who was not a full-fledged officer, the administrative career field not being considered 'really' diplomacy. In his mid-forties, Cornelius had a round face with perpetually reddened cheeks, and faded blue eyes that stared at the world through thick gold-rimmed spectacles. His light brown hair was thin on top of his round skull, giving him the look of a slightly rumpled and constantly perplexed professor.

The chair to his right, at the end of the far side of the table, was empty. This place was reserved for the dragon lady, Vera Cotton, the ambassador's secretary, who also took notes for the meetings. Her appearance was the signal that the ambassador was on his way, and everyone was to stand until he was seated.

The only woman in charge of anything at the embassy sat in the chair next to Cotton. Laura Pettigrew was head of the consular section. A slightly heavy woman with a round face, framed by dark brown hair that feathered at the ends, she had dark brown eyes that were always moist as if she was about to cry. Her doleful look, though, masked a personality that was as tough as tempered steel, forged from fifteen years of dealing with foreigners who sought entry into the United States by hook or by crook.

Carlton Raine, the chief of station, sat next to Pettigrew. As usual, his brown face betrayed nothing about what was going through his mind, although, he made discrete eye contact with Morgan from time to time.

The last man at the table, sitting directly across from Morgan, was Joseph Wade, the embassy's economic officer. Like Larson, he was a grade one officer, though only recently promoted. His six-six frame sat uncomfortably in the chair made for someone much shorter, and Morgan knew that his knees were wedged against the edge of the table. Ghoulishly thin, with a receding hairline that terminated in a widow's peak at the top of his narrow head, and looking over the tops of his bifocals, he looked like an economist who had wandered into the wrong classroom.

Morgan knew everyone around the table; except for Raine, Cotton, and the defense attaché, he did the performance reviews on them, so he had made it a point to get to know them and what motivated them. He visited each of them daily in their sections, listening to their gripes, giving them his interpretation of the ambassador's instructions, which were becoming increasingly erratic, and assuring them of his concern for them as individuals. This was something that had been stressed in the training for deputies, but something he would have done even without instruction, having learned it long before becoming a diplomat.

The room was silent, except for the occasional clearing of a throat. No friendly chatter. It had been different with the former ambassador. First, she was always on time, or early, for meetings, and she encouraged freewheeling discussion. Ellingsworth, on the other hand, preferred a quiet room; a room full of bobbing heads as he issued instructions. Ever since he'd arrived, a chill had descended over the embassy.

Morgan looked at his watch. It was ten past eight. Damn, he thought, the bastard plans to keep us sitting here until half past. He signed deeply, and then, the door swung open, and Vera Cotton made her regal appearance, the herald announcing the arrival of the king, except that, in the one piece black dress she wore, with her straw colored hair pulled back severely, and a sharp nose that turned downward over her thin lips, she looked like the broomstick-riding witch from *The Wizard of Oz*.

"Lady and gentlemen, the ambassador," she said, in the reedy, nasal voice that made Morgan's teeth tingle.

Everyone stood, Duggan at a military attention that would have looked good on a parade ground, but in the confines of the conference room, only looked like the parody Morgan knew it to be; the colonel hated the ambassador with a passion that could not be described in mere words.

Robert Ellingsworth, Ambassador of the United States of America to the Socialist Republic of Dagastan, dressed in his usual somber dark – today a very dark gray – suit, white shirt, and red tie, knotted perfectly with a little dimple under the knot, and black wingtip shoes shined to a high gloss, entered the room behind his hag-like secretary, his shoulders back, and his chin lifted like Caesar strutting into the forum.

Ellingsworth was a short man, just a shade over five feet. He had rounded shoulders and a sunken chest that sloped down to a volleyball gut. His round head and tiny, close-set eyes, sitting to either side of a slightly bulbous nose, along with the stringy look of his nondescript hair – which was either reddish brown or brownish red depending on how the light struck it – made him look like a dressed up garden gnome.

Like many men of short stature, who are aware of how they look in comparison to just about everyone they encounter, he compensated by being a completely arrogant, overbearing, bullying asshole. Making people await his arrival was just one of his little compensation techniques. The other was the way he offhandedly ignored the greetings of 'morning, Mr. Ambassador,' and 'good morning, sir' as he walked along the wall from the door to his seat at the far end of the room, or the way he regarded everyone with a cold gaze, standing beside his chair, knowing that they would remain standing until he sat.

After what seemed to be a longer than usual pause, Morgan thought, punctuated by the soft swishing sound of shoes scuffing against the carpeted floor of the conference room, or the quiet clearing of throats, Ellingsworth sat.

"You may take your seats," he said, in his high-pitched voice. "Mr. Morgan, would you care to start."

Ellingsworth never addressed anyone on the staff by their first name, and to everyone, he was 'Mr. Ambassador.' Morgan had been told that the relationships between many ambassadors and their number two were formal in public, but more relaxed in private. He hadn't found that to be the case with Robert Ellingsworth; even in the privacy of his office, on those rare occasions when he deigned to allow Morgan to enter, he remained stiffly formal.

Morgan would have preferred having the other members of the team to speak first, with him and the ambassador going last to sum things up, but Ellingsworth had his own way of doing things.

"Not much to report, sir," he said. "I'd like to recommend, though, that we start including the RSO in country team meetings."

Ellingsworth looked at him, his expression glacial. "For what earthly reason?"

Morgan cleared his throat and took a deep breath. "I just have a sense that the security situation here is becoming tense, and having the security perspective in our meetings might be useful."

"I completely agree," Duggan said. "My military contacts have been acting antsy lately.

Something's brewing, and having the RSO keeping us posted on the security situation from his perspective would be a great help."

Morgan appreciated the colonel's support, but found himself wishing the man had remained quiet. Duggan's dislike for the ambassador was, unfortunately, reciprocated in full. If Duggan thought it was a good idea, Ellingsworth was likely to veto it on general principle.

"I disagree," Ellingsworth said. "We don't need to clutter up this meeting with any more junior staff than necessary." He looked down the table at Cornelius, and then let his gaze drift to Pettigrew. Upon his arrival, he'd moved to exclude them from the country team meetings, only relenting when Morgan stood his ground and reminded him that the administrative and consular functions were the ones most likely to generate problems, and it would be extremely useful to have them at the meetings. Ellingsworth hadn't forgiven his deputy for what he viewed as an act of defiance, he just hadn't decided on the proper response. "No, the RSO will not be included in our meetings."

"I think that's a mistake," Carlton Raine said. He seldom spoke out in meetings. But, his expression now was firm, as he looked down the table at Ellingsworth. "I'm getting hints of trouble brewing as well. If the lid blows off, it would be useful to know about it just before it blows, not as it's crashing down on our heads. Pete Jeffers and his crew have excellent contacts among the local police and could be our early warning."

Raine was the only person present, other than the defense attaché, who could defy Ellingsworth without immediately endangering their careers. They could, if he so decided, be removed from country, but even Ellingsworth was reluctant to take such a step, as it would impact negatively on his relationship with their home agencies, and would be seen in the corridors of power in the State Department as a kind of failure. Ellingsworth disliked Raine only slightly less than the army officer. As he looked at Raine, his puffy cheeks reddened, increasing the garden gnome resemblance.

"I . . . have . . . made . . . up . . . my . . . mind," he said. "The RSO will *not* be included in these meetings. Do you have something else, Mr. Morgan; hopefully something useful?"

Feeling like a whipped dog, Morgan shook his head. That was another thing he really disliked about Ellingsworth; the man's habit of debasing people in front of others.

"Very well, then," Ellingsworth continued. "Does anyone else have any pearls of wisdom to offer? No? I didn't think so." Cotton was scribbling away on the legal pad she brought to meetings. "You are of course right." He glanced disdainfully at both Duggan and Raine. "There are things happening in Dagastan at the moment; things that you can't hardly appreciate. My instructions to each of you are simple: keep your ears and eyes open, and inform me of anything new or out of the ordinary immediately."

"Should we be reporting this to Washington, sir?" Dennis Larson asked; a hopeful look in his eyes.

Ellingsworth regarded the hapless political officer with a patronizing sneer. "Not yet; Mr. Larson, not yet; still your eager writing finger until I tell you it's time to report something. It wouldn't look good for us to be reporting information before we fully understand the import of it."

Raine made a low snorting sound, looking down at the table top. Ellingsworth shot him an angry glare.

"You have something to add, Mr. Raine?"

"No, Mr. Ambassador," Raine said evenly. "Not a thing."

"Well, in that case," Ellingsworth said. "I guess this meeting is at an end."

He stood, and so did everyone else. As he slid out of his chair and started making his way around the table, Morgan followed him. He signaled Larson to hold the others there; they would hold a proper country team meeting as soon as the ambassador was out of earshot. Usually, Morgan conducted them, but he had a more urgent errand on this morning.

The short man was several feet down the hallway in the direction of his office, when Morgan turned the corner behind him.

"Mr. Ambassador," he called. "I need to speak with you."

Ellingsworth turned; a look of annoyance on his face. "Whatever for, Mr. Morgan? You had a chance to bring up whatever is on your mind in the meeting."

Vera Cotton hovered protectively between Morgan and her boss.

"This is a private matter, sir."

"The ambassador is quite busy this morning," Cotton said. "Perhaps I can arrange an appointment for some time this afternoon?"

"This is urgent, and can't wait."

"Very well, then, Morgan," Ellingsworth said. "We'll go to my office, but, I warn you, don't waste my time."

Morgan followed him, past the spacious outer office where Cotton sat, and into his inner sanctum. His desk, a large oak executive desk with rounded corners, sat in the far corner, flanked by to large, low vases containing lush palm ferns that had the effect of obscuring Ellingsworth from view unless one was standing directly in front of him. In the corner nearest the door, were a French provincial sofa, two matching chairs, and a teak coffee table. Here was where Ellingsworth held court when he had visitors.

Without waiting for Morgan, Ellingsworth took a seat on the sofa, sitting in the center, and looking up, his close-set eyes narrowed.

Morgan sat in the chair more directly opposite him.

"Okay, Mr. Morgan, what's on your mind?"

Morgan decided that his career was probably going to take a hit from this little martinet anyway, so he might as well plunge right in. "It's your analysis of the current situation, sir. I think you're maybe misreading things, and that we need to take a few more precautions."

Ellingsworth closed his eyes to narrow slits and pursed his lips. "You obviously weren't listening at the meeting just concluded, Mr. Morgan. In the first place, I do . . . not . . . misread things. And, secondly, I think I made myself clear; we will continue to do things as we've always done them. There is no need for any special measures."

"But, sir; the assassination of the First Secretary's cousin; surely that signals something happening in the government. We should really look into that."

"That was merely an unfortunate incident, and one that I don't think we should squander the embassy's meager reporting resources on. There's nothing there to look into."

Morgan knew that he was on shaky ground confronting the man, but he couldn't believe what he was hearing. "I respectfully disagree, sir."

Ellingsworth laughed mirthlessly. "Whenever a subordinate says that he 'respectfully' disagrees, it seems he always proceeds to be disrespectful. Correct me if I'm wrong, Mr. Morgan, but you recently applied for consideration for promotion into the senior service, right?"

"Yes, sir," Morgan said, nodding. "But, what does that have to do with our situation here?"

"Perhaps everything. My assessment of your potential will carry significant weight with the board when it meets this summer. It wouldn't look good for you should I have to say that you lack loyalty to your superiors, now would it?"

You son of a bitch, Morgan thought. "I'm not being disloyal, sir. In fact, I believe I'm doing my duty. If I think a course of action is incorrect,

I'd be derelict in my duty not to point it out."

"Very well then; you've pointed it out. Now, my instructions still stand. We will *not* waste time investigating the unfortunate incident involving the First Secretary's cousin, and we will *not* change the embassy's security policy. Have I made myself clear?"

"Crystal, sir. If I may, though, I do have one other question?"

"Okay, but make it brief. You've wasted enough of my time as it is."

"What or who are the White Dragons?"

Ellingsworth's eyes widened. His face paled. "W-where did you hear of that?"

Got you, you bastard; you know something about it. Morgan could tell from the stiffness of Ellingsworth's posture that the name meant something. "It doesn't really matter, sir. Let's just say that it came to me from a reliable source; the same source who informed me that you've been meeting regularly with Milosevic Dragov. Is there some reason that you've never shared that with me?"

Ellingsworth took several deep breaths to compose himself. "Mr. Morgan, you are sticking your nose into matters that do not concern you, and that you could not possibly understand. I strongly advise you to forget you ever heard the term 'White Dragons,' and as for my meetings, if you're prying into my affairs, you will cease immediately."

"Mr. Ambassador; your safety and the security of this mission are my concerns. If there is something going on, I think I should know about it."

"Drop it; I don't want to hear another word about any of this."

"Okay, sir; you're the boss. If that's the way you want it to be, so be it. My apologies if I upset you."

Ellingsworth nodded. "Is there anything else?"

"No, sir, not a thing," Morgan said.

He rose and left, leaving Ellingsworth sitting on the sofa glaring at his back. David Morgan had no intention of leaving anything alone. There was something going on, and his instincts told him it wasn't good. If it was the last thing he did in his career, he intended to get to the bottom of it.

Chapter 14

Wednesday, May 14, 1975, Washington, DC

To Kennedy's surprise, Rachel was not at all put out by his bringing Alison Chambers home. The two, in fact, hit it off immediately.

While he got blankets from the closet to make his bed on the sofa; and, he had to convince Alison that it wasn't him being a gentleman, but because if he slept in the living room he'd be more able to protect them if the assailant had managed to follow them and made another attempt. This, of course, prompted a flood of questions from Rachel, who wanted to know what they'd done on a date to cause someone to attack them. Kennedy gave her a sanitized version, converting the man in black to a common mugger. Her wry look as he related the quickly improvised details of the night's events told him that she didn't believe any of it, but she simply smiled.

Alison slept fitfully, partly, a reaction to someone trying to kill her, partly from guilt at evicting Kennedy from his own bed.

Her guilt was compounded the following morning when the smell of bacon frying woke her.

She went into the bathroom and brushed her teeth, splashed cold water on her face, and then ran a brush through her tousled hair. She then padded into the kitchen, where she found Kennedy pouring little circles of batter into a large skillet.

"Are you making pancakes?"

"Yeah; Rachel loves 'em. I like to get up early and fix breakfast for her before she leaves for school."

Alison found herself warming to him all over again. Despite his gruff exterior, she could detect warmth at his core. He clearly adored his daughter, and Allison had learned from the conversation she had with Rachel until nearly one in the morning, it was a love that was reciprocated.

"You amaze me. A tough cop who can also cook. Do you have any more secret abilities?"

He smiled at her as he idly flipped the saucer-sized ovals that had browned on the bottom. "Well, let's see; I can leap tall buildings in a single bound, I'm faster than a speeding locomotive, and I make a mean hash brown potato."

Alison laughed. Despite the events of the

preceding evening, she felt comfortable and safe here. She hadn't thought about it much before, but she also felt a sense of belonging, a feeling of warmth unlike anything she'd felt since leaving home. An analytical person by nature, she quickly ran this confusion through the logical filters of her mind, and just as quickly came to the conclusion that what she felt was a sense of not being alone; she'd not thought of herself as lonely, but being here, so close to a close-knit family group, she realized that she had been.

"My super hero; what's your weakness?"

"Up to now, I would have said I didn't have one," he said. He looked at her, his eyes bearing an expression that she couldn't read. "Now, I'm not so sure."

She could feel a warmth, in her cheeks and elsewhere. She knew she was blushing.

"Uh, I think I'd better get cleaned up and ready for work."

"Don't dawdle," he said, laughing. "These flap jacks don't last long once Rachel gets at 'em."

Had Alison's extrasensory perception matched her ability to analyze things logically, she would have seen that Kennedy's inner feelings were similar to her own. He hadn't felt anything toward a woman since receiving the telegram informing him nonchalantly that his former wife, Michelle, was leaving him. At that time, he'd been conflicted. For the fourteen years of their marriage, he'd loved Michelle unconditionally, and had assumed that she felt the same. His frequent postings to places where family members weren't allowed, he'd taken as part of the career he'd chosen, a career he'd been in when they married, and thought she understood and felt the same. The sense of loss that hit him as he read her telegram – and, he thought, what kind of person sends a 'Dear John' letter by telegram? – was like nothing he'd ever experienced. Her abandonment left an empty place in his heart, a void that was only partly filled by Rachel, that he thought would never be filled again. Now, as he stood at the stove, sliding the cooked pancakes into three plates, he felt a warm glow. It was nice that Alison and Rachel had hit it off, and he sensed a degree of sexual tension between Alison and himself. She was a bit withdrawn and hesitant, as was he. But, his mind played with the possibilities of something developing.

Before he could pursue the relationship, though, he had to make sure he could keep her alive.

Breakfast, with the three of them sitting around the tiny table in his dining nook, was a pleasant affair. Rachel kept up an endless chatter, asking Alison about her job, where she grew up, and regaling them with tales of the kids in her class at the junior high school she attended.

Afterwards, Alison helped him wash the dishes and clean the kitchen while Rachel got ready for school.

They piled into his car and he dropped Rachel at the school, which was on Washington Boulevard, and then drove across the Roosevelt Bridge to the District. Kennedy was fortunate that his DSS position entitled him to parking space in the State Department's underground garage, although it was halfway across the building from the elevators.

He and Alison rode in silence to her floor. He got out of the elevator with her.   "Do me a favor," he said. "Unless you absolutely have to, stay in your office, but under no circumstances leave the building without me."

She smiled and laid a hand on his arm. "You surely don't think someone in the building would try to harm me, do you?"

"I don't know what to think. Something's going on, and until we get to the bottom of it, you need to take extra precautions. I think after work today, we should stop at our place and pick up whatever you might need."

"Wha-,"

"That's right; you're staying with me until I know you're safe."

"But, Lee, are you sure that's a good idea? I mean, I don't want to impose on you and Rachel."

"You're not imposing. Besides, Rachel likes you." She started to open her mouth, but he held up his hand, shushing her. "Not another word. You're not getting killed on my watch, so there. Now, I've got to get to my office. I completely forgot to call Al Murphy to inform him about last night; he'll be pissed at me about that."

"Murphy; that's the policeman you work with?"

"Yeah, and he'll probably want to talk to you about it as well."

A worried look caused Alison's brow to wrinkle. "Lee, this might sound crazy, but you don't think last night's incident has anything to do with Lesley's murder, do you?"

"Probably not, but best not to take chances. Now, you get on to work; see you at lunch?"

"Yes, sir," she said, smiling broadly at him as she gave him a mock salute. "You're the boss."

"And, don't you forget it."

He watched until she was behind the cipher-lock door before turning and going to his own office. Once inside, he dialed Murphy's number.

When the policeman answered, he gave him a summary of the incident of the previous evening.

"You sure the guy was going after her?" Murphy asked when he'd finished.

"Yeah, I'm sure. He was waiting in the bushes near her steps."

"Might have just been a mugger."

"Al, the guy had a knife, and he was dressed all in black. That sound like a garden variety mugger to you?"

"Hey, this is the District; anything's possible in this town. Maybe it's a mugger with fashion sense. Why would someone want to go after this Chambers woman?"

"Beats the shit out of me; but then, why would somebody want to knife Lesley Carter?"

"Good point. You know, when we found the purse, and it was pretty clear it wasn't a robbery; I was thinking maybe a jealous lover or something. But, the ME says she had a single stab wound, and it was precisely placed to penetrate her aorta. It if had been a crime of passion, there would have been more wounds. Whoever killed her was good at what he did – a real pro with a blade."

"The guy last night; he was holding the knife down along his leg, like he knew how to use it."

"Aw, come on; you're not saying you think it was the same guy?"

"Dammit, Al; I'm not sure what I'm saying. I just know some asshole tried to kill Alison last night. I don't know why, but I'm not resting until I find out, and nail him."

"Alison, eh? Sounds like our Miss Chambers is more than just a name on a file to you, my friend. Getting a bit sweet on her, are we?"

Kennedy cleared his throat. "Maybe, maybe not; oh hell, yeah, I kinda like her. She's a real sweet woman, and smart as a whip. But, it wouldn't matter, Al; when I became a DS agent, I took an oath to protect the people of this department along with the one about protecting and defending the Constitution. I don't plan on letting anything happen to her."

"Okay, bucko, I got you. I'd like it if you could arrange for me to talk to her, though. Get her version of what happened, and maybe a description. She might have seen something you missed."

"You got it. I'll also be sending you a list of names of the people who knew or had contact with Lesley Carter sometime today. You want me to arrange interviews with them as well?"

"Be nice if you would," Murphy said.

Chapter 15

In her office, Alison opened the safe and her filing cabinet, and, sitting at her desk, began making notes of everything she knew about Dagastan.

She began with a history of the tiny, landlocked country, its history, inhabitants, and geography. Nothing particularly remarkable there. During the time of the Russian czars, it had been a backwater kingdom, ruled by a prince who was related to the Russian royal house. After the October Revolution, the Communists, a small minority of the country, mainly ethnic Rus, had overthrown the prince and established a centrally-controlled state on the Soviet model and thrown their lot in with the new rulers of what was to become the Soviet Union.

Possessing no known resources of value to the soviet state, a small population, and having had little contact with the outside world, it was seldom given much thought by anyone, soviet or otherwise. As an 'independent' country, however, it had received ambassadors from many Western countries, including the United States, the United Kingdom, and the Federal Republic of Germany, all countries with contentious relations with Moscow. With few resources, and a national budget that could barely support its own people, it sent out few ambassadors itself, so relations were mostly one-way.

Most of the information Alison found consisted of single-page information sheets, prepared almost as an afterthought by researchers doing analyses of the Soviet Union, always the last page of whatever study she read. Dagastan was, to all intents and purposes, an insignificant backwater; a country that wasn't important to anyone.

There was, she felt, something missing. Most of the information she found readily available was five or more years old. She needed more current information, and recent reporting from the American embassy in the capital, Kazbektun, wasn't very helpful.

She went out to the bank of cabinets containing the central files for the region, and looked for the biographic summaries of important political and military figures. It took some searching, but she finally found three folders marked DAGASTAN-BIOS, and took them back to her office.

The top folder contained the brief biography

of Dmitri Kovasc, the mercurial first secretary of Dagastan's Communist Party. Kovasc, a Rus whose father had been a minor functionary in the party, had surprise everyone and joined the security service after completing his studies in philosophy and religion in Russia at Moscow University. He'd risen quickly through the ranks, and thanks to a series of timely, and some speculated, well-arranged, accidents, had within ten years become the director of state security. In 1968, he'd engineered a palace coup against then first secretary Vladimir Renkov, and replaced him at the top of the Dagastan pecking order, a position he'd held onto, again, the writer of his biography surmised, through a series of 'accidents' that removed any likely rivals for power. Kovasc was thought to be strongly pro-Soviet in his loyalties.

Vasily Shermov's biography listed him as the number three official in the bureau of economic planning, the agency responsible for control of Dagastan's moribund economy. Little was known of him, other than that he'd received a degree in metallurgical engineering from Kim Il Sung University in Pyongyang, North Korea, and that he was rumored to be Kovasc's first cousin on his mother's side of the family, and fiercely loyal to him.

The biography on Milosevic Dragov was the scantiest, consisting of a half-sheet. He was thought to be of mixed ethnicity with a Rus father and a Kazbektuni mother. He'd joined the security service after finishing high school and risen steadily through the ranks, finally being appointed deputy director by Kovasc when he took power in 1968. Rarely seen in public, little was known of his background or political loyalties.

Alison hadn't worked on Dagastani politics much, and she found it strange that even such a small country would have such a scanty file of biographical reporting. In fact, she found it strange *because* the country was so small. In most of the smaller nations, embassy people often knew just about everyone in government and politics, and, tended to clog the system with reports on everything from political affiliation to pet's names. Dagastan, she thought, must be a real backwater for there to be so little reporting.

Stranger still to her, though, was the fact that the embassy had not reported on the assassination of a relative of the top man in the country. Such an incident could have repercussions, and most embassies would want to have their backsides covered should something happen.

Her analyst's sense of filling in all the blanks, and understanding the meaning of events, along with an innate curiosity, compelled Alison to dig deeper into what was going on.

She put a sheet of paper into her typewriter and drafted a quick cable draft for the embassy, asking for information on the Shermov incident. She got up and took her draft to Earline, the secretary, asking her to prepare it in final form for transmission.

She then went back to her office and began working on her other projects; unaware of the wheels she'd just set into motion.

CHARLES RAY

Chapter 16

After getting off the phone with Murphy, Kennedy took a chance that Pete Jeffers might still be in his office at the embassy in Kazbektun. It took a while for the call to go through Dagastan's antiquated switching system, but the younger agent's voice finally came over the line obscured only a little by static.

"RSO's office, Jeffers speaking."

Kennedy identified himself and filled Jeffers in on what had been happening in Washington.

"Shit, Lee," Jeffers said when he heard of the attack on the INR analyst. "You think there's any connection between what's happening there and the shit going on out here?"

"I don't know, bubba; but, you need to keep your head down. Who you got out there you can trust?"

"Dave Morgan, the DCM's a righteous guy, and my security office employees; other than that, I'm not sure."

"What about the agency guy?"

"Guy named Raine, Blood Raine; can you believe it? I don't know, Lee. Sometimes he seems like an okay fella, then at other times . . . well, I just don't see how the ambassador can be moving around like he does and the spooks don't know anything about it."

"Well, you keep your head down. One other thing, Pete; could you quietly provide me the details on that assassination? I have a feeling it's somehow the key to what's going on."

Jeffers was silent for a while. "Yeah, I think I could probably do that. The ambassador's been pretty firm about it not being reported, but, he never reads my stuff, so I could bury it in a long and boring security report."

Kennedy laughed. "Okay, you do that. Get it to me as soon as you can."

He rang off, and as he did, he sensed that he wasn't alone in his office. He looked up to see Melvin Broadbent, a senior DSS agent who was in charge of overall security for the building, and basically his superior, standing in the door. He had a frown on his vulpine face.

"That Jeffers out in Dagastan you were just talking to?"

"Yeah, it was."

"Mind telling me what you two were talking

about?"

He did mind; in fact, he resented the senior agent's tone, and was curious as to why he'd want to know. It wasn't normal to monitor or ask about another agent's phone calls like this.

"Just some routine security stuff."

Broadbent's eyes narrowed to slits. "Why would you be discussing security with the RSO at a post? You're responsible for liaison with the local police."

The hairs on the base of Kennedy's neck tingled. He'd been in enough hairy situations to recognize that his subconscious sensed danger; just what it was he couldn't know, but common sense said he had to play things close to his vest until he knew more. "Pete was friends with the woman who was killed, Lesley Carter, and I was just updating him on the investigation."

Broadbent walked into the office, close to Kennedy's desk. He leaned forward, supporting his weight on his hands, and looking down at Kennedy with his thin lips pursed.

"I heard you say something about an assassination; why should that concern you?"

Clearly the man had been eavesdropping longer than Kennedy knew, so lying probably wouldn't work. "Yeah, the embassy hasn't done a report on it, and Carter, the desk officer, was working on it when she was killed."

Broadbent laughed. "She was killed her in DC, and some insignificant official gets himself killed halfway around the world; why would you think they're related?"

For one thing, you asshole, Kennedy thought, because you just made the connection. "It's probably not connected," he said. "But, my local cop connection asked me to run down anything she might have been doing just before she was killed, and this was one."

"Well, events in Dagastan are of no concern to a DC cop, or you either for that matter, so stand down."

"Huh? What the hell do you mean, stand down?"

"Just what I said, Kennedy, leave it alone. The ambassador out there's decided not to bother with it, and there's no reason for us to."

"The ambassador has his reasons for what he's doing; I don't know what they are, and frankly, I don't give a damn. My job is to help the police investigate the murder of a State Department employee, and to do that, I need to track down every lead, no matter how tenuous it might seem."

"I don't think you heard me clearly, agent," Broadbent said. There was ice in his voice. "You are to leave this issue alone."

"Sorry, but I don't think I can do that."

"I just gave you an order."

"One that you have no authority to give. My job description says that I'll cooperate with local law enforcement to the fullest, and I plan to do just that."

Broadbent raised a bony finger and waved it in Kennedy's face. "You're making a mistake. You don't know what or who you're dealing with."

Kennedy could feel his anger rising. "I know exactly what and who I'm dealing with," he said. "I'm dealing with a bunch of pussy bureaucrats who're afraid of their shadows, and whose main mission seems to be to cover their asses. Well, I have a job to do and, if you're not good with that, then fuck you."

Broadbent's face went red, and his thin lips opened and closed. "How dare you! You can't talk to me like that; I'm senior to you. I'll report you to the assistant secretary."

"Report me; I don't really give a damn. Now, get the fuck out of my office before I throw your bony ass out."

Kennedy stood. He was Broadbent's height, but wider in the shoulders, and, as he leaned forward, Broadbent backpedaled toward the door, his face now going pale.

After the man had gone, Kennedy sat at his desk and brooded. There was something about what was happening that smelled like three-day-old fish wrapped in newspaper. Too many people were telling too many other people to ignore an incident that, while not important on a global scale, was nonetheless an incident worthy of paying some attention to. In his time with the Diplomatic Security Service, Kennedy had seen people try to step on reporting; but, it was usually something that impacted on some sacred cow, like a report criticizing a government that some senior official wanted to make nice to. But, this didn't seem to fall under that category.

The death of a desk officer who had inquired about the incident; the attack on Alison after she began looking into it; and, now, him being given orders to leave the incident alone; Kennedy didn't believe in coincidences. Things happened for a reason, and when you had three situations, all connected by the same factor, then, that factor was important.

He didn't know what he would, should, could do next, but knew that do something he must. He was also aware that whatever he did would have repercussions; professionally and personally. Pissing off the people above you in the pecking order by ignoring their orders, he knew, was never a good career move.

On the other hand, if Alison was harmed, and he could have done something to prevent it, he knew he couldn't live with himself.

THE WHITE DRAGONS

CHARLES RAY

Chapter 17

Saturday, May 17, 1975, Dagastan

Morgan liked coming into his office on Saturdays. Except for the Marine on duty at Post One, the security guards at the gate, and one or two workaholics who had nothing else to do on weekends, the place was quiet, giving him time to go over paperwork and plan the week to come. A bachelor, he had nothing to do at home but sit around and read, so he'd decided early on in his tour that even though it set a bad precedent for his subordinates to see the boss working on Saturday, he might as well make productive use of his time.

The only drawback of working on weekends was that he never insisted that Mary Sung, his secretary, also come in, in fact, he had ordered her not to unless there was an emergency requiring her special skills; something that had never happened. Being alone in the front office meant he had to brew his own coffee, a skill he'd never quite mastered. What he brewed could be drunk, but it was like drinking brake fluid compared to her coffee. He was staring down at a cup of the coffee he'd brewed upon arriving, debating whether or not to drink it, when Montgomery Cornelius rapped on his door, and stuck his head in.

"Hey, Dave," he said. "You busy?"

Morgan waved the administrative officer in. "No, Monty; just sitting here debating whether to inflict pain on my stomach with this gunk I brewed. What's up?"

Cornelius ambled into the office and straddled the chair sitting next to Morgan's desk. "I was just in going over reports from the warehouse, and I got tired of looking at rows of numbers. I knew you'd be here, so I thought I'd pop in just to shoot the bull."

Morgan knew that Cornelius wasn't the type to 'shoot the bull.' He was probably one of the most dedicated officers in the embassy, but he was also humorless. He had something on his mind, and Morgan intuited that it was serious, but of a such a nature the man couldn't approach it directly. He decided to play along.

"I know what you mean. I was sitting here staring at the list of reports we're required to submit, and wondering how to do it with the small number of reporting officers we have. It's a losing battle. We put some things on the shelf to meet rush deadlines on one bunch of reports, and then take it in the shorts for the things we didn't do. I could use a break, frankly. What's on your mind?"

Cornelius draped his arms over the back of the chair and rested his chin on them. He had a doleful look in his eyes. "Well, I was also looking at the motor pool reports; you know, we've been hit with a cut in funds for fuel, and I have to watch vehicle use carefully. Anyway, I noticed some oddities in vehicle usage."

"Someone on the staff misusing vehicles?" Morgan knew that from time to time, people would use embassy vehicles for social trips because most of them hadn't shipped a car of their own. He'd signed a memo forbidding such unofficial use without prior approval, and with appropriate payment for personal use, the previous month.

"No, no, nothing like that at all; the staff's been going through the dispatcher and making payments for personal use." Cornelius took a folded sheet from his jacket and spread it on the desk. He ran a finger down the rows and columns of crabbed writing. "This is about the ambassador's use of his official vehicle. Now, I know he has the right to use his vehicle anytime, unlike the rest of us . . . and, I wasn't looking for anything . . . in fact, I missed it at first. But, something about the entries caught my eye."

Morgan leaned forward, his brow furrowed with impatience.

"Okay," Cornelius continued. "It's this. His driver has been filling out his trip log and turning it in every week, just as he's supposed to. And, for the past month, the ambassador has been making some strange trips."

"What makes you call them strange, Monty?"

"Well, for starters, there's one or two; sometimes three; trips per week, when the driver drops him off at a location, and then picks him up about two hours later. I know some of these addresses; they're in some really seedy parts of town, and when I call a place in Kazbektun seedy, you can imagine it's bad. Then; there are the times; some of these trips are after midnight. Now, Dave, I know I'm just a lowly admin officer, and I'm not supposed to have an understanding of the high policy shit you *substantive* types get up to, but, what the hell is the ambassador doing in rundown parts of town by himself at midnight, huh?"

What indeed, Morgan thought.

"I don't know, Monty. I'm sure he has his reasons."

"Yeah, but isn't it dangerous? What if something happened to him?"

Morgan knew that, if Ellingsworth was meeting with the deputy head of Dagastan's security service each time, he was probably well protected. The question wasn't 'what if something happened to him?,' but, 'what the hell was he up to?'

"Good point," he said. "I'll talk to Pete about it. In the meantime, I want you to take all of the ambassador's driver's logs and put them under lock and key. No one, and I mean no one, but you and me are to have access to them."

Cornelius nodded, but he was now looking nervous. "Dave, what the hell's going on?"

"I don't know, but I'm damn well going to find out."

Cornelius folded the log sheet and put it back into his coat. He stood. "Oh, before I forget; I came in to talk to you about one other thing; some of us are playing a little pickup basketball at the Marine House this afternoon. We were wondering if you'd like to join us."

Morgan smiled. A little physical activity might relieve some of the stress he'd been feeling lately, and he always liked visiting the little compound on the edge of town where the embassy's Marine security guards lived. They always had the latest movies, a well-equipped bar, and a complete gym. In the depressed social milieu of Kazbektun, it was like Club Med, and was where most of the embassy's single Americans hung out on weekends.

"Sounds great; I'll see you around two."

Cornelius smiled and left. Morgan turned his

attention back to the papers on his desk, but his mind was really on Robert Ellingsworth. Without knowing just what the man was up to, Morgan still was convinced that he was playing some kind of dangerous game; a game that could have severe consequences, not only for himself personally, but for everyone else in the embassy. He didn't know how he knew, but he trusted his instincts.

What he did not trust was his ability to make a cup of coffee that wouldn't turn his stomach, so after allowing the noxious looking brown liquid in his cup to become too cool to drink anyway, he poured it in the toilet, rinsed his cup, emptied the coffee maker, and went back to his office. He was beginning to reassess his rule on not making his secretary work on her off hours.

When his stomach started growling, he looked at his watch. It was already nearly half past twelve. He decided to grab a bite from the bar at Marine House; they had great chili dogs and fries, so he called the Marine Guard at Post One, the main entrance to the embassy, and asked him to have his driver meet him in front of the building. He put the papers he'd done very little work on back in his filing cabinet. He then dug his shorts, a sweat short with the sleeves torn off, a pair of white socks in need of washing, and his sneakers from the closet behind his desk, where he kept a few changes of clothing for those times when he had to go to an event after work, but didn't have enough time to make it to his residence. He folded the sweat around everything else, and, tucking the bundle under his arm, turned off the lights and went downstairs to the main entrance.

The Marine guard on duty, a young redheaded corporal from Kentucky, gave him a friendly wave when he passed the glass-enclosed booth.

Achmed, his driver, was waiting at the bottom of the marble steps, standing next to the rear door of the '73 Ford Galaxie that was his official car as the embassy's number two. Although only two years old, the car, in basic black, had almost as many dents as a demolition derby car, and the black finish was scratched and spotted with rust spots from the wind-driven sand that was ever-present in Dagastan's air. The shocks had long since ceased cushioning the vibrations from the potholes which constituted the majority of the surface of Kazbektun's streets.

"Meester David," Achmed said, his nicotine-stained teeth displayed in a broad smile. "You finally go home?"

"No, Achmed, we're going to Marine House for some fun."

"Is what kind fun weeth Marines today?"

"Well, after a lunch of hot dogs and French

fries, we're playing basketball."

The driver's brown face wrinkled in concentration, and then he smiled. "Ah, yes, I know game. Besketball, was invented by Russian, no?"

Morgan laughed. "No, Achmed, I'm afraid your Russian friends didn't invent the game of basketball. It was actually invented in 1891 by Dr. James Naismith, a Canadian while he was working at the YMCA Training School in Springfield, Massachusetts. So, you have to say that basketball is a completely American game."

"This Dr. Nazmeeth, he was probably Russian I think."

This back and forth with Achmed had become a routine part of Morgan's day. He never knew when the driver, an ethnic Kazbektuni of about fifty, was joking, though he suspected that most of the time he was. Achmed had credited the Russians with the invention of everything from baseball to penicillin, each time with an absolutely straight face.

Morgan sat back, his head against the back headrest, idly watching the landscape rolling past through the slightly tinted windows. There wasn't much to see, even in the country's capital. In the area near the embassy, the best part of town, were a few blocky buildings, many with the red and green flag of Dagastan, with a golden hammer and sickle in the upper left corner, flying over the entrances, marking them as government offices, the main industry of the country. Sandwiched between the government buildings were older structures, gray and depressing; mainly shops with empty display windows and almost bare shelves, except for the large, multi-story Government Department Store about half a mile down the street from the embassy. It was here that the few luxury goods available in the country were for sale, mostly to high-level officials and foreign diplomats, at inflated prices for the diplomats, and greatly reduced rates for local officials. Needless to say, even the few Dagastani who had the funds to buy such goods weren't permitted to enter the establishment unless they were among the lucky ones who worked as sales clerks or janitors.

The most ornate structure, located near the center of the city, was the headquarters of the Central Committee and Presidium, where the First Secretary had his office, and from which he ran the country with an iron hand, and the help of the dreaded security service. Morgan had heard that First Secretary Dmitri Kovasc had a luxurious, walled resort to the north of the city, in a valley flanked by jagged hills, atop which sat guard towers and anti-aircraft emplacements, but neither he nor any other foreigner in Dagastan had ever seen it. The road to Kovasc's residence was blocked off more than ten miles from the reported location of his residence, and guarded around the clock by uniformed security force troops supported by armored vehicles. No one, foreign or Dagastani (except for a select few) was allowed to pass the checkpoints.

The streets in town were almost deserted. A few pedestrians, dressed in drab gray and brown, moved in shambling gaits from empty shop to empty shop, mostly old women, their heads covered with shawls, carrying burlap sacks into which they put the few items they were able to find. Traffic was light, for other than government cars and embassy vehicles from the five foreign missions, there were few motorized vehicles in the country.

Farther out from the downtown area, the traffic picked up, but it consisted mainly of horse drawn carriages from the surrounding farms, rickety trucks carrying pigs or sheep to the central market, and tractors donated to Dagastan by their Soviet masters. Even on Saturday, farmers and herdsmen were out in their fields tending their meager stock, or working the hard gray earth trying to scratch out a living.

What the hell are we doing here? Morgan asked himself as the somber scene rolled past outside his window. *This place has nothing of interest to the United States. It can hardly feed itself, and it poses no security threat. Hell, the army of Dagastan would be hard pressed to hold out against a determined troop of boy scouts armed with camping knives. Except for the security force, which was targeted primarily against internal threats to the current government's hold on power, there's no one who cares enough about this place to invade it.*

But, he knew the answer to his question. Universalism; the policy of having an embassy in every sovereign country on the planet; from the newly independent states in Africa to a backwater like Dagastan, if it called itself a country, and had a seat in the UN, the U.S. had an embassy. Often little more than an ambassador, a secretary, and a communicator, but the Stars and Stripes, like the British Union Jack, flew all over the world.

Lulled to inattention by the dreary scene, Morgan didn't at first notice Achmed's nervous glances in the rear view mirror. But, after the third or fourth time that the driver glanced up at the mirror and frowned, Morgan sensed his unease.

"What's the problem, Achmed?" he asked.

"I not sure, Meester David," the driver said, but there was tension in his voice. "But, black car follow us for last few minutes. I think we being followed."

Morgan glanced over his shoulder. There was a black ZIL with darkened windows about five car lengths back, keeping pace with them.

"Do you think it's the security police?" Morgan knew that the security force kept tabs on all foreigners, but he'd never been followed before. Besides, they knew that the only place he could be heading, the only place of any interest in this direction was the Marine security guard residence, and that was under surveillance around the clock.

"I don't know," Achmed said. "Maybe security police, but it don't have government license plate."

That, Morgan thought, was strange. The thugs of Dagastan's security service usually wanted their victims to know who their tormentors were. But, if wasn't the security service, then, who was it, and why were they following *him*? "Can you go fast enough to lose them, Achmed? Once we get out of this area and nearer to Marine House, we should be okay."

The driver looked at Morgan in the rear view mirror, his bushy eyebrows raised as if to say, 'are you joking, on this road?' He shrugged. "I don't know, Meester David. The ZIL, she's ugly, but got big engine. This car pretty, but got power like old horse with bad leg."

Morgan knew, too, that the Galaxie's suspension couldn't cope with high speed driving over the roads, but, he didn't want to be trapped by unknown assailants in such an isolated area. "Give it a try; let's see what this baby's got."

Achmed jammed his foot down on the gas pedal, and the old car lurched forward hard enough to press Morgan into the seatback. The jostling as they bounced from one irregularity in the pavement to another was almost painful. Morgan hung onto the door handle to steady himself. As he looked back, through the cloud of dust thrown up by the Ford, he saw that the black ZIL had increased speed, and seemed to be closing on them.

"Can you go any faster, Achmed? They're gaining on us."

Achmed shrugged, his white knuckled hands tightly gripping the wheel. "Is going as fast as she can, sir," was all he said.

There was a loud bang, followed by a sudden vibration of the car, and Morgan was thrown forward against the front seat, barely avoiding colliding with it face first. He turned and looked out the back window. The ZIL, it's front bumper dented, had closed on them, and was now preparing to ram them again. Achmed was swinging from one side of the street to the other in a zigzag pattern, but the driver of the black car was skillful; he matched Achmed's every move. The black car leapt forward, hitting the Ford solidly, and again throwing Morgan against the seat.

Morgan could imagine what the rear end of his car looked like. The ZIL's front bumper was crumpled and looked as if it would soon fall off. The black car was larger and much heavier than his, and was sure to win the game of bumper tag they were playing.

The black car surged again, making contact with the rear of the Ford. Only, this time, it hit just as Achmed was zigging to the right. The glancing blow caused the Ford to skid sideways and then shoot off the road into the recently plowed field. It's momentum took it over a hundred feet into the field, destroying the neatly plowed rows, until it came to a stop, its nose buried in a mound of earth.

Morgan looked out the rear window. He saw four black-clad figures emerge from the ZIL and start walking across the field. They all carried deadly looking weapons, AK-47s Morgan thought.

"Achmed," he yelled. "Get out the right side and try to find cover."

He looked around, but through the dust-smeared windows, the closest cover he could see was an adobe farmer's house about a quarter mile further up the road. They'd be cut down before they'd gone halfway. But, if they remained in the car, they'd be slaughtered too. Morgan didn't like the idea of going down without a fight, but his options were limited.

The four men were taking their time approaching the car. Suddenly, there was a popping sound, and a geyser of dirt spouted up in front of them, and they stopped, looking to their right. Two more popping sounds and two more eruptions of dirt; only this time, closer to the men. One of the men started to raise his weapon, but his companion put a hand on his arm.

The four men conferred for a moment, and then, lowering their weapons, turned and walked back to their car. The ZIL did a three point turn and sped back toward the center of town.

As Morgan and Achmed got out of the Ford, Morgan saw Pete Jeffers, wearing an armored vest and holding a large handgun in his right hand, a shotgun in his left, flanked by two of his local security guards, walking across the field toward him.

"Dave, you all right?" Jeffers asked.

"Yeah, just a bit shaken. Good thing you came along when you did."

As Jeffers holstered the .357 magnum Smith and Wesson, he gave Morgan a guilty look. "Well, uh, I'm not exactly here by accident, Dave. I've been shadowing you for the past few days. Sorry I didn't warn you in advance."

Morgan walked over and clasped the young security officer's shoulder. "No need to apologize, Pete. I'm glad you were here."

"Who the hell were those guys? None of my guys recognized them."

"I wish I knew. At first, I thought they might be from the security service, but Achmed pointed out that their car didn't have government plates. I'm at a loss as to why whoever they were, they'd come after me."

"They picked you up about a block from the embassy. When we saw them, I thought they might be security goons, too, but my guys said the same thing; if they'd been security, they would have had official plates."

Morgan scratched his chin. He hadn't shaved that morning, and his hand made a scratching sound. "Damn, this is puzzling. Something's going on, but I can't figure out what."

"Me either, but whatever it is, it's serious. From now on, I'm putting one of my guys with you around the clock - - don't argue with me. The ambassador wants to be stupid and not have security; damned if I'll lose both of you."

"I'm not complaining, Jeff; but, what can your guys do? They aren't armed."

Jeffers cheeks turned red. "Well, uh, I know they're not supposed to be, but under the circumstances, I've issued .38s and shotguns to each of them, except the guy on the front gate. One Marine at Post One with his riot gun and .45 might not be enough, so I'm putting two guys inside the chancery with shotguns after hours, and I'll have one at your residence. He'll ride shotgun in your vehicle whenever you move. I hope that's okay."

Morgan knew that this was technically a violation of the rules, and the agreement they had with the government. He also wasn't sure how the ambassador might react should he learn what they were doing. But, he was still shaken by the incident, and decided that discretion was the better part of valor. If things went bad, he'd just have to deal with them. "I haven't seen a thing, Pete. Just make sure your guys are careful. It wouldn't do to have them arrested; it could cause an international incident."

Jeffers laughed. "If things get that bad, an international incident will be the least of our worries."

Chapter 18

Monday, May 19, 1975, Washington, DC

For Lee Kennedy, the weekend had seemed endless. He was still puzzled by his supervisor's reaction to him looking into the Carter killing, and his questions about what was going on in Dagastan.

A routine had been established in the Kennedy household; Rachel and Alison had taken to each other, and his daughter hung around Alison like they'd been friends forever. He had to admit, he too liked having Alison around.

After dropping Rachel at school, Kennedy and Alison drove across the river to Foggy Bottom. Over her objections, not too forcefully expressed, he walked her to the door to the INR suite of offices and waited until the heavy metal door had closed behind her before going to his own office.

He avoided Broadbent all morning, but kept an eye on the man's office door, while idly flipping through the folder of correspondence on his desk. Mostly routine reports and security notices, he found it hard to focus on the papers. From time to time, he got up and refilled his mug from the large coffee urn that was kept in the corner near the photocopier.

By a quarter to noon, his stomach was grumbling from too much coffee, and he was having difficulty focusing on the white and green sheets of paper. He leaned back in his chair, and was rubbing his eyes, when he saw Broadbent come out of his office for the first time. The man looked around the outer office, and then walked over to the duty secretary and, leaning over, mumbled something to her that Kennedy couldn't see.

When the door had close behind him, Kennedy went out to the secretary's desk. "Did Mr. Broadbent say where he was going?" he asked nonchalantly. "I had some documents I wanted him to take a look at."

The woman, a middle-aged civil servant with prematurely graying hair, didn't even look up at him. "He said he had to meet someone, and that he might be late coming back. He didn't say who he was meeting, or where."

Kennedy mumbled his thanks and hurried back to his office. He called Alison and told her to eat in the building's cafeteria, and that he'd check with her before the close of the business day. Before she could ask him any questions, he rang off and hurried out into the hallway. He saw the elevator doors closing on Broadbent, and noticed that the indicator above the door showed that it was going down. Taking the stairs two at a time, Kennedy hurried down to the second floor, beating the elevator by a few seconds. The doors opened and closed; a few people got on, but Broadbent remained inside, standing in the back corner looking down at the floor.

So, Kennedy thought, he must be planning to go out the C Street entrance instead of the employee entrance. He reentered the stairwell and loped down to the first floor. As he emerged from the stairwell and walked around the corner, he saw Broadbent exiting through the glass doors and across C Street and down Twenty-First Street toward Constitution Avenue.

Kennedy followed, hanging back near the doors until Broadbent was well down Twenty-First Street. He followed, staying on the opposite sidewalk so that should Broadbent turn or backtrack he wouldn't be seen. It proved, though, an unnecessary precaution. The man forged steadily toward Constitution Avenue without once looking back, or even taking much note of his surroundings. At Constitution, he waited for the light and then crossed, stepping across the low cable that ran along the sidewalk, and crossing the grass toward the west end of the Reflecting Pool.

Kennedy barely made it across Constitution before the light changed and impatient drivers sped into the intersection. He crossed the sidewalk, and hung back in the evergreens that line the National Mall, watching as Broadbent approached three men standing on the marble edge of the pool.

Even from a distance, Kennedy recognized one of the men; a tall, patrician looking man of about sixty, with a flowing mane of white hair that he wore combed back, accenting his high, broad forehead and aquiline nose. He was wearing an expensive looking dark gray suit, and Kennedy assumed he also wore his signature powder blue shirt and red, white, and blue striped tie. The Honorable Carlton Longroux, a Republican who was junior senator from the state of Alabama, was a familiar figure. A member of the Senate Foreign Relations Committee, he was one of the Department of State's fiercest critics, accusing it of being weak and caving in to America's enemies at every opportunity. Longroux stopped just short of the tactics of 'Tail Gunner' Joe McCarthy, the senator from Wisconsin who, in the fifties, had gone on an anti-communist witch hunt, alleging that Communists had infiltrated every department of the executive branch, but no one missed the implication of his inflammatory speeches.

The second man was also on the older side, probably late sixties based on stance and the wispy white hair that lay plastered across his sunburned skull. He too wore a gray suit, somewhat lighter than Longroux's, and paced nervously as Broadbent approached.

It was the third figure, though, that most interested Kennedy. A youngish looking man, slender build, with glossy black hair, parted in the middle, he was dressed in black; black shirt, black pants, and black shoes. He stood apart from the other two, watching them, but at the same time, watching everyone who came near them. The man radiated menace, even at that great distance, and Kennedy found himself wondering if this was the man who had tried to attack Alison.

There wasn't enough cover for him to get near enough to hear what they were saying, so Kennedy used the time to commit to memory every detail of the two unidentified men.

As Broadbent joined the waiting trio, the unidentified older man stepped forward and began talking to him, and, from the way he waved his finger under Broadbent's nose, it was clear to Kennedy that he was administering a tongue lashing. Broadbent stood, his shoulders rounded and his head bent like a school boy caught smoking in the boy's toilet. Senator Longroux entered the conversation from time to time, sometimes pointing to the man in black, but the other man was clearly in charge. The man in black didn't seem to join in the conversation, and except for the movement of his head as he scanned his surroundings, did not move.

The conversation at the Reflecting Pool, mostly dominated by the elderly man, lasted for thirty minutes. Then, Broadbent, his shoulders still rounded, turned and headed back toward the State Department building. Kennedy beat a hasty retreat across Constitution, and turned left toward Twenty-Third Street, hoping he wouldn't be spotted. He walked up Twenty-Third to the employee entrance on the E Street side of the building and got back to his office five minutes before Broadbent arrived. The man's face was pale; he looked as if he'd just received news of a death in his family. He walked past the secretary, ignoring a folder she held up for him, went into his office, and closed the door.

Kennedy called Murphy and gave him a description of the man in black, telling him that he thought this was the man who had tried to assault Alison. Murphy informed him that it wasn't much to go on, but he'd put the description out to street patrol officers, especially those patrolling in the vicinity of Alison's house. He then called Alison and told her he'd pick her up at five-thirty for the ride home; he was still insisting that she not return to her own place. She objected, but there was no force in her objection. She, too, was beginning to warm to the new relationship;

Kennedy could hear it in her voice.

Now, he only had to keep her alive.

CHARLES RAY

Chapter 19

After dinner, with Rachel in her room doing homework, Kennedy and Alison took coffee on the patio. They sat in a pair of folding lawn chairs, almost close enough for their shoulders to touch, and watched the fading light of dusk through the towering trees behind his house.

"What did you do for lunch today?" she asked.

Kennedy laughed and took a sip of coffee. "Actually, I completely forgot to eat lunch."

"What? What on earth could you have been doing that was so important you'd neglect to eat?"

He told her about tailing Broadbent to the Mall, and the meeting with Senator Longroux and the other two men. He gave her a detailed description of the other two. When he described the man in black, she felt a cold shiver.

"Oh, my God; that sounds like the man with the knife at my house."

"That's what I thought, too; but, I didn't get

a good look at him from the street. Do you remember anything else about him that might help identify him?"

"I was so scared, I couldn't focus. All I remember is that knife; I could see the light reflecting off it. Oh, and his eyes; I remember his eyes. They were cold; not like human eyes at all. They were like the eyes of a moccasin when it's stalking a mouse."

"Afraid the cops probably don't have snake eyes in their data base. If you remember anything else, let me know, and I'll pass it to Al Murphy. What about the old guy? Anything about him that rings a bell?"

"Not really; but, you said he was with the senator, and he seemed to be in charge. I can check the files we have, and news files. Maybe there'll be a photo of him with the senator in one of them."

"Hadn't thought of that. Good girl."

She reached over and laid a hand on his arm. "Just in case you haven't noticed, Lee Kennedy, I haven't been a *girl* for a few years now."

His face reddened. He could feel heat in his cheeks. "Uh, yeah, I mean . . . of course . . . you're all . . . uh . . . woman."

She laughed. Her hand tightened on his forearm, sending a current of feeling up his arm. "Just don't you forget it," she said.

Kennedy spent an uncomfortable and sleepless night on the couch.

Chapter 20

He was uncharacteristically silent during breakfast the next morning; said little as they drove Rachel to school; and, stared at the street ahead on the drive into the District. He walked beside her from the elevator to her office, and mumbled something incoherent as she entered.

Alison was confused. Suddenly, Lee Kennedy had become withdrawn; almost sullen. The one time she'd touched his shoulder, as they were walking from the elevator to her office, he'd shrunk back as if burned.

Oh well, she thought, I guess there's no figuring men. She put his strange behavior aside and set about trying to identify the strange old man Kennedy had seen the previous day.

She went to the file room, a cavernous space at the back of the office area, filled with filing cabinets and large map folder storage containers. Her destination was the large cabinets in which clippings from world media organizations were kept. She started with the files of the *Washington Post* and *New York*

Times, which were most likely to have articles and photos of congressional figures, and looked in the index for files relating to Senator Carlton Longroux and the Senate Foreign Relations Committee. She ignored the articles containing no photos, and focused on those with pictures. Fortunately, Longroux was something of a publicity hound, always looking for a chance to display his southern charm for the camera, so there were dozens of photos of him at one event or another, or head shots of him speaking to the press. She concentrated on photos of groups, paying particular attention to whether or not other people in the photos were identified.

She'd been at it for more than an hour, her fingers stained black from the musty old newsprint, before she came upon a photo of Longroux with five other elderly men, at a retreat near his home just outside Mobile, Alabama. One figure in the photo, standing near the back and ignoring the others, caught her eye. An ascetic looking man, with thin white hair combed over his skull, dressed in a dark suit, resembled Kennedy's description of the man at the Reflecting Pool. He was identified as Niles Hitchcock, a State Department official who at the time was on loan from State, serving as an assistant to the President's National Security Advisor.

Taking the paper to the large photocopier in the corner, she made a copy. The resolution was poor, but Hitchcock was still recognizable.

Alison returned to her office. She put the photocopy in an envelope, which she put in her purse. She then called the department's central personnel office.

A man with a bored sounding voice answered, and when she identified herself and asked for information about an employee named Niles Hitchcock, asked why she wanted it.

"There's a project in INR at the moment that I understand Mr. Hitchcock might have some expertise in," she said. "But, I don't have his current assignment."

"So," the bored voice said. "You just want to confirm his assignment? Well, I guess that's allowed. Let me check."

There was a long pause, and she could hear the rustling of papers and muted voices in the background. She held the phone to her ear for ten minutes before the voice came back on.

"I'm sorry, Miss Chambers, but somebody must have given you wrong information. Niles Hitchcock is listed as having retired ten years ago. Could it be you have the wrong name?"

"You might be right," she said quickly. "Let me double check and I'll get back to you."

She quickly broke the connection. There was

no way she would be 'getting back to personnel.'
She got the information she wanted. She could
tap into her other connections around the
building to get other information on Hitchcock.
If he'd been seconded to the National Security
Council, others in the building would have
heard of him; corridor gossip was what made
the building work; everyone knew something
about everyone else, and most were more than
willing to talk about what they knew. It was
puzzling, though. What was a retired diplomat
doing with a senator, a senior security official,
and the mysterious man in black?

She would have to consult Lee on it. She
hoped that whatever had put him in a snit had
passed.

Chapter 21

Monday, May 19, 1975, Dagastan

Although Morgan had been rattled by the incident on the way to the Marine House, a hotdog and fries, washed down with two beers, had settled him. He'd sided with two of the taller marines and the three of them had swept the pickup basketball matches. By the time the sun was setting, he'd exhausted himself.

Jeffers had arranged for a tow truck from the embassy motor pool to retrieve his car, and with the uncommunicative guard from the embassy security force sitting in front with Achmed, Morgan had gone home, showered, had a light supper, and slept until mid-morning on Sunday.

He spent all day Sunday at home, reading the papers he'd brought from his office, catching up on the world news. None of it was interesting. By evening, he picked at the light supper his cook prepared, and decided to turn in early.

When he entered his office Monday morning,

just after six, the weekend's events were hazy in his mind. He quickly got caught up in the busy start-of-week routine.

Around ten, Mary Sung came in and stood in the door. "Dave, there's a local here insisting he talk to you."

He looked up. She had a look of frustration that he usually associated with some disgruntled visa applicant seeking his intervention to get a visa denial reversed. "Did you tell him to speak to the chief of the consular section, because I don't do visas?"

"Yes, I did. But, he said it had nothing to do with visas, and was extremely important. I don't know; he might be pulling my leg, but he seems sincere."

Morgan sighed. The creativity of people seeking entry into the 'Land of Opportunity' was endless, and they wouldn't hesitate to lie to achieve their dream of going to America.

"Okay, bring him in; but, the minute he starts talking about going to visit his cousin in Detroit, the meeting's over."

She disappeared, only to reappear a few minutes later with a small, narrow-shouldered man, dressed in a dusty brown coat that was two sizes too big, followed in her wake. He had a narrow face, watery brown eyes, a narrow nose, and stringy brown hair flecked with white.

Morgan couldn't even begin to guess his age.

"Mr. Morgan, this is Anton Vechkov," she said.

Morgan stepped forward, extending his hand. The man's grip was firm. His hands were calloused. He was either a worker or a farmer, Morgan thought.

"What can I do for you, Mr. Vechkov?"

The man looked over his shoulder at Sung, and then back at Morgan. "I hef very important matter to discuss with you, Meester Morgan; is confidential."

Morgan nodded at Mary Sung. "That's okay, Mary. Would you like a cup of coffee or tea, Mr. Vechkov?"

"Tea vud be fine," the man said. "Tsenk you."

"One tea, one coffee, coming right up," she said.

Morgan waved his visitor to the sofa in the far corner of his office, away from his desk. He took the chair facing, a slight smile on his face. Mary Sung brought a tray containing a little pot of tea, a cup, and containers of cream and sugar, along with Morgan's Chicago Bears coffee mug. She put the tray on the table between the two men and quietly withdrew.

"Now, Mr. Vechkov," Morgan said. "What can I do for you?"

Vechkov poured tea into the cup, and then carefully measured two tablespoons of milk and one of sugar into the brown liquid, stirring it until it was the color of chocolate milk. He took a sip, sighed, and put the cup down.

"A very nice cup of tea," he said. Morgan's face creased in a frown. "Yes, why I must see you. Is matter of urgency for my country, and I am believing is maybe for your country as well."

Despite his accent, Morgan sensed that Vechkov was more than a mere laborer or farmer. He nodded for the man to continue.

"As you know, Dagastan is poor country. We have no natural resources, and must rely on our friends the Russians for energy. Is what I believe you Americans call shotgun wedding, only in this case, is groom who has shotgun."

There was no doubt; the man was definitely not what Morgan had first assumed. Thoughts of the attempt – to do what, he still wasn't sure – on him came flooding back; now this. *Could this be the government trying to entrap me? Well, if so, let them try; I wasn't born yesterday.*

"I'm aware of Dagastan's economic situation; but, how does this affect my country?"

"You must also know that many of us here wish to see change in government; more democracy. The Kazbektuni, especially; they are the many, but have no power, no say; and, many of us who are Rus agree that they must be allowed to share more in what we have."

"So, you're part of the Dagastan Democracy Movement?"

Vechkov looked around nervously, licking his thin lips. "Is safe to talk here?"

As safe, Morgan thought, as anyplace. Of course, the security goons saw you come in here, so they'll be on to you about your visit. But then, he figured Vechkov already knew that and would have some cover story.

"Yes, it's safe to talk here," he said.

"Yes, Meester Morgan; I am member of group that wants to see my country more free. But, we wish to achieve this freedom peacefully. Unfortunately, First Secretary Kovasc does not like any opposition, and he does not hesitate to use violence to put it down. Many of my comrades have disappeared; to where we do not know."

"Then, you must know coming here is very risky."

"Living in this country is risky. Life is not without risk; one must be prepared to take risk for things of worth. Freedom is worth risk. But, what I must tell you is what you do not know. There are rumors that Dagastan might not be as poor as we thought. Something of value has been found that the government can use to pit the great powers, the Soviet Union and your country against each other."

"Do you know what this thing of value is?"

"No, and I do not know where it is. But, I trust the source of information. It is also said that Vasily Shermov, the cousin of our first secretary, knew, but now that he has been killed, no one knows who possesses the information."

"Surely, the first secretary," Morgan said.

"But, you see; that is the interesting thing. My source informs me that Shermov died before sharing the information with his cousin."

"Well, if the information died with him, I fail to see the problem."

"The information did not die with him. My source did not know who, but he tells me that someone else in government also has this information, and plans to use it. First, against Kovasc, and then in, how do you call it, a bidding war between the Americans and the Soviets."

"Can you tell me who your source is, or at least, how he came by this information."

"Please forgive me, but I don't think it wise to do that. Just know that this is someone who is in position to know. I trust, and I ask you to believe me; I have no reason to lie to you."

"I'm not accusing you of lying, Mr. Vechkov. It's just that the more details I have, the easier it is for me to evaluate what you're telling me."

Vechkov wiped at his lips with his fingers, and took another sip of tea. "I cannot tell you name of source, but I can tell you this; someone in the government has been meeting with Americans and Soviets secretly, without first secretary knowing. The aim, my source says, is to remove Kovasc, and then money from this thing of value goes to country with highest bid."

"Do you know the identity of the Americans this person, or persons, have met with?"

"I do not know name; but, Americans represent organization called White Dragon."

Morgan's senses went on high alert. The name 'White Dragon' had been heard during Ellingsworth's meeting with Dragov. He'd have to have Jeffers check with his people in Washington to see if anyone knew this organization. This was also something Raine should be working on; provided, Morgan thought, he could be trusted. He still wasn't ready to write the agency man off.

"Did your source learn the nature of this White Dragon?"

"No; is thinking it is maybe American

company that is part of your military-industrial complex. Everyone is knowing that your Pentagon is always sleeping with defense companies."

"You mean, in bed with?"

"Yes; is different, what I say?"

Morgan chuckled. In a way, it probably wasn't so different, except in the often unholy alliances between governments and rich private companies, the ones getting screwed were the taxpayers. He wouldn't, of course, say any of this to Vechkov. The man probably wouldn't understand it anyway; no one in Dagastan paid taxes.

"No, it's not different. So, this American organization has been approached by someone in the government, who you can't name, to make an offer for this thing of value, which has not been identified? Do I have it about right?"

"Yes, you have right. I know is not much information, but I am promising you, this is danger for both our countries. If America and Russia argue over small country like Dagastan, it is Dagastan which will suffer most, of course, but I think your country does not need such problem after Vietnam, no?"

Cut off from the world, Dagastan might be, but some news filtered in. The humiliating defeat of South Vietnam by the northern

Communists; photos of North Vietnamese tanks rolling into Saigon, and the hordes of Vietnamese scrambling for space on the aircraft evacuating the remaining Americans, was known from the great capitals to the tiniest hamlets. The great American army, with all its firepower, defeated by tiny Vietnam, with many of its soldiers equipped with little beyond assault rifles and rifle propelled grenades. Of course, there were also Soviet tanks and artillery, but it was a David and Goliath matchup, and David's slingshot sent the giant Goliath to the mat.

After more than a decade of being mired in the jungles and rice paddies of Southeast Asia, with most of the American population up in arms against it, another foreign adventure in some unknown part of the world, for interests too vague for the average citizen to understand, didn't make sense. More to the point; why would the U.S. Government be making moves in the country without involving the embassy? It didn't make sense. Nothing that had been happening of late made any sense.

"This is all very well, Mr. Vechkov; and, I thank you for sharing it with me. But, what is it you think I can do?"

"That I am not knowing, Meester Morgan. I am trusting that you will think of right thing to do."

CHARLES RAY

Chapter 22

Tuesday, May 20, 1975, Washington, DC

"What the hell is a retired FSO doing messed up with these guys?" Kennedy asked.

He and Alison were sitting on the grassy slope to the north of the Reflecting Pool, not far from where he'd seen his boss conferring with the others.

"You could ask the same about a U.S. Senator," Alison said.

Kennedy shook his head. "It's even worse. I heard from Pete Jeffers out in Dagastan; some goons attacked the DCM, and he thinks it might be connected somehow with all this."

"I hope he's okay, but how can it be related?"

"Well, the DCM's incident was on the weekend, and then on Monday some local comes in to see him, talking about Americans and White Dragon. Now, it could just be coincidence, but I don't believe in coincidence. If it looks like a damn duck and quacks like a duck, it's no turkey."

Alison winced at his mangled metaphor. "It is strange; this White Dragon coming up here and there as well. I wonder if somehow the Chinese are involved."

"What brought the Chinese into this?"

"I don't know," she said. "It's just that the dragon is an important figure in Chinese culture. It doesn't often crop up in ours, and I've never known the Russians to use it. Another thing; Dagastan *is* in the far eastern part of the Soviet Union, nearer to China than to Moscow, and most of its people are descended from Mongolian stock."

Kennedy stared out at the Reflecting Pool, at a flock of ducks swimming lazily across its placid surface. He was reminded of a joke that he'd heard often during his initial training as a diplomatic security agent; something about DS agents being like ducks in a pond, all peaceful looking on the surface, but paddling like hell under water. He was, at that moment, like one of those ducks. Maintaining a calm expression so as not to alarm Alison; and, because he'd been taught from childhood to keep his emotions in check; while his mind was buzzing like a disturbed wasp nest as he tried to make sense of what was going on around them.

"Man, that's all we need; the Chinese sticking their oars in the water."

"I wouldn't put it past them. They're still a bit put out at the Russians over a number of issues, not least of which was the way the Russians out-maneuvered them with the Vietnamese."

"Yeah, and I imagine they don't like us too much either."

Like Kennedy, Alison found herself conflicted. Too many inexplicable things were happening, and she didn't like unsolved puzzles or unanswered questions. Her passion for order was what had drawn her into the intelligence profession in the first place.

"Not much we can do about that, though, until we solve our own little mystery."

"Mysteries," he said. "We have more than one problem to deal with. First priority is to identify and stop that guy who attacked you. Which reminds me, I need to hook you up with Al Murphy so you can give him a description; maybe we can do that today."

"Okay, I guess you're right." She nodded, and then held up three fingers of her left hand. She folded one down. "Next, we need to figure out what Niles Hitchcock's role is in all this." She pulled a second finger down. "And, then; how does all of this relate to what's happening in Dagastan, because I'm convinced that they *are* related."

Kennedy held a hand up. "You're forgetting one other thing; why are our bosses so nervous about us looking into what's happening in Dagastan?"

"You mean, your boss. I haven't spoken to mine about this yet."

"Really; you think he might be helpful to us?"

"I'll let you know after I brief him. He's not been in charge of the unit very long; and, I haven't had much contact with him, but he seems a decent sort."

"I thought all you people in INR were civil servants, permanently assigned. Where'd this guy come from?"

"He was overseas somewhere. For your information, we have a number of FSOs in INR. Dudley Lakeworth, my boss, is one of them."

Kennedy shook his head. He was learning more than he'd ever known about the organization, but none of it was helping him solve his problems.

"But, if he's new, how can he help?"

"He might know Hitchcock. If so, it might shed some light on what's going on. Can't hurt to ask."

After finishing their lunch of tuna sandwiches and chips that Kennedy had made for them before leaving home that morning, they walked back to their offices. Kennedy again escorted Alison to her door and waited until she was inside before going to his own office.

Her independent streak made her want to object to his treating her like some fragile person incapable of taking care of herself, but another part of her enjoyed the attention. Never before in her life had she had to contend with such conflicting emotions.

In her office, she left the door open so she could see the door to Dudley Lakeworth's office. The secretary, Earline, told her he'd gone to lunch and had said he might be late returning. Every few minutes, Alison would get up and peer around the door. After the eighth time, the secretary looked at her, exasperation on her face.

"Alison, girl, you're going to wear a rut in the carpet jumping up and down like that; and, you're about to drive me crazy. I'll tell you when he gets back. Don't worry; I won't let him leave before you see him."

Alison's face reddened. Of course, Earline would keep her word. Everyone knew who really ran the office. When she said you had an appointment, you had an appointment; when she said, go back to your office and quit acting like an expectant father waiting for his first child; you went back to your office and found something to occupy your mind while you fretted. Alison killed time by going back over the notes she'd made from the newspaper clippings.

After finding the picture of Niles Hitchcock with Senator Longroux, she'd specifically searched for any news references to just Hitchcock. There hadn't been many; just the occasional reference to him attending some conference or other. Although, she suspected that a few articles she'd seen that referred to some 'senior government official' were actually reporting on him. The statements were usually of the hardline variety, and in line with the position held by Longroux. She couldn't prove it, but her gut told her she was right.

She had almost forgotten about her plan to talk to Lakeworth when Earline rapped on the door frame. She was standing in the doorway smiling. "Langhorn's back; and I told him you needed to see him, so get your butt on in there."

Alison almost fell getting off her chair. She squeezed past the secretary. "Thanks, Earline. I owe you one."

"No, honey; you owe me a lot, but, who's counting?"

She knocked on the door to Lakeworth's office. "Come in," a muffled voice said.

He was sitting behind his desk, a neat stack of paper precisely centered before him. Small of build and small featured; Dudley Lakeworth had the look of someone who had been raised with a silver spoon in his mouth, held by an expensive nanny with a plummy British accent. His reddish brown hair was combed straight back from a high forehead, and he looked at the world with watery brown eyes over the top of gold-rimmed spectacles. Even behind his desk, he sat with his jacket buttoned.

"Thank you for seeing me," Alison said.

"Of course, Miss Chambers," he said. His voice had a hint of New England; not Boston, but somewhere along the Massachusetts coast, probably one of the exclusive communities inhabited by those who claimed descent from the Mayflower. "I haven't had the opportunity to get to know everyone in the unit since my arrival, so it's nice of you to take the initiative to introduce yourself."

Alison noticed that, unlike most of the other Foreign Service people she encountered in her work, he didn't immediately address her by her first name. Instead of being impressed, though, she found it rather off-putting; as if he was establishing some kind of social distance.

"Uh, yes, welcome to INR," she said. "I hope you're settling in well."

"Yes. It's different from what I'm accustomed

to, but I find it interesting. Tell me, Ms. Chambers, what is it that you do here?"

Damn, Alison thought; he hasn't even bothered to read the staffing pattern or the office directory. Either of those two documents would have told him her job title, which described her area of responsibility.

"Oh, I do a number of things. Mostly, I've been doing analysis of agricultural production and weather impacts on food production in the central Asian region. Right now, I'm doing some biographic analysis."

"My, my, that sounds interesting. I look forward to seeing some of your work."

Sure, she thought; and, you'll love sitting around watching paint dry. "Actually, I was hoping you'd be able to help me with a project I'm working on right now."

His thin eyebrows arched upwards; the eyes regarding her with a faint look of surprise. "Really? I've only just arrived; how could I possibly know enough to help you?"

"In my research I ran across a name that I thought you might be familiar with."

"I seriously doubt that; I've never been in Central Asia, or anywhere else in Asia for that matter."

"Oh, it's not an Asian name. The person who

I'm looking for information on is a retired American diplomat. His name is Niles Hitchcock. I was wondering if you'd ever encountered him in your career, or heard anything about him."

"Niles . . . Hitchcock; why, I think the name is familiar. Uh, he once worked in the White House, I believe. I don't recall ever seeing his name linked with Central Asia either. In what context did you encounter his name?"

She almost blurted out what she'd learned, then, she realized that she didn't know this man, and her experiences of the past several days had taught her one thing; Lee Kennedy was the only person in Washington she could trust.

"Oh, it was in a couple of reports I read. I believe in being thorough, so I'm following up on every name."

"Well, that's certainly commendable. I don't think, though, that you'll find Niles Hitchcock to be really involved in anything of significance in Dagastan."

Alison clinched her teeth to stifle the impulse to gasp. She'd never said anything about Dagastan; only Central Asia, which was a vast region. So, Lakeworth wasn't as ignorant of what she did as he pretended to be. She suddenly felt cold.

"Yes, you're probably right," she said, standing and backing toward the door. "I'm just a bit anal retentive about such things. Well, anyway, just wanted to welcome you to INR. If there's anything you need, I'm just down the hall."

She backed out and pulled the door shut. She was almost back to her own office before she began breathing again.

Chapter 23

When she had her breathing under control, she called Kennedy and asked to meet him, suggesting the Lincoln Memorial.

She left the building by the employee entrance and walked around to Twenty-Third Street, knowing that he was likely to take the shorter route through the ceremonial entrance on C Street. This way, she thought, maybe no one would see them together; at least, no one in the building.

She was breathing hard by the time she arrived at the bottom of the marble steps leading up to Lincoln's statue. Kennedy was waiting, leaning against the marble, a half smile on his face.

When he saw the worried look on her face, though, his smile faded. "What's wrong, Alison? You look like you've seen a ghost."

She described her meeting with Dudley Lakeworth.

"You sure you didn't mention Dagastan

somewhere in there?" he asked.

She glared at him, her hands on her hips. "I'm absolutely, one hundred percent positive. I never mentioned the country, and at the start, he acted as if he didn't know what I was working on."

"That is strange." Kennedy rubbed his chin. "Did you ask him about White Dragon?"

"Uh, no; I was so shocked when he mentioned Dagastan I just got the hell out of his office. Should I have?"

"No, it's probably best you didn't. Say, I got a phone call from Pete Jeffers; must have been the middle of the night out there when he called; he says his DCM got a strange visitor, and the name White Dragon came up again during the conversation."

"I think I see what you meant about coincidence. It simply cannot be coincidence that that term would come up in both places if there wasn't a relationship."

"Yeah," Kennedy said. "But what the hell does it mean?"

A part of Alison's mind had been mulling that very question, even as she talked with Kennedy. "Well, I thought it might be some kind of foreign gang, but it appears it's American. My guess is that it's either a company, or some kind of organization."

"What kind of American organization has a name like that? I mean, we have the elks and the moose, but I've never heard of an American organization taking an Asian name."

"You'd be surprised at what some people do in this country," Alison said. "There was an organization that had members here, in England, and in mainland Europe, called Ordo Templi Orientis. It was even more secretive than the Masons, and supposedly had all kinds of occult practices. My guess is this White Dragon bunch is probably organized along similar lines, but rather than occult practices or religion, is probably economically based; or, given the involvement of such high level people in government, maybe even political."

Kennedy put a hand on her shoulder. His touch sent shivers through her body, but, it his touch wasn't meant to be seductive. He gazed into her eyes, his expression somber. "You're not seriously telling me you think some kind of secret society is involved in what's going, are you?"

"Oh, I'm must thinking out loud. But, there are things about what's happening that keep diverting my mind back into that channel. Think about it, Lee; the secrecy, the efforts to keep us away from the whole thing. And, don't forget the attack on me. This kind of thing's not new to this country, you know. During the Civil War, there was an organization called the

Knights of the Golden Circle; John Wilkes Booth and Jesse James were both members. The Knights were very pro-slavery and supported the Confederacy, and not just through secret handshakes and rituals; they robbed stagecoaches, and even tried to block San Francisco harbor. So, you see, American secret societies aren't strangers to violence."

Kennedy thought about Lesley Carter. Could she have accidentally stumbled across some forbidden knowledge, for which she forfeited her life? Was that behind the attack on Alison? And, what had she – they – learned that put their lives in danger. What frustrated him almost as much as not knowing who was after her; or, based on the reports from Pete Jeffers, the deputy chief of mission at the embassy in Kazbektun, was not knowing what they knew.

He'd never paid much attention to such things. In school, history hadn't been his favorite subject, and he didn't recall the few times he stayed awake in class that secret societies had been even mentioned. He had heard talk about groups like Yale's Skull and Bones Society after he joined DSS, but hadn't paid much attention.

Well, he thought, guess I have my work cut out for me. I have to keep a bunch of guys whose identities I don't know from killing a woman I just met and think I'm seriously falling in love with.

"If you're right," he said. "We'll really have to watch our backs, and so will the guys out in Dagastan. I'll get word to Pete. And, here I was thinking this assignment was going to be boring."

Alison looked at him, and her eyes widened. He was smiling again. *My God,* she thought, *I think he's enjoying this.*

CHARLES RAY

Chapter 24

Wednesday, May 21, 1975, Dagastan

There's something about an office building at night. Regardless of its function, no matter how noisy it gets during the day; at night, when the only sound is the hum, clank, and buzz of the machinery that keeps it running, the elevators, the water pipes, miles of electric wiring, when it's almost empty except for the graveyard shift of night workers, mostly cleaning crews, night guards, and the workaholics, when it takes on a menacing appearance.

Embassies are just office buildings, and they take on the same transformation.

No matter how many times he worked late, David Morgan found himself stopping every few minutes to listen to some stray sound that he hadn't noticed before. Some whisper or buzz that during the day, when the place was filled with the sound of hushed voices and soft footfalls and rustling paper, he'd failed to notice. And, he had to admit that on occasion it unsettled him.

With everything that had been happening of late, the night sounds were even more unsettling. But, he'd been preoccupied with a minor emergency during the day, the main water pipe had burst, and he had to work with the administrative section to reshuffle people around the building so that work could continue while emergency crews repaired the pipe and restored full water supply. Washington didn't care about the embassy's minor emergency, the bureaucracy wanted its pound of flesh; or, in this case, several pounds of paper, come hell or high water. So, here it was, almost nine at night, and he was at his desk, doggedly moving documents from his IN tray to his OUT tray, so that Mary Sung, his secretary, could get them in the outgoing pouch first thing the next morning.

He found that he could only apply part of his mind to the task; paperwork had never been his favorite part of the job. Morgan was fortunate, however, in being able to absorb the main points of papers without paying much attention, of reading whole blocks of text at a glance rather than having to read word by word, or even sentence by sentence. This made it possible for him to move paperwork off his desk with astonishing speed, but still maintain a level of quality. He wasn't a fan of bosses who rewrote everything submitted to them by their subordinates either. If a memorandum or dispatch didn't communicate clearly, he'd merely scribble that fact across the top and send it back to the author to be redone. After a few weeks, the word had filtered down: the new deputy won't do it for you, so if you don't want to have to be doing it over and over again, get it right the first time.

When Pete Jeffers poked his head around the door frame, Morgan welcomed the intrusion. His eyes were beginning to sting from poring over page after page of the jargon that passed for in-depth, perceptive reporting on inconsequential events that even the participants had forgotten about almost before the acts were concluded.

"What's up, Pete?" he asked. "I know why I'm working late, but why are you burning the midnight oil?"

"Same as you, boss; feeding the beast. I had some security reports that will soon be overdue, so I figured I'd hang around and do 'em tonight. I also had to call Lee Kennedy in DC."

Morgan pushed the last stack of papers before him aside. "What's the latest from Foggy Bottom?"

Jeffers filled him in on his conversation with Kennedy. At the mention of Hitchcock's name, Morgan's brow furrowed.

"What's up, Dave?" Jeffers asked. "You know this guy?"

"I know of him. A couple of my instructors in the orientation course mentioned him. He was apparently a real climber in the Foreign Service, but he ran into some kind of problem in the late sixties and retired. Funny thing is, the people who mentioned him seemed conflicted; I could never tell if they admired him or feared him; and, they'd never give us the details of what kind of problem he had. Sounds like he still has his fingers in things."

"What worries me," Jeffers said. "Is that Lee said he saw him with a guy that looks like the person who assaulted his friend from INR."

"Something tells me there's more to this than we know. Maybe I should ask Raine if his agency can get us any information on these guys."

"Are you sure you can trust him? I'll tell you; right now you're about the only person in this place I trust."

Morgan put his hands flat on the desk and looked at the young officer with a wan smile on his brown face. "I have a feeling we *can* trust him, so I'm going with my gut. If I'm wrong, though, you'd better be prepared to watch your back, because we're in deep shit."

After Jeffers had gone, Morgan sat for a while before picking up the phone and dialing an internal extension.

"Regional Affairs, Raine speaking."

"Blood, this is Dave Morgan; glad I caught you still in. Can I come up and talk to you?"

There was a pause. "Sure, Dave. I just happen to be here by myself, but come on up. Just buzz when you get here and I'll come out and let you in."

Morgan looked at his the much diminished stack of paper in his IN tray and decided he could clear it all if he came in a bit earlier the next morning. He took both trays and secured them in his safe. He turned out the light in his office, and walked around the reception area outside his and the ambassador's office to make sure no sensitive material had been left unsecured, knowing that the marine guard on the graveyard shift, to combat boredom often did an extra thorough check of the front office in hopes of finding a stray classified document left unsecured, or a safe not securely locked. The young marines loved it when they could issue pink slips, their reports of security violation, to the ambassador or deputy.

He made his way down the hall to the unmarked door at the end. Punching in the code for the cipher lock, he opened it and entered into a well-lit alcove with stairs rising up toward a metal door at the top. Behind that door was the station, the intelligence officers assigned to the embassy. Carlton Raine was the senior intelligence officer, or chief of station, and while he ostensibly worked under the ambassador's authority, Morgan knew that the man had other tasks to perform that neither he nor the ambassador had the required clearance to be briefed on.

At the top of the stairs, he pushed the black button near the cipher panel and then positioned himself directly in front of the door so that he could be seen through the peephole set about head high in the thick steel.

The door made a hissing sound as it swung inward. Raine stood there smiling. He waited until Morgan had entered and then pushed the door close, waiting until it was firmly settled in the metal frame before speaking.

"What's up, Dave?" he asked, walking toward his office which a windowless cube in the corner just behind a desk where normally a bull of a woman who was the station's secretary sat.

After Raine had seated himself behind his paper-littered desk, Morgan sat in a leather upholstered chair across from him. He filled him in on what he'd learned from Jeffers, as well as the incident when he'd been chased by the four men the previous weekend. He noticed that Raine didn't seem surprised at any of this.

"Can you or any of your guys tell me what the hell's going on, Blood?"

Raine stared across the space between them, his brows furrowed until they almost met at the top of his nose. He put a finger against his nose. Finally, he sighed. "I can't tell you much, Dave; in fact, I could get my ass in a sling for what I'm about to tell you now. Something's going on here; something's about to pop, and when it goes down, it won't be pretty. My sources can't tell me exactly what it is, but they all say there's outside involvement, and a couple of them have even hinted that there's American involvement."

"You aren't telling me anything I don't already know," Morgan said. "Do you have any leads, for instance, on the guys who came after me?"

"Only that I'm pretty convinced they weren't from the security service." Raine shook his head. "At least, not the part of the service that we work with."

"What's that supposed to mean?"

"This is the part that's really sensitive, and I mean *really* sensitive, Dave. I'm picking up hints that there's some fissures in the service; that people are lining up on one side or another, and that could lead to a fight."

"I'm assuming one of the sides is Dmitri Kovasc?"

"Yeah; but, I can't figure out who the other

side is."

"I thought you guys were wired into every level of this government?"

Raine laughed harshly. "So did I until this current shit started happening. Turns out, we've only scratched the surface. These people have had centuries of playing off stronger against weaker forces, dancing around with the Russians; I guess dealing with us was relatively easy for them."

"So, tell me this; how does the ambassador fit into all this, and what the hell is White Dragon?"

Raine's eyes widened slightly. After a heartbeat's hesitation, he spoke. "I'm trying to figure out what our good ambassador's up to. He and Dragov have been meeting, but no one can tell me what they discuss. I've been reluctant to ask him without having more background information. As to White Dragon, one or two of my sources have mentioned it, but I have no idea what it is."

"The name's come up in Washington, too," Morgan said. "It sounds like an American organization."

"Well, if it is, it's kept pretty far below the radar. I've never heard the name before, and I can't find reference to it in any of our files."

"Have you checked with your people at

Langley?"

"Yeah, but they haven't gotten back to me yet. If I can, I'll let you know if they find anything. Anything else?"

"There is one thing. When are you going to tell me how you got the nickname Blood?"

CHARLES RAY

Chapter 25

Wednesday, May 21, 1975, Washington, DC

Alison Chambers was sitting at her desk, a stack of papers in front of her, which she couldn't concentrate on, when Earline walked into her office.

"Alison, there's a man out here wants to talk to you. He won't give me a name or why he wants to see you, but he must have clearance, because he came in unescorted."

"Does he look dangerous?"

"No, he just looks weird."

"Well, in that case, show him in."

Alison laughed. If only, she thought, you knew just how weird my life has been the past few days.

Earline disappeared, only to reappear a few seconds later with a thin, hawk beaked man with receding gray hair and a gray suit in tow. She ushered him into Alison's office, gave her a raised-brow look and departed.

"Please," Alison said. "Won't you have a seat?" She indicated the chair near her desk. The man walked over and sat in the other chair near the filing cabinets. "Who are you, and why did you want to talk to me?"

"My name is of no importance, Miss Chambers." The man's voice was gray; lifeless and without feeling. "It is the information I have for you that is important."

Alison felt heat in her cheeks. She didn't know what game the stranger was playing, but her patience with the bureaucratic maneuverings in the building was almost at an end. Something about having a stranger with a knife lurking about your doorstep in the dark did that to you, she thought.

"Look, whoever you are; I'm not in the mood for fun and games right now. If you can't tell me who you are, I don't think there's anything you have to say that I'm interested in hearing, so just get the hell out of my office."

A tiny hint of color appeared in the pale face. The gray man reacted as if struck. "They said you were likely to be aggressive. I fear they underestimated your emotional state. Very well, if you must have a name, you can call me Mr. Jones."

Even though the stranger showed no emotion as he spoke, other than the momentary discomfiture from her outburst, Alison knew somehow that his name wasn't Jones. He was an accomplished liar, which also told her who he likely worked for.

"Okay, *Mr. Jones*; what is it you have to say to me?"

The man placed his narrow hands on his lap, entwining his bony fingers and looking, not at her face, but at a space on the desk in front of her. When he spoke, his voice was soft, but there was a note of menace in it. "You have recently been looking into events in Central Asia, in Dagastan to be precise, have you not?"

"As an intelligence analyst, it's to be expected that I would be doing that."

"But, in this particular research, we understand that you've run across the White Dragons."

Alison felt a strange tingling on the backs of her hands, and a fluttering in her chest. This stranger seemed to know more about her than she was comfortable with him knowing. Why, she wondered, would her browsing through the news files be of interest to him or anyone else, and even more important, *how* did he know?

"Yes, that name has popped up once or twice." She tried to keep her voice level, but her pulse was racing. "Why; is it of interest to your organization?"

"Let us just say that it is important to people

in this town that you would be well advised not to run afoul of, Miss Chambers. What have you learned about this White Dragon?"

Now, she could feel the heat in her cheeks, but the feeling wasn't fear – she was angry. How dare these people, whoever they are, send this mousy little man to threaten her! She breathed deeply to control her raging emotions. Now was not the time to let her stubborn Georgia personality leap to the fore. After silently counting to ten – and, then, counting to ten yet again, she gazed steadily at the little man who sat as still as a gray statue, not even a sign of movement in his eyes as he regarded her.

"I haven't learned a thing," she said finally. "It's just a name that has popped up a couple of times. The only reason I've even been interested is because it came up in connection with some kind of American involvement in Dagastan, and that's just unusual enough to arouse my curiosity."

There was some movement in the stranger's face; not quite a smile, but the ends of the lips did rise up fractionally. "You know the old saying, Ms. Chambers; curiosity killed the cat. Your curiosity has taken you into some rather dangerous territory."

"Are you threatening me, Mr. Jones?" She leaned forward, her hands planted flat on her desk, glaring at him.

"Oh my, not at all," he said, leaning back in his chair as if to ward off a blow. "We don't make threats. You might call this a bit of friendly advice. There has already been one casualty that should have been avoided. We would not like to see another."

Alison suddenly felt as if a window had been blown open somewhere and an icy cold draft of air admitted. She clinched her muscles to keep the tremors she felt from showing. "Y-you're talking about Lesley Carter?"

The man nodded. "Unfortunately, we did not learn of her involvement until it was too late."

"Are you here to warn me to stop looking into this?"

Now, the man was definitely smiling, although, it did nothing to ease the ghostlike look of his narrow, pale face; in fact, the smile only made him look more grotesque to Alison. "No, Ms. Chambers," he said in that soft, almost seductive voice. "If we thought it would do any good, perhaps we would recommend that you drop your inquiries. I have a feeling, though, that it would do no good. Instead, I will merely tell you to proceed with extreme caution. And, one final thing; don't trust anyone."

With that, the stranger stood, brushed at the fronts of his trousers, adjusted his jacket, and left.

Alison sat there staring at the door. Trust no one. The words echoed in her mind. That had been a warning she hadn't needed. She didn't trust anyone; well, she did trust Lee Kennedy, but other than Lee, she now looked at everyone else in the building with suspicion. And, most of all – no, strike that, she thought, *least* of all did she trust the little man in gray who had just left her office.

Chapter 26

When her breathing has slowed enough that she felt she could speak without rambling, Alison called Kennedy's office and asked him to meet her in the cafeteria on the building's first floor.

They arrived at about the same time, and after getting large containers of the noxious brew being served, paid and found an empty table in the far corner near the large glass windows looking onto the interior courtyard. There were few people in the place at that time of day, and the tables around them were empty.

"Okay, what's so important that I have to risk my stomach in this place?" Kennedy said when they'd seated.

Alison told him of her visitor and his warning.

"You took him seriously?"

"He knew too much about what I was doing for me not to," she said. "I don't trust him; in fact, right now, I don't trust anyone in this building but you. I just don't know what to do next."

Kennedy played with the coffee cup, picking it up and sniffing at it, then putting it back on the table. "Well, he's right about one thing; you need to be careful. You might also consider contacting the DCM in Kazbektun, David Morgan; Pete Jeffers says he's a straight up kind of guy. Tell him what you've found out, and see what he might know."

"I guess you're right." Alison nodded. "This is so strange. I mean, having to hide things from co-workers and supervisors. It's like we're in some perverted version of *1984* or something." Kennedy gave her a puzzled look. "That's a novel by George Orwell. It's about this society that's under the control of Big Brother, where independent thought is prohibited. It's all about secret societies and conspiracies and the like."

"Oh, yeah," Kennedy said. "I sort of remember hearing about it, but I never got a chance to read it. It was banned in my high school."

"Mine too, but I got a bootleg copy from my English teacher and read it. Anyway, I should get back to the office and call Dave Morgan. With the time difference, if I wait until noon, he'll likely not be in the embassy, and I want to talk to him over the secure phone."

"Good idea. I'll come by and pick you up for

lunch."

She smiled at the prospect. She felt a flutter in her chest at the thought of spending time with him. At least, she thought, some things are normal.

"Aren't you going to drink your coffee?"

"Are you kidding?" He pushed the cup toward the center of the table. "That's another piece of advice. Never drink the coffee in the State Department cafeteria."

CHARLES RAY

Chapter 27

Wednesday, May 21, 1975, Dagastan

It was just about eight in the evening, and David Morgan was securing the papers in his office when he heard the unfamiliar warble of the secure telephone in the cabinet against the wall behind his desk.

Finding the key that enabled secure communication took a few minutes. In the entire time he'd been in Dagastan, the thing had never rung.

"American Embassy, Kazbektun," he said. "This is DCM Morgan speaking."

"Mr. Morgan," the distorted female voice said in his ear. "My name is Alison Chambers. I'm an analyst in INR, and I'm currently working on Dagastan. I hope I haven't caught you at a bad time."

Morgan put his hand over the mouthpiece and laughed softly. Typical of a Washington bureaucrat to be unmindful of the time difference when something was wanted from the field. It wasn't even lunch time yet in DC. "That's quite all right, Ms. Chambers. I was closing up the office to go home, but we're always happy to be of service to the department."

He knew that his voice on the other end was as distorted as hers had been, so his sarcasm was probably missed.

"I know it's late there, and I do apologize for that, but it's important and couldn't wait. And, please, call me Alison."

Alison then filled him in on what had been happening in Washington, leaving out no details. As Morgan listened, he regretted his sarcastic tone, even if she hadn't picked up on it.

"Okay, Alison; I'm Dave by the way; I got a lot of this from my RSO, but it's good to hear it from a different source. We've been picking up the name White Dragon here, too; that, and the involvement of Americans somehow." He told her about his visitor.

"This man Vechkov; he didn't say what the thing of value was?"

"He claimed not to know. But, whatever it is, it's apparently important enough to have us and the Soviets involved."

"When you say us, you mean us as a nation, not the government, right?"

"Until I heard about the involvement of a U.S. Senator and this retired diplomat meeting with a senior official of the State Department, that's what I would have meant. Now, I'm not so sure."

Alison then told him about the visit she'd received from the man in gray.

"What do you want to bet that your visitor was from a certain unnamed agency across the river?"

He could hear a sound that indicated Alison was laughing, and then her voice, somewhat garbled and tinny, "No bets on that. I'm just puzzled at what their role is in all this."

Morgan, too, was puzzled. He still trusted Carlton Raine; thought of him as a friend; but, he also knew that the man's loyalty to his agency and his profession might take precedence over personal relationships. "I have the same problem with my ambassador," he said. "He's been acting strangely lately; clandestine meetings that he refuses to describe, or even tell us about, banning reporting on certain issues; I can't help but think that he knows what's going on, that he knows who or what this White Dragon is."

"I think," Alison said. "That if we can answer that question, we'll have the key to what's going on, both here in Washington and there in Dagastan. But, Dave, you have to be careful.

Whatever this is, there seems to be someone who doesn't want us prying into it, and I don't know what they might do."

"I've a pretty good idea. After all, you've already had one person murdered there, and you yourself attacked. I think we know that there's nothing they won't do; so, you be careful yourself."

For a long moment, the only sound Morgan heard from the ear piece was the whistling static. "I guess," Alison's voice said. "That means we all have to be careful." She gave him two phone numbers. "The first is my office line, and the second is the home of Lee Kennedy. Since the attack, I've been staying at his house. If you need anything, or learn anything, regardless of the time of day, call me."

Morgan recited the phone number of his residence. "Same goes for you, Alison. If you can't get through to me at home or the embassy switchboard, leave a number and I'll get back to you."

The line went dead as Alison broke it at her end. Morgan had a somber look on his face as he removed the code key from its slot on the front of the device and placed it back in the top drawer of his safe. Alison's news had cast a chill over him. The thought of senior U.S. government officials involved in some clandestine deal, a deal so sensitive they seemed willing to kill to keep it from being known, was frightening.

Had he been able to see Ellingsworth standing just outside the door to his office, his attention focused on the just-concluded phone call, a dark and angry look on his face, he would have been even more frightened.

CHARLES RAY

Chapter 28

Wednesday, May 21, 1975, Washington, DC

As Alison put the secure phone handset back into its cradle, she looked up to see Dudley Lakeworth, a scowl on his face, standing in the door of her office.

"Who were you just talking to?" he asked.

Alison felt the heat in her cheeks. She felt somewhat embarrassed at the thought that he probably had overheard her conversation, but, at the same time, she felt anger that he would so brazenly eavesdrop on her. This just wasn't done in polite society; and the analysts of INR were a very polite society; a group of introverts who left each other a significant radius of personal space; not 'empty bundles of good manners,' as senior diplomats were often described, more orbiting stars, careful not to perturb the orbits of others.

After she'd had time to compose herself and calm her breathing, she looked up at him, a noncommittal look on her face. "That was the DCM out in Kazbektun," she said. "I was just checking with him regarding a few questions I had on some embassy reporting."

"And, just what does Niles Hitchcock or White Dragons have to do with reporting from an obscure embassy in the middle of nowhere?"

He had been listening to her entire conversation, she thought. That he wouldn't even try to conceal the fact worried her. She took another deep breath. "That's what I was asking him. The two names keep popping up, and it makes no sense. I was hoping he could shed some light."

Lakeworth moved into the office, standing just inside the entrance. He had a worried look on his face. "Are you sure this is the best use of your time?"

"I'm sorry, but I don't understand. Aren't we supposed to gather and analyze information that might have an impact on our policy?"

"Of course we are." He laced his fingers, holding his hands in front of his crouch defensively. "But, we shouldn't be wasting our time chasing phantoms. In addition, there's the question of the propriety of poking our noses into the affairs of American citizens, especially an individual with a distinguished record of public service."

"By that, I assume you mean Mr. Hitchcock?"

"Niles Hitchcock served this nation honorably, Ms. Chambers. I simply do not see how your prying into his affairs has any bearing on some obscure incident in a country that most Americans have never even heard of."

Alison knew that her cheeks were reddening; she could feel the heat. Could this little popinjay really be that dense, she thought, that he would presume to tell her how to do her job? She hadn't gone looking for Hitchcock. He'd presented himself to her when he met with Lee's boss, the senator, and the mysterious man in black; the man she was certain had been the same one on her steps with a knife.

"I'm not prying into his *personal* affairs, Mr. Lakeworth." She fixed him with a steady gaze. "But, as I investigate the situation in Dagastan, his name keeps cropping up. I don't know what's going on out there, but whatever it is, it doesn't seem good for this country to be involved in it. I'm just following the leads that I find. If Mr. Hitchcock has done nothing wrong, the more I know, the easier it will be to prove that."

"You're not seriously suggesting that he's involved in wrongdoing, are you? That, I can assure you, would be a mistake on your part."

"I'm not *suggesting* anything. I'm just telling you what I've learned. I think I'd be derelict in my duties not to pursue this to its conclusion."

Lakeworth squared his shoulders. His face took on a stony look. "I'm telling you that your duties are to do analysis of information that is related to our policy. Niles Hitchcock's affairs are not, and I'm ordering you to cease your prying forthwith."

She couldn't believe what she was hearing. Never in all the time she'd been in INR had anyone told her not to gather and make sense of information, particularly about a situation as murky as Dagastan and what seemed to be transpiring there.

Her instinct was to tell him to shove his order. She would have liked nothing better than to see the look on his face, should she tell him to go to hell. She bit her lip and glared at him, her eyes glistening with tears that she stubbornly refused to shed.

Lakeworth stood, looking down at her, for several moments. Finally, when it was clear that she would not respond – couldn't really, he thought to himself – he turned and walked away.

Alison got up and swiftly crossed the distance to the door, pushing it shut. She then turned and rested her back against the smooth wood and slid down until her hips touched the floor.

She folded her arms across her knees and rested her forehead on her arms. And then,

Alison Chambers quietly wept.

Chapter 29

At six, Alison was waiting at the elevator in the basement parking garage, when the doors slid open and Kennedy emerged with a worried look on his face. When he saw her, he smiled and grabbed her shoulders.

"You were supposed to wait for me at your office," he said. "I really don't think you should be wandering around here without an escort."

She'd been able to get her emotions under control, sitting alone on the floor of her office, but his nearness, the heat she could feel from his hands resting on her shoulders, brought it all back. The words poured out, as did a new torrent of tears.

Kennedy pulled her against his chest, rubbed her back, and let her talk. He could feel her body trembling as she spoke. When she'd finished, she'd also stopped crying, although the tremors continued. She lay her head against his shoulder.

"Will you drop it?" he asked quietly. "Will you stop trying to figure out what's going on?"

She pulled back and looked up into his eyes. "When hell freezes over. I'm not letting that little weasel intimidate me."

He kissed her gently on the forehead. "That's what I wanted to hear; now, why don't I take you home?"

She knew that by home, he didn't mean her house in DC; and, that made her feel good.

Chapter 30

Thursday, May 22, 1975, Dagastan

Morgan was back in the embassy at six, after a sleepless night. The call from Alison Chambers, an INR analyst he'd never met, worried him. It's bad enough to have strange things happening on the ground, but when things start to go wrong back in Washington, he thought, it doesn't leave much room for maneuver. He'd always had the comfort of knowing that no matter how bad things got in a country, he could always depend on backstopping from the country desk back at the State Department. So far, there'd been no announcement of a desk officer to replace the slain Lesley Carter, and the country director, James Whitman hadn't communicated with him either.

Morgan vaguely remembered Whitman from the orientation meetings he'd had in Washington before coming to Dagastan. The man had briefly dropped in on a meeting he was having with the then desk officer, a young man named William Courtney, a shy, retiring type who spoke seldom, and who seemed to avoid contact with people outside his office unless directed to do so. Courtney had been replaced by Carter, and until her untimely death, she'd made it a practice to contact him or the embassy political officer at least once a week, sometimes for nothing other than filling them in on Washington gossip. He had a sinking feeling that the powers that be would assign another bureaucratic drone to the position, some young officer looking to get his Washington assignment out of the way while he looked for a good overseas job.

That, of course, was the least of his worries. As he sat at his desk, staring at the pile of documents Mary Sung had dumped into his IN tray, he was doing a mental juggling act; trying to decide how much could be ignored, what could be delegated to someone else, and which items he'd have to personally attend to. With the news from Washington, and their own local mystery weighing on his mind, filling in the bureaucratic blanks of his job was low on his list of priorities.

A rap at his door was a welcome diversion. It was Pete Jeffers, standing in the door holding a small green bag. "Dave, got a minute?"

"Always, Pete, come on in."

The security officer carefully and quietly closed the door behind him when he entered.

This got Morgan's attention. Unless he was having a sensitive meeting, or reaming someone out for screwing up, he seldom closed his office door, preferring to leave it open so people felt free to come and see him. He knew that Jeffers was aware of that, so, he obviously had a reason. When he crossed the room and opened the green bag, Morgan saw why. Jeffers pulled a large, black, lethal looking revolver from the bag and slid it across the desk.

"I've been thinking," he said in a quiet voice. "I got guys shadowing you, and I try to stay pretty close myself, but, you need to be able to protect yourself. You know how to use one of these things, right?"

Morgan recognized the .357 magnum. He didn't own a gun; wasn't much in favor of having them around; but, he'd been exposed to them during his time in the military. He'd been an expert marksman with both rifle and handgun, but after leaving the military, hadn't touched one. He hefted the weapon, noting that the cylinders were empty. Jeffers pulled a box of shells from the bag and placed them on the desk.

"I know how to use one," Morgan said. "But, are you sure this is a good idea? The ambassador's only authorized you and the chief of station to have weapons."

"Yeah, I know what the ambassador's

firearms policy is, so technically this is breaking the rules, but, the situation we're in now isn't normal. I want to make sure we're ready for anything that might happen. I can trust you to keep this thing out of sight unless you absolutely have to use it, can't I?"

Morgan put the gun back on the desk, staring down at it. *Has it come to this? Must I now arm myself, in violation of the ambassador's policy, because I don't trust the ambassador?* Of course, he knew the answer. He couldn't trust the ambassador. The man was playing some kind of shadowy game, and if what he'd surmised from his phone conversation with Alison Chambers was correct, a deadly game. He wasn't sure by what train of logic he'd come to the conclusion, but he was convinced that the death of Lesley Carter in Washington was somehow connected with events in Dagastan, and furthermore, there were people in Washington, in the organization he'd come to love, who were behind it. *This is the kind of stuff that's only supposed to happen in the movies or pulp novels.* But, it was happening, and if he let his guard down, he could be a casualty. Worse, if he slipped, someone else in the embassy could become a victim.

He picked the pistol up again, and put it in the top drawer of his desk. He then picked up the box of ammunition and placed it beside the weapon. After closing the drawer, he looked at

Jeffers and sighed. "Damn, Pete, I hope I never have to use this thing. What have we come to, when I have to consider having a gun in my office and home?"

Jeffers shrugged. "I don't know, Dave, but, do me a favor; if you have to use it, shoot to kill. Our asses are gonna be in a sling if you shoot somebody, but at least I want you to be alive to face the music."

Morgan laughed. "You mean, if I get myself killed, you'll have to explain why I had a gun I couldn't use, right?"

"Damn straight. I'd much rather explain why you popped somebody who was trying to kill you, and have you standing next to me when I did it."

CHARLES RAY

Chapter 31

Thursday, May 22, 1975, Washington, DC

Alison felt much better after a good night's sleep. She'd sat on the sofa, with Kennedy's arms around her until midnight, when he finally, and she was sure, reluctantly, urged her to go to the bedroom and get some sleep.

After dropping Rachel at school, Kennedy drove Alison to Metropolitan Police Headquarters to meet with Al Murphy so that she could give him her account of the assault at her house. She could add very little to the description of the assailant, other than he had close-set, light-colored, lifeless eyes – like a snake. In the dim light, she'd been unable to get a good look at any other features, describing his hair, for instance, as either close-dropped or comb close to the skull. As he had done with Kennedy, Murphy bluntly informed her that it was highly unlikely they'd find the suspect with the sketchy description they had, but the police would keep trying.

It was nearly nine when they arrived at the door of the suite where Alison worked.

She paused at the door, looking at his breastbone, rather than meeting his eyes.

"What's wrong, Alison?" he asked.

"I was just thinking . . . I mean, I'd like you to come into my office with me," she said. "Just a thought, but, I'd like that little weasel Lakeworth to know I have someone behind me."

"I don't mind doing it, but it doesn't make any sense. You think this guy's a threat to you?"

She shook her head and looked up into his eyes. "No, not really, but, I'm still steamed at the way he spoke to me yesterday. I - -"

He put a finger on her lips. "I get it. Don't worry, I'll try to look appropriately intimidating."

She smiled as she punched in the numbers that opened the cipher lock. Kennedy held the heavy metal door as she walked through, and then he followed her toward her office.

As they came abreast of the secretary's desk, the woman looked up. When she saw Kennedy, her brown face brightened in a broad smile.

"Well, well, Alison, what do we have here?"

"Earline, this is Lee Kennedy. He's with Diplomatic Security. He's providing me with additional security."

Kennedy winced at giving out so much information, but tried to maintain a stoic look.

"Aren't you a long drink of water?" Earline said. "You could provide security for me any day." She gave Alison a wink as she spoke, causing her cheeks to redden.

"Is Mr. Lakeworth in?" Alison asked, trying to change the subject.

"No, he's late this morning. You need to talk to him?"

Alison shook her head.

"I'd better be going," Kennedy said. "I'll pick you up at lunch."

He gave Alison's shoulder a light squeeze, turned, and walked away. Both women's gazes followed him.

"Now, that is one fine looking man," Earline said after the metal door had sighed shut. "So, he's your bodyguard?"

Alison told her about the attempted assault, and about Kennedy's suspicion that the murder of the desk officer might somehow be related. "He's looking out for me until we find out what's going on."

"Girl, if you're smart, you'll have that man looking out for you after you find out what's going on."

Alison shook her head and laughed. She went to her office and began the process of ignoring Lakeworth's injunction to drop the Dagastan case.

She made several trips back and forth to the file room, lugging stacks of dusty manila folders and newspapers. When she ran out of space on her desk, she started spreading documents on the floor.

Her first step was to do a quick analysis of Dagastan, its history and geography, which yielded little useful information; certainly nothing that would point to the events of the recent past. The country had been a backwater for its entire existence. It hadn't been on any significant trade route, commanded no strategic crossroads or strongpoints, and had never been fought over by any of the invading armies that had, over the centuries, crossed this region of the world. In fact, except for the poor souls who had, for reasons lost to history, chosen to settle here, most groups had simply bypassed it.

Nor did her study of the ethnic groups provide any clues to the mystery. While the Kazbektuni had a numerical majority, but no political power, this had been the case throughout the country's history. There had never been even a hint of ethnic discord, or potential for rebellion. Like the feudal societies of ancient Europe, everyone in Dagastan seemed to accept the status quo.

There might, Alison thought, be something in the backgrounds of the current political and military leaders of the country, but the biographical reporting was thin. Dagastan's notables had apparently not come to the attention of those in the intelligence establishment who compiled such dossiers. She made a note to ask the embassy to begin doing reports on individuals in the country.

This left her with only the domestic side of the enigma. Fortunately, there was a large amount of reporting on at least two of the individuals involved; Senator Carlton Longroux and Niles Hitchcock.

Longroux, the junior senator from Alabama, had originally come from Louisiana. He'd been a student at the University of Alabama during the 1950s, graduating at the height of the McCarthy hearings, when the irascible senator from Wisconsin had been accusing half the executive branch of being soft on communism and of being infiltrated by communists. The absolute fear McCarthy inspired in many of his victims had impressed the young Longroux, who began working for a congressman within whose district the university was located. Two years after graduation, he ran against his former boss, defeating him soundly, and then went on to serve four terms in the U.S. House of Representatives before his election to the senate. He was completing his second term in that body, but was considered a sure thing for re-election.

During his time in the House of Representatives, and later as a senator, Longroux had made his reputation as something of a firebrand; often parting ways with his own party on issues, particularly regarding foreign affairs. He had been a thorn in the side of every administration, Republican or Democrat, since being elected to congress, often arguing for stronger positions on foreign affairs issues than the occupants of the White House, and even many in congress, thought prudent.

Niles Hitchcock was harder to pin down. A native of Gloucester, Massachusetts; Hitchcock came from a well-to-do family with antecedents dating back to the founding of the Massachusetts Colony. The sketchy files on him indicated that he'd had a privileged upbringing, attending private preparatory schools and then graduating *magna cum laude* from Harvard in the early 1950s with a degree in international relations. He'd entered the Foreign Service upon his graduation from Harvard, and had risen quickly through the ranks, serving in high level positions within the Department of State, including an assignment to the National Security Council as a special advisor just before his retirement from government service. Alison noted, though, that, despite his rapid promotions and positions of responsibility, he'd never been appointed ambassador, the premiere assignment for career diplomats. The few positions listed in the files indicated that he had always been an *advisor* or *special assistant,* positions that in the right hands could be just as influential or powerful as being the number one. Better in many ways, she thought, as she read. He'd been in a position to determine the direction of policy without ever having to bear any responsibility for such policy. From all that she could see, he was still pulling strings from behind the curtains.

Nowhere in the increasingly untidy pile of papers, though, did she see any reference to White Dragons, except for one tiny memo buried in a thick stack of documents; a memo written in the late 60s by a mid-level analyst. The cryptic memo referred to a cabal of senior people within the Foreign Service, primarily Ivy League people, who viewed themselves as the *raison d'etre* for having a career service in the first place. The final sentence caught her eye: MY SOURCE, WHO I SHALL NOT NAME, TOLD ME THAT THE CAREER FOREIGN SERVICE WAS IMPORTANT; BUT, IT ONLY EXISTS SO THAT THOSE OF US WHO REALLY MATTER CAN BE MADE AVAILABLE WHEN THE COUNTRY NEEDS US.

Could that refer to the White Dragons, she thought? Could this unidentified group of men – and, she was absolutely sure they were all male – be the cryptic group involved in the current crisis? A shadowy group of people with common backgrounds setting themselves apart from all others; Knights Templar with a mission to set the world right? She thought of the often sarcastic comments she'd heard in conversations around the building, when the few women who, by virtue of remaining single, were allowed to remain on active service, describing the Foreign Service as, pale, male, and Yale. While she knew this to be only partially accurate, it did in fact describe a large percentage of the diplomatic service; a service that had few women, fewer minorities, and whose top levels were dominated by a coterie of Ivy League graduates. The Foreign Service was, as far as Alison had been able to see during her time in INR, mainly a good old boys' club whose upper ranks were restricted to a chosen few.

She flipped open the steno pad in which she'd been making notes as she pored through the documents scattered around her, and made a few notes. As a last sentence, she wrote, ARE THE WHITE DRAGONS A SUBSET OF THE SERVICE?

She closed the pad and stuffed it in her purse, and began shuffling the papers into neater stacks.

"Miss Chambers, do you mind telling me what you're doing?"

Lakeworth's voice startled her. She hadn't heard him open the door to her office. When she looked up, she saw him standing in the doorway with his hands on his hips, an angry expression on his face. She clutched at her purse.

He moved into the office, looking down at the scattered papers. His brow furrowed.

"I thought my instructions were quite specific, and clear," he said. "You were to cease your work on Dagastan and your snooping into Niles Hitchcock's background."

His foot was on a news clipping that had a blurred photo of Hitchcock in a group of somber looking men in dark suits at some international conference in Europe. Trying to deny that she'd defied his orders was useless, and she knew it. She decided to try to brazen her way through it.

"I know what you said, but, I believe the incidents taking place in Dagastan are important."

"Important enough to risk your career over?"

She looked up at him, wide-eyed. "W-what do you mean?"

"I mean, Miss Chambers; that you have deliberately and flagrantly disobeyed a direct order given to you by me. Effective immediately you are on administrative leave pending a decision on what to do about you. If you're lucky, Personnel won't fire you, but I can assure you that you'll no longer be working in

INR."

Alison's mouth dropped open. Her brain was having difficulty processing his words.

"Y-you can't do that. I've only been doing the job I was hired to do."

He laughed; a mirthless, rasping sound. "Your job is whatever I say it is, Ms. Chambers. It is also *not* what I say it's not, and I told you it was *not* your job to stick your nose into matters in Dagastan. You chose to disregard my instructions. I am, therefore, totally within my rights to take action against you for act of disrespect. Now, please remove your personal things from this office, and remove yourself from this suite immediately."

He folded his arms across his bony chest, and stared down at her over the tip of his nose. Alison looked around. She wasn't in the habit, as so many were, of decorating her office with personal items, and she didn't choose to display her photos or certificates. Her sole personal item was the scuffed brown purse she carried, and in which she kept her wallet, house keys, and spare change; and, at the moment, the steno pad containing all her notes on Dagastan and the White Dragons.

Brazen hadn't worked. She'd hoped he would back down if she pushed the issue. He'd surprised her. Whatever was happening, it was serious enough to cause people to act completely out of character.

She eyed him warily as she tucked her purse under her arm and slowly stood. She decided to give it one more shot. "I feel it only fair to warn you; I plan to file a grievance with personnel over this. I think you're exceeding your authority."

Lakeworth didn't blink. He just continued to stare at her. The mere mention of grievances was usually enough to make most supervisors seek another way to handle problems. He seemed not to have even registered her threat.

"Time is running out, Miss Chambers," he said. "Now, are you going to do the civilized thing and leave, or must I call security and have you escorted out."

Alison knew when she was beaten. He'd won this round. Now, she had to conduct a dignified retreat if she was to help Lee finish the battle, which, as far as she was concerned was far from over.

CHARLES RAY

Chapter 32

On her way out, Alison stopped at Earline's desk long enough to give her instructions to forward any personal correspondence to Lee Kennedy's office. The secretary had overheard Lakeworth's words, and was fighting back tears as she wrote. Alison, too, felt like crying, but not from sadness. She was fighting mad and determined to strike back. But, she knew she would need help to do it, and at that moment, the only person she could rely on was Lee.

The two women hugged briefly, and Alison left without looking back. She walked down the stairs to Kennedy's floor, and followed the long hallway to the obscure corner office where he worked.

None of her anger had faded by the time she got there, but the tears had started to flow.

Kennedy, red-faced with his own anger, considered going up to INR and having it out with Lakeworth, but his own good sense and Alison's urging held him back. She convinced him that they needed to bide their time and fight smart, rather than trying a frontal assault against an unknown enemy.

When she asked if he could drive her home, and this time, both of them knew what she meant, he informed the secretary that he was leaving the building early to work on a case, and probably wouldn't be back.

They were silent in the elevator to the basement parking; silent throughout the drive to his house. It was still early afternoon when they arrived, and Rachel was still in school. As soon as Kennedy closed the front door behind them, Alison turned and collapsed against his chest, sobbing uncontrollably. He spoke softly and rubbed her back until her crying subsided. Then, he lifted her chin and kissed her, gently at first, but as she responded, with more urgency. They clung tightly to each other, the pressure that had been building over their days of such close proximity under such intense pressure, finally seeking release.

They were still clinging tightly to each other as he guided her to the bedroom.

Chapter 33

Alison and Kennedy had showered and dressed, and were in the kitchen preparing supper when Rachel came home from school. They tiptoed around the fact that the two of them were home before her. Kennedy tried to change the subject by asking her about her day at school, but a knowing look on her bright young face told him that she knew – but, her half-smile didn't tell him what she thought about the whole lash up.

Rachel put her books in her room, and, instead of her usual, doing homework, or watching TV, she came into the kitchen with them. She placed herself equidistance between them and just stood there, looking from one to the other, saying nothing, but with the little half-smile still on her face.

Alison blushed, her cheeks bright red, and Kennedy felt his own face getting warm. Both tried to ignore it and concentrate on what they'd been doing when she walked in; Kennedy grilling steaks and Alison tossing a salad.

"Okay, which one of you is planning to tell

me?" Rachel said; her hands on her hips.

"Tell you what, honey?" Kennedy said.

"I don't know what you mean," Alison said.

Rachel folder her arms across her just-budding breasts and cocked her head back, looking as stern as a teacher who has just caught students skipping class. "You two don't make very good liars," she said. "I know you're a couple now, so why don't you just 'fess up, okay?"

"Uh, uh," Kennedy said.

Alison just stood there, her mouth open, blushing a deep red.

"B-but, Rachel honey, I don't . . . I mean, I uh - -"

"Daddy, I'm not a baby. You two have moping around here for days, trying to avoid each other. Now, I come home and you're all domestic. I even heard you humming when I came in, so I know you've finally realized that you love each other, so stop trying to pretend around me."

"Rachel, dear," Alison said. "I don't want you to think - -"

"That my dad loves you; and, that you love him. Alison, it's as plain as the nose on your face; which, by the way, is quite red right now.

Why shouldn't I think it? I think it's great by the way."

"You do?" Alison and Kennedy asked in unison.

Rachel rushed into her father's arms, hugging him tightly. "Of course I do, silly. I think you two are cute together." She released him and walked over to Alison, hugging her. "And, I really like you, Alison; uh . . . I guess I better think about calling you mom, eh?"

"Whoa there, young lady," Kennedy said. "Let's not rush things. Alison practically just met, you know. I haven't even asked her to . . . I mean, well . . ."

"What are you waiting for?" Rachel said, giving him a stern look. "Neither of you are getting any younger, you know. And, I'll be in high school soon and am gonna need a mother's advice about a lot of things you don't know anything about, daddy."

Somehow, the three of them ended up in a tangled embrace, with Kennedy smiling helplessly at Alison over the top of Rachel's head.

"Looks like she has us in a corner," she said, and shrugged.

"Is that a yes?" Kennedy asked.

She shrugged again, but her broad smile

was all the answer he needed. Damn, he thought, this has got to rank as the strangest proposal ever.

The rest of the evening was just as topsy-turvy, with Rachel bugging Alison about what she should wear for the wedding, and Alison trying to explain that there had to be a longer period of courtship before the nuptials, and Rachel countering with 'nonsense,' and Kennedy sitting on the end of the sofa wisely keeping his mouth shut.

It was well after eleven by the time they were able to calm Rachel down enough to get her to go to bed.

Sitting on the sofa, their shoulders touching, Kennedy and Alison gazed into each other's eyes.

"Did I actually propose to you tonight?" he asked.

"In a backdoor kind of way, I think you did," she said. "Did I accept your proposal?"

"Yeah, I think you did."

"Well, I guess that's that. Uh, now that we've got that little detail out of the way, we need to discuss tonight's sleeping arrangements."

Kennedy smiled. "Well, we are getting married, and we've already sort of . . . you know . . ."

Alison punched his shoulder. "I know, but, it's a little sudden, and for all her trying to act adult, Rachel is still just a child. I'm not sure the reality of it has sunk in for her yet, so for tonight at least, I think we shouldn't change our sleeping arrangement."

"You mean I have to sleep on the couch again?" Kennedy looked crestfallen.

"Just for a while longer."

"Promise?"

She leaned forward and kissed him. "Promise."

They took turns in the bathroom, with Alison going first. When Kennedy had finished brushing his teeth and was padding back toward the living room and his bed on the sofa, he couldn't see any light in the crack under her door. Sighing, he stretched out on the sofa and pulled the blanket up to his chin, staring up at the gray rectangle of ceiling for what seemed like hours before finally drifting off to sleep.

In the bedroom, although she'd turned the light off, Alison was, at first, unable to sleep. She was regretting her insistence on the two of them sleeping apart. Their afternoon encounter had reminded her of just how starved she'd been for that kind of closeness, and her body ached for more. But, she knew, it was the right thing to do. She really liked, no loved, Rachel.

She was a bright, engaging child, who hadn't been permanently scarred by her mother's abandonment. And, Alison could tell, Rachel liked her too. Whether it was a a kind of big sister, or even potentially a step-mother, Alison couldn't tell, and in truth, she knew it didn't matter. Her feelings for Kennedy, though, were unambiguous. She'd been physically attracted to him from the first moment she'd encountered him.

She lay there in the dark, the light blanket pulled up to just cover her breasts, staring up at the ceiling, and thinking thoughts that her mother would have definitely not approved of. The sound of joints settling in the house, and the low whisper of the central air system, circulating air through the house, finally lulled her to sleep.

The sound of the curtain fluttering jerked her awake. It was still dark, but she could see a dark shadow against the rectangle of the open window. *I thought that window was closed when I came to bed.* The shadow moved slowly toward the bed, as if feeling its way through the room's darkness. At first, she thought it must be Lee, having changed his mind about maintaining chastity, and deep within the recess of her will, she welcomed it. She reached up and started to slide the blanket down toward her waist, when her brain started to process what her eyes were seeing.

As her eyes grew accustomed to the low level of light, she realized that the shadow was much too small to be Lee, and too large to be Rachel. As her mind began to focus on what she was seeing, she felt her throat tighten, and a fluttering in her stomach.

She stopped moving her hand downward, lying still and focusing on the shadow, which had now covered half the distance from the window to the side of her bed. Part of her wanted to flee, but the rational part of her mind knew that there was nowhere to run. The shadow was between her and the door.

Slowly, she snaked her left arm from beneath the blanket and toward the lamp on the bedside table. As her fingers bumped the porcelain base of the lamp, she slipped her hand slowly upwards until she felt the protruding switch.

Tensing, she braced herself with her right hand, narrowed her eyes to slits, and twisted the switch. Light flooded the room. The figure, a wicked looking knife in its right hand, halted its forward movement, its left hand covering its eyes against the sudden flash of light. It was the man in black, the man who had come after her on the steps of her house. Her vision was only slightly blurred, but the figure was unmistakable, as was the knife, glinting in the light from the lamp.

Before the man in black could recover his balance, Alison grabbed the pillow from beneath her head and started swinging it across her body. And, she screamed, a loud, piercing yell. "Help! There's someone in the house. Lee, please, come help me!"

Alison's scream, only slightly muffled by the closed bedroom door, yanked Lee Kennedy from a fitful sleep. It took only a second for his brain to register what she was saying. He rolled off the sofa, grabbing for his .38 revolver which he'd taken to keeping near since the assault on Alison. Dressed only in a pair of boxer shorts, he swiftly ran for the bedroom. As he reached the door, he could hear scuffling inside the room.

Kennedy shoved the door open and, crouching, with the pistol held before him in a two-hand grip, he stepped through the doorway. What he saw sent a wave of anger through his body.

Alison was sitting on the bed, her back against the headboard, frantically waving a pillow from side to side and up and down, still screaming. Kennedy heard footsteps behind him. He turned his head to see Rachel, her eyes wide with alarm, coming out of her room.

"Rachel," he shouted. "Get back into your room and lock the door until I tell you to come out."

The child ducked back inside her room.

The man in black was waving a knife from side to side, trying to cut through the pillow that Alison was using as a shield and weapon all at the same time. At the sound of Kennedy's voice behind him, he stopped and turned, his snake-like eyes widening.

"Drop the knife," Kennedy ordered.

There was a momentary flash of confusion on the man's face, and then he snarled and whirled around, holding the knife waist high.

In all his time as a diplomatic security agent, Lee Kennedy had only fired his weapon for qualification. He'd never before shot at a live person. But, his training had been good. With the weapon in a two-hand grip, he aimed at the man's chest, and squeezed the trigger three times.

The sound of the three shots, so close together they were like the continuous backfire of a car, only louder in the confined space of the bedroom, rang in his ears.

The stranger stopped, and looked down at his chest where a dark stain was spreading from the three holes; grouped in a space that could have been covered with a child's hand; and then back up at Kennedy. His face took on a puzzled expression. The knife slipped from his limp fingers and thudded against the carpet.

The man's eyes rolled up in their sockets, and blood gushed from his mouth, as he sank to the floor, falling forward. His legs twitched once, and then he was still.

Chapter 34

Friday, May 23, 1975, Dagastan

At the end of the work day, deciding to go home early for a change, Morgan got an attaché case from the supply room located near his secretary's desk in the outer office, and secured the .357 and ammunition. As he was leaving, he bumped into Pete Jeffers.

"Pete; you here to escort me home?"

"Yeah, but there's something I need to tell you first. I just got a call from Lee Kennedy in DC. The guy who tried to assault the INR gal, Alison Chambers, tried again. Only this time, Lee was there and popped the guy."

Morgan smiled. "Well, it would seem their troubles are over back there at least."

"Not really. Lee says the Virginia cops shared information with the cops in DC, particularly the knife the guy was carrying. Looks like the same knife that was used to kill Lesley Carter, our desk officer."

"That doesn't sound good." Morgan's brow

creased. "Why would the same guy go after two people working in different offices?"

"Working in different offices," Jeffers said. "But, the same subject. Alison Chambers is looking into the assassination of Vasily Shermov too. Seems Lesley sent her a note about it the same day she was killed."

"Damn, that doesn't sound coincidental to me. I wish I knew what the hell was going on."

"Oh, it gets better. Lee said he saw the guy he killed talking to his boss, a senior agent named Broadbent, along with a senator and a retired guy - -"

"Niles Hitchcock?" Morgan said.

"Yeah, that's right. What do you think it means?"

"It means we have people in our own government playing some kind of double game, and they're willing to kill to cover it up. I think somehow our ambassador's in it up to his neck, and we need to talk to him."

"His car and driver are out front, so he's still in the building," Jeffers said.

Morgan knew that meant he would be in his office; the man never went to any other part of the embassy other than the big conference room.

"Well, let's go see what he has to say."

Robert Ellingsworth looked up, his eyes widening in surprise as the door to his office swung open. Morgan and Jeffers entered without knocking or requesting permission to enter. His lips turned down in a frown. "What's the meaning of this intrusion?"

"Mister Ambassador," Morgan said. "We have to talk."

Morgan knew that he was treading on dangerous ground. He'd already violated every rule of bureaucratic and diplomatic behavior in his encounters with Ellingsworth. As ambassador, the man held all the cards, and now, sitting behind his massive desk, the expression on his face said that he knew it. He was smiling, a slight upturn of his lips, like a man who is holding four aces while his opponent has just drawn three cards.

"I'm not sure I like the tone of your voice," Ellingsworth said. "Who are you to tell *me* when we have to talk?"

Well, Morgan thought, in for a penny, in for a pound. "As your deputy, sir, I feel it's my responsibility to tell you when I see something that I think is wrong."

"And, you see something wrong?"

Jeffers stepped forward, but Morgan put a hand on his arm, stopping him. "Yes, sir, I do.

You've been holding meetings with the deputy head of security services without sharing this information with me or the rest of the staff, and, you've been going about without security."

Ellingsworth's smile became cold. "The last time I checked, *I* was the president's senior representative here in Dagastan. As such, I believe it is *I* who has the authority to decide what behavior is or is not appropriate."

"But, Mr. Ambassador, wandering around this city without security is just plain foolish," Jeffers blurted out before Morgan could stop him. "As RSO, it's my responsibility to ensure the safety of everyone in this mission, and that includes you."

"Mr. Jeffers," Ellingsworth said, his voice dripping with menace. "Unless you wish to be on the next plane out of here, you would be advised to remain silent until you're asked to speak."

"Sir, Pete is only doing his job," Morgan said. Ellingsworth's icy stare turned to him. "And, for the record, I completely agree with him. I think it was a mistake for you to dismiss your security detail, and I think your meetings are ill advised."

Ellingsworth toyed idly with a sheet of paper on the desk in front of him. His eyes narrowed in concentration. He looked up at Morgan. There was a strange glint in his eyes. "Why do you think they're ill-advised, Mr. Morgan?"

"Well, sir, suppose something happened to you while you're out there without security. If I don't know what's going on, how am I to answer to Washington should they inquire? I'm your deputy, and in your absence, I know you expect me to keep the embassy running the way you want it to. I can't do that if you insist on keeping me in the dark."

Ellingsworth continued to stare up at Morgan, but he seemed to be looking at something beyond him. "Very well, Mr. Morgan, your point is taken. I have my doubts about your ability to understand what's at play here, but I suppose you're right about the need to be kept informed. I'm meeting with Colonel Dragov tomorrow. I will allow you to accompany me to that meeting."

"I should go along as well, sir," Jeffers said. "It's not a good idea to have both of you out in town without some security."

Ellingsworth smiled again. Then, he sighed. "Oh, very well; if you insist." He took a gold pen from his shirt pocket and scribbled on the sheet of paper that he'd been toying with. "This is the address and time of the meeting. Your driver will know how to get there."

He slid the paper across the desk. Morgan picked it up and glanced at it. He vaguely recognized it; a street in one of the crowded slums of a town that looked like one giant slum, a warren of narrow alleyways lined with adobe hovels and shops. Why on earth would the ambassador agree to meetings in such venues? He folded the paper and put it in his pocket.

"Thank you, sir. We'll be there."

Ellingsworth wasn't listening. He had already dismissed them from his mind. Morgan nudged Jeffers and turned away. He pulled the door shut as they exited Ellingsworth's office.

"I don't like this," Jeffers said, when they were in the hallway outside the front office. "I got a glance at that address, and that's not a place I'm comfortable going into without at least a full security detail."

"I don't like it either," Morgan said. "But, it at least gives us a chance to find out what's going on."

"Just what is going on?" Carlton Raine's deep voice said from behind them.

They hadn't heard him approach from down the corridor in the direction of the door up to his office on the top floor, so quietly did he move.

Morgan was hesitant at first to share the information, but his gut told him he should trust the man. He took out the paper and showed it to Raine, and told him of the ambassador's agreement to allow him and

Jeffers to accompany him to the meeting with Dragov.

"You've got to be kidding," Raine said. "That part of town is nothing but a den of thieves. You'll be lucky not to be killed and stripped of everything five minutes after you get out of your car. The ambassador's meeting someone here, and at night?"

Raine returned the paper to Morgan. "What else can I do?" Morgan said. "It's the only way I can find out what he's up to."

"And, I'll be going with him," Jeffers said.

Raine smiled at the young security officer. "You're a scrappy kid," he said. "But, the two of you don't stand a chance in that part of town alone, you know that."

"You got a better idea?"

"Yeah; I'm going with you."

"But, the ambassador only agreed to allow Pete and me to go."

"Don't worry. If nothing goes wrong, he'll never know I was there. But, if the shit hits the fan, you'll be glad I am." Raine chuckled. There was a cold menace in his laugh.

"I'm not sure that's a good idea," Jeffers said.

"Maybe not," Raine retorted. "But, it's a hell

of a lot better than letting you two go down there alone."

He turned and walked back toward his office. As Morgan watched him go, he felt doubt creeping into his mind. He wanted to trust the man, but so many strange things had been happening, he frankly wasn't sure anymore who he could trust.

"I don't like the way this is turning out," Jeffers said.

"I hope you know a good prayer for the protection of fools," Morgan said.

Jeffers patted his hip where he wore his own .357 magnum. "I have six of them, and a fast loader for backup. And, I strongly recommend that you carry yours as well."

"With that, and Raine backing us up, how can we lose?"

Chapter 35

Morgan spent Saturday puttering around his residence. He picked idly at the meals his houseman prepared for him, but the thoughts of what lay ahead that evening preoccupied his mind.

He'd tried reading on the patio, but that proved boring. He'd listened to some of his records, but after a while, he found himself losing track of the song being played. He cleaned, loaded, unloaded, and reloaded the wicked looking revolver several times. For the entire day, he did what he'd done on many occasions when he'd been in SOG in Vietnam; he killed time waiting for the go order for a mission. In those days, it had been for missions that he knew he might not return from. Today, he knew, was no different.

Pete Jeffers arrived just before six in the evening. The houseman showed him to the patio where he found Morgan sitting sipping coffee from one of the official china cups that had come with the residence.

"Come on in, Pete," Morgan said, waving idly

at the empty patio chair. "Have a cup of coffee."

"Sure, boss," Jeffers said. "But, we ought to move out a little early. I'd like to get there well ahead of the time the ambassador said, so we can do a little recon."

They had an hour to spare, but Morgan saw the wisdom in the young man's idea. After quickly gulping a half cup of coffee, Jeffers urged him to go. Clipping the holstered pistol to his left hip and putting ten spare rounds in his pocket, Morgan followed him out to the front where his driver, Achmed, was waiting standing by the car.

"Meester Morgan," Achmed said. "Meester Cheffers tell me where we are going. That is not good neighborhood. Many thieves."

"I know, Achmed," Morgan said. "That's why Mr. Jeffers is going with me."

"I am thinking only two is not enough."

"Don't worry, we'll be fine."

But, the driver's dour expression and shaking of his head as he made his way down the hill from Morgan's house, said that he didn't believe they would be fine. In Achmed's view, if things could go wrong, they would go wrong, and they would do so in the worst possible way.

At the bottom of the hill, as they turned toward the center of town, Morgan was reminded that it was the first day of Dagastan's spring festival. Spring came late to this part of the world. The frozen ground, icy sometimes down to three feet below the surface, was still difficult to work and hostile to plant life through most of the month of April. Now, though, in late May, all the below-ground ice had melted. The earth was black and pliable, and farmers had spent most of the first days of the month turning the soil and planting their crops.

Now, though, was time to stop and celebrate their good fortune. Everyone, from townsman to peasant, took out their finest garb, faded garments that had lain folded in chests for the entire year, were unfolded, dusted off, and donned for a week of celebration.

The narrow, potholed street was clogged with pedestrians and carts jostling each other for space. The pedestrians were mostly peasants from the surrounding countryside, men of all ages, some wearing turbans with their gaunt bodies wrapped in dark colored coats to protect against the chill of the evening air, women with large pendulous breasts and broad hips, wrapped in colorful shawls and carrying large baskets of fruits and vegetables, and children of various ages and sizes, darting in and out of the crowds, enjoying a respite from the rigors of farm work for the one week out of the year when chores are put aside to celebrate the end of the bitter winter, and before the rigors of planting, tending, and then harvesting their crops for the coming year. Many of the men were already red-cheeked, not from the chill, but from the noxious beer made from barley that they consumed in large quantities to fortify their bodies against the combination of back breaking toil and harsh climate that was their lot.

The carts, mostly rickety horse-drawn affairs with two large wheels, were laden with the leftovers from the past year's harvest, destined for the many outdoor banquets that were the hallmark of the spring festival. Some of the cart drivers, bent old men wrapped in coats and shawls, their heads covered with turbans or fur caps with ear flaps that flopped as the carts bounced over the rough street, held musical instruments; stringed guitar-like devices made from gourds with strings of sheep gut; that they would use to entertain the crowds that gathered in any convenient open space for their impromptu parties.

As Morgan's car penetrated deeper into the city, it passed the gray-brick shops in the main local shopping district, its shops lit up with candles and lanterns, windows filled with local handicrafts brought in by craftsmen who lived in a nearby district in adobe hovels, which would be traded for what goods the peasants could afford to part with. Over the doors of many of the shops, Dagastani flags, rectangular banners of green, white, and red stripes, with a golden sun in the upper left corner of the green stripe, hung limply from canted poles, only flapping when someone passed near and brushed under them.

They passed party headquarters, the building from which every facet of Dagastani life was controlled, a large, sprawling complex of buildings dominated by a pink stucco building with a domed roof. Uniformed guards, armed with AK-47 assault rifles, stood guard at the massive wrought iron gates. The compound was brightly lit by large flood lights sitting atop the twelve-foot-high stone fence that enclosed it. It stood out like a bright jewel amidst the dimly lit surrounding area, thanks to the large industrial generators that guaranteed constant electrical power to the country's leaders. No dim single bulbs or candles for the elite. A large Dagastani flag hung limply from a tall pole in front of the domed building. The flag was lit by a single floodlight set at the base of the pole. Morgan noticed, as his car drove past the gate, that none of the pedestrians glanced in the direction of the compound as they shuffled past, and the guards paid no attention to the crowds.

Less than a mile past party headquarters, they were plunged into semi-darkness as they entered the main residential part of town. A few of the finer houses showed lights, and the hum of generators could be heard over the murmurs and scuffling footsteps of the crowd, but most were either unlit, or showed the dim glow of lanterns. The narrow street was enclosed by the brick and adobe dwellings on each side, and even with the car windows closed, Morgan could smell the cloying odor of roasting lamb, sweat, and stale beer. It hung over the area like a cloud.

As they approached their destination, the crowd grew in size. No one paid their vehicle any attention as the driver leaned on the horn to clear a way.

Finally, the densely-packed crowd had closed the street off completely. Achmed brought the vehicle to a halt. "Sorry, Meester Morgan, but I think I can drive no further. Not to worry; is close." He pointed to a serpentine dirt path, too narrow for the car, which wound about a hundred yards up a slight incline between the buildings, ending at a block-like structure that showed a flickering light in two square windows. "I wait here with car."

"Jesus Christ," Jeffers said. "We got to go up there in the dark? I don't like it."

Morgan felt for the .357 at his hip. "Not much choice, Pete. At least the crowd doesn't seem to be going up that way. We'll just have to keep a sharp lookout."

"I wonder where Raine is."

Morgan looked around. On the road with them, the crowd continued to shuffle past, still ignoring them, but the chief of station was nowhere to be seen. "Maybe he changed his mind about coming. Come on, let's go."

They got out of the car, and began making their way up the path. Dark shadows from the buildings made the going difficult as they felt their way over the irregular surface. By the time they were halfway to their destination, the enclosing buildings had masked the sounds from the street below until they were little more than a faint murmuring. Both men kept their hands on their weapons as they continued walking.

About ten yards from the building at the top of the hill, Morgan saw a door between the two windows open, and a figure, outlined by the flickering light, appeared in the opening. As they approached closer, he could see that it was Ellingsworth, dressed, as usual, in his dark suit.

"You're early," Ellingsworth said. "Dragov hasn't arrived yet."

Morgan and Jeffers stopped ten feet from the building, looking up at Ellingsworth. In the dim light the expression on his face couldn't be seen. He looked to his right and nodded.

"When is Dragov due?" Morgan asked, looking in the direction Ellingsworth had looked, but in the dark shadows of the buildings he saw nothing.

"Don't worry, in a few minutes our problems will be solved."

Morgan looked at Jeffers, who was still peering at the darkness to their left. The young man tensed, and then swiftly drawing his weapon, grabbed at Morgan and shoved him forward. "Dave, move," he shouted. "There's someone over there."

As Morgan stumbled forward toward the building, he heard a popping sound. Geysers of gravel and dirt erupted around him. Jeffers was still shoving him with his left hand while aiming at the darkness and squeezing of shots as fast as he could. "Move it, man," Jeffers said. There was no panic in his voice, but he was clearly agitated. "Someone's shooting at us."

Morgan didn't need to be told that. He'd been under fire before. Reflexes, honed by a year fighting the North Vietnamese and Viet Cong in the jungles of Cambodia kicked in. He pulled his weapon and, firing as he ran, added his own firepower to Jeffers.

They reached the building at the same time, pushing past a shocked looking Ellingsworth, who stood there with his hands on his chest. Morgan grabbed the man and pushed him inside as he and Jeffers dove into the building. The sound of several AK-47s was clear now, as were the thuds of rounds impacting the stone building, and the tinkling of window glass as more and more rounds knifed into the building.

Jeffers dropped to his knees and scuttled to a table near the center of the room upon which sat a flickering lantern. He grabbed the lantern and extinguished it, plunging the room into sudden darkness. He then crawled back to the door where Morgan lay, trying to locate whoever was shooting at them.

The initial ambushed having failed, the shooting had diminished, only an occasional shot in their direction, well above their heads and impacting the rear wall of the room. Morgan saw winks of light from the shadows. Taking careful aim at the last position from where he'd seen a flash, he squeezed off a shot. He was rewarded with a grunting sound, telling him he'd aimed correctly, but the firing picked up again. He saw what seemed like dozens of flashes of light, and bullets slammed into the outer walls and the inside back wall of the building, kicking up a cloud of dust from the stone walls.

"They have us pinned down," he said. "There must be at least five or six of them out there."

Jeffers, lying on the floor on the other side of the door, looked at him and smiled. "Yeah, looks like it, and I don't think we have enough ammo to hold 'em off until morning. Well, boss, it's been fun."

"Hey, pal," Morgan said. "We're not dead

yet."

Then, Morgan heard the sound of another weapon. Not the familiar pop of an AK, but a deeper sound. Single shots, well-spaced, and each was followed by a cry of agony. The AK-47's began firing again, but he heard no impacts on the building.

"Sounds like someone else's out there shooting, and not at us," he said.

"You think it might be Raine?"

"Who else could it be? And, from the sounds, he's got the advantage."

The shooting continued for several minutes. The loud boom, followed by more grunts and screams, and much diminished AK fire. Finally, there was silence.

Morgan peered into the darkness. He saw a single figure, broad shouldered and dressed in black, emerge from the shadows. He took aim, but held his fire as the figure neared. Then, as the figure walked into a pool of light from a nearby building, Morgan saw that it was Raine, carrying a short rifle with a large clip, walking nonchalantly toward them. As he came close, he held the rifle across his chest.

"Hey, guys, you can come out now," his deep voice echoed off the surrounding buildings.

Morgan and Jeffers stood, brushing the rock

dust from their clothing. Jeffers retrieved the lamp and relit it as Raine entered the building.

"Who the hell was that shooting at us?" Morgan asked.

"Sorry, I didn't have time to ask for ID," Raine said. "There were six of them, and they were loaded for bear."

"Did you get them all?" Jeffers asked.

Raine just looked at the young man and smiled. Morgan then knew how he'd come by the nickname, Blood.

"Where's the ambassador?" Raine asked.

In the excitement, Ellingsworth had been forgotten. The three men looked in the far corner of the room. Ellingsworth sat on the floor, his legs splayed out before him. A dark stain was spreading across the front of his white shirt. He was staring blindly at them. His lips were moving.

"Holy shit," Jeffers said. "He's been shot."

They rushed to him. Morgan knelt beside him feeling for a pulse. It was weak and thready. A string of blood trailed from his pale lips, and as he breathed, he made a bubbling sound.

Raine knelt and peered into his eyes. "He's been shot in the lungs. He's lost a lot of blood already. I don't think there's anything we can do for him."

Ellingsworth weakly lifted his right hand and placed it on Morgan's wrist. He turned and looked into Morgan's eyes. "This . . . not . . . supposed . . . to . . . happen," he said weakly. Bubbles of blood pulsed from his lips with each word.

"Mr. Ambassador," Morgan said. "Hang on; we'll get you to a hospital."

"Too . . . late . . . for . . . that." Ellingsworth's head dipped forward, but through some will of effort, he managed to raise it again. He struggled for breath. "No . . . matter . . . The. . . White . . . Dragons . . . will . . . pre - -" Then, his head slumped forward. His body shuddered, and a stream of bright red blood gushed from his mouth.

Raine felt for a pulse at the side of his neck. He pulled his hand away and put a hand on Morgan's shoulder. "Sorry, Dave. He's done."

"Shit, shit, shit," Jeffers said. "That can't be. I don't want to be known as an RSO who got an ambassador killed."

"Don't beat yourself up, kid," Raine said, turning to the young security man. "You didn't get him killed. He brought this upon himself."

"What do we do now?"

"Well, that's up to the man in charge," Raine said, turning to Morgan. "But, I recommend we get the body out of here and back to the embassy. Then we'll have to come up with a suitable story for Washington."

CHARLES RAY

Chapter 36

Friday, May 23, 1975, Washington, DC

The Arlington County Police had spent the rest of the night investigating the shooting at Lee Kennedy's house. There'd been some anxious moments when they first arrived, until Kennedy showed him his DSS badge and ID, which authorized him to have a weapon. The corpse on the bedroom floor, with the wicked looking knife at hand also helped.

When he told the detective in charge his suspicions about the dead man, Arlington contacted the DC metro police. Sharing information back and forth, it was discovered that the knife the man was carrying was a 99% match with the weapon that had killed Lesley Carter.

The dead man's fingerprints were taken and within five hours he'd been identified as Gawan Hart, a wanted felon from Louisiana who was the principal suspect in a string of knife murders along the Gulf Coast from New Orleans to Pensacola during the early 1970s. He'd dropped out of sight in 1973, but the warrants for his arrest were still outstanding. Kennedy didn't mention to the police that he'd seen his boss at the State Department in the man's company. This was something he felt he had to deal with himself.

Alison was still shaken by the night's events, but by the time he'd taken Rachel, who was herself a bit shaken, to school and returned to the house, she was calmer, but frustrated at not having anything to do. Kennedy promised her that he'd look into the situation with her boss, but first he had to deal with his own boss.

He kissed her lightly on the lips and left. As he drove away, he saw her standing in the doorway watching him. The sight gave him a warm feeling.

That warm feeling lasted throughout his drive across the Roosevelt Bridge an on to Constitution Avenue, through the left on Twenty-Second Street and into the underground parking at the State Department. He was still feeling good as he took the elevator up to his floor, and walked down the corridor to his office.

The feeling evaporated as soon as he walked through the door.

Melvin Broadbent, a frown on his face, was standing at the door to Kennedy's office. When he saw him, Kennedy's first instinct was to walk up and smash his face. Instead, he took a deep breath and calmed himself.

"Keeping bankers hours now, are we?" he said, his reedy voice dripping with sarcasm.

Kennedy brushed past him. "I was tied up with local police regarding an attempted murder," he said simply. He fought to keep his voice level.

Broadbent didn't react to Kennedy's words, nor did he seem to notice that Kennedy had roughly pushed past him, shoving him against the door jamb. It was as if he hadn't heard, or, Kennedy thought, he already knew about it and just didn't care.

"There was another attempt to kill a State Department employee," Kennedy said. "Only, this time, it was at *my* house."

Broadbent's face creased momentarily, in confusion or shock, Kennedy couldn't tell, but that had clearly meant something to him.

"Well," Kennedy continued. "Aren't you even interested in what happened?"

"Uh, yes, of course. Someone tried to kill someone at *your* house? Not you, was it? A department employee? I thought you lived alone with your daughter."

Kennedy explained about the previous attempted assault on Alison Chambers. "I decided she'd be safer at my place," he said.

"Apparently, though, the assailant had her under surveillance, and tracked her there. He had another go at her last night."

"You said attempted murder. That means the assailant was captured?" Broadbent's brow creased further. He looked worried, Kennedy thought.

"No, I shot him. But, the cops were able to identify him; a wanted hit man from Louisiana. The knife he had appears to be the same one that killed that desk officer two weeks ago."

"That's terrible," Broadbent said, but the look on his face was one of relief. "Why would this person be targeting employees of this department, I wonder?"

"That's my thought, too. More importantly, though, is why senior people from this department would be associating with him?"

Broadbent's brows arched upwards and his eyes widened. "W-what? What senior people? How do you know this?"

Kennedy fixed the man with a glacial stare. He was nervous, but not as much as he would have expected. But then, he was a senior DS agent. He would have been trained to control his reactions under stress. Maybe, Kennedy thought, he needs more prodding. "You, Melvin," he said. "I saw you on the Mall the other day, talking to a group of men, and this guy was one of them. A slight build, dressed in black; remember him?"

"How could you - -? Have you been following me? How dare you!" Broadbent's face paled.

Got you, you son of a bitch. Kennedy was feeling anger now. He wanted nothing so much as to smash the bastard's face in. "Yes, Melvin, I followed you. You met with Senator Longroux, some retired diplomat named Niles Hitchcock, and the guy in black; his name, by the way, was Gawan Hart. He's wanted in Louisiana, Alabama, and Florida for a string of unsolved murders. Now; you want to tell me why you were meeting him?"

"I, uh, well yes, I recall meeting with the senator and Mr. Hitchcock. There was another man there, but we were never introduced. He just stood there and never said a word. I had no idea."

Kennedy laughed; a harsh barking sound. "You really expect me to believe a lame story like that? You're an experienced security agent. There's no way you'd be meeting with someone and not try to find out who they were."

Broadbent's face was now the color of faded parchment, and a muscle in his left cheek twitched. "Believe what you will, Lee. I tell you, I wasn't introduced to the man, and I'd never met him before. I was asked to come to that meeting by Niles Hitchcock. I met him once just before he retired. He's a respected former officer, so when he called, I went."

"What did you talk about?"

"I'm sorry, but that's confidential."

"Dammit, Melvin; we've had one person killed, and another nearly killed. Moreover, my daughter was in the house when this bastard tried for Alison, so now it's personal. If you know something, you'd be well advised to tell me now, because trust me, I *will* find out what's going on."

"I . . . don't . . . know . . . *anything*, and *you'd* be well-advised to heed my previous instructions and drop this. Lee, you don't know what you're getting yourself into. This is bigger than the both of us."

"Does this have anything to do with the White Dragons?"

Broadbent looked as if he'd been punched in the gut. His mouth dropped open. He looked at Kennedy as if he was a deadly viper about to strike. His eyes darted from side to side. Then, he spun on his heel and nearly ran from Kennedy's office. He entered his own office and slammed the door. Kennedy heard the click of the lock.

Chapter 37

After Kennedy had driven away, Alison went back into the house. Her stomach still felt queasy. She couldn't get the image of the man in black and wicked looking long blade of his knife. The dead look in his eyes as he tried to stab her through the flailing pillow floated in the front of her consciousness. She shivered at the thought of how close she'd come to being killed.

To take her mind off things, she went into the kitchen and busied herself tidying the place. But, Kennedy was a neat housekeeper for a man. He never left dirty dishes in the sink, and always cleaned up after himself when he cooked. As she looked around the gleaming kitchen, warmer thoughts of him began to overlay the grim images of before. She even found herself humming as she took the garbage bin out and put it at the back gate.

As noon approached, though, she found herself suffering from cabin fever. She wondered how women could remain cooped up alone in a house all day, every day. Her mother had been such a woman, never complaining, but Alison wondered if at times she hadn't suffered the same thoughts that were currently flitting through her head – if I don't get out of here and find something interesting to do, I'll go crazy. But, she'd been put on administrative leave. She couldn't go to her office. She'd never been fond of wandering through stores, looking at things she had no intention of buying.

Finally, she decided to challenge her boss and the system. She dialed the number to her office. Earline answered.

"INR, how may I help you?"

The woman's contralto voice was like a beacon in the fog to a drifting sailor. Alison realized that she *needed* to be back where she belonged, and she was willing to do anything to get back.

"Earline, this is Alison. May I please speak to Dudley?"

She was willing, if necessary, to debase herself if it meant going back to work. If the damned man wanted her to stop working on Dagastan, she'd gladly do it. She would even apologize to him for her insubordination if he demanded it.

"I'm sorry, girl," Earline said. "But, he hasn't come in yet this morning."

"Did he call and say when he was coming

in?"

"No, but you know how these guys can be. They always got something important to do, more important than keeping us poor peons in the loop. I reckon he'll come drifting in sometime around mid-afternoon with some lame story about an important meeting, and he'll never apologize for not calling me."

Damn, Alison thought. I can't wait around here that long. Then, she thought maybe it would be worth trying to see if Lakeworth was at home. She asked Earline for the number, hastily scribbling it on a grocery receipt she'd found in the top drawer of the cabinet next to the sink. For good measure, she asked for his address, noting as she wrote that it was only a few blocks from her own house.

When she broke the connection with Earline, she immediately dialed Lakeworth's number. The phone rang and rang, but no one answered. Unlike many people, he didn't seem to have an answering machine. In frustration, she jammed the handset back into the cradle.

Okay, she thought, if I can't get you on the phone, I'll get you in person. She picked the phone up again and called a cab. Within minutes, a Red Top cab was in front of Kennedy's house, the driver leaning on the horn impatiently. Grabbing her purse, Alison ran out and jumped into the back, giving him the address in DC, not far from George Washington University.

It was not yet noon, and the traffic was still light. The trip only took fifteen minutes. Lakeworth's neighborhood was a bit more prosperous looking than Alison's, with newer houses and with the older, nineteenth century structures having been renovated and kept up well. The brick townhouses, with pink and green shutters, and large porcelain vases containing shrubs and flowers reeked of wealth. If Lakeworth owned his house, he obviously had money. If he rented, he was shelling out a monthly amount that would have knocked a huge hole in Alison's salary.

The cab pulled to a stop in front of a three-story town house with white trim, coral pink shutters, and small evergreens in large green pots to either side of the front door. Alison gave the driver a twenty and told him to keep the change. Getting out of the cab, she walked slowly up the walk toward the front door, a dark green, almost black door with brass-rimmed arched windows in the top, and a large brass lion's head knocker. As she mounted the steps, she noticed that the door was slightly ajar.

"Hello; is anyone home?" she called as she approached the door. She pushed the brass button to the left of the door. From within the recesses of the house she heard the sound of an organ echoing off the walls. She rapped on the door, but no one answered.

Curious about the open door, Alison pushed it open and stepped inside. She was in a vestibule with doors on either side that opened into a sunken living room. Large double glass doors, the curtains pulled to reveal a walled in garden outside, were at the back of the room. As she moved through the vestibule and down into the living room, she noticed a strange, unpleasant odor in the air. It was a metallic smell, but with the acridity of ammonia, and mixed with the rankness she remembered as a child when a rat had died in the rafters of their house.

She saw a narrow hallway to the right. As she moved toward it, the odor became stronger.

She entered the hallway. At the end were two doors; one to the left and one at the very end. The one to the left was open. She continued to walk forward, holding her hand over her nose to try and block out the noxious smell, which was so strong now it stung her eyes.

When she turned into the doorway, what she saw at first refused to register on her brain. She had never seen violent death before. What lay on the floor of the bedroom didn't even look human.

Lakeworth's body; and Alison finally recognized him from what was left of the right side of his face, lay face down, a halo of blackening, congealed blood surrounding the head, shoulders, and upper torso. The left side of his skull had been cracked open like a ripe melon, and the left side of his face down to the jawline was mangled almost beyond recognition. Bits of brain matter, flesh, and bone, and splatters of darkening blood, were all over the area around the body.

The smell of blood and expelled body wastes was overpowering. Alison fought the urge to throw up. She put her hand over her mouth and backed from the room. When she was in the vestibule, she whirled around and ran for the door. As she bolted through the door into sunlight, she collided with a young uniformed police officer.

"Hold it, lady," he said. "What's the rush?"

"Uh, er, there's a dead . . . I mean, so much blood - -"

The cop, a young white man with bright red hair and freckles covering his face, held Alison's shoulder, not squeezing hard, but preventing her from moving. He turned to his partner, an older black cop with a dusting of gray at the temples of his tightly curled hair. "Bob, maybe you should check inside," he said. "I'll try and make sense of what she's saying."

The black cop entered the doorway. As the smell hit his nostrils, his face wrinkled. "Jeez, something smells awful. Yeah, you hold her there." He disappeared inside the house.

"Now, lady," the young white cop said. "Maybe you're calm enough to tell me what's going on."

"Dead man," Alison said. "In house." Her mind was still having trouble processing what she'd seen. She felt faint, but fought against it, trying to stand upright and focus.

"Dead man; what dead man?" the cop asked. "Who are you?"

"Alison . . . Alison Chambers." She focused hard on her own name. Everything else was blurry.

"You live here?"

"No. Came to talk to Dudley - -"

"Ray, you get to the car and call for backup," the black cop said as he came through the door. He glared at Rachel. "Lady, you got some explaining to do." He encircled her wrist with a massive right hand, as he reached for his handcuffs with his left.

"What's up, Bob?"

The black cop took deep breaths. "There's a stiff inside," he said. "He's had half his head knocked off, looks like. Call for detectives, a crime scene unit, and the meat wagon." He turned his attention back to Alison as his partner dashed toward the waiting patrol car. "Now, lady, you want to tell me what's going on?"

He slipped the cuffs over her wrists. The feel of the cold steel against her flesh snapped Alison back to reality.

"What, why; why are you putting handcuffs on me?" she demanded.

"Sorry, lady, but there's a dead guy inside, and we bumped into you running out. Until we figure out what happened, you're in protective custody."

Chapter 38

DC police lieutenant Murphy and Kennedy arrived at the scene at the same time. They found Alison sitting cuffed in the back seat of the patrol car.

"Why is she cuffed?" Kennedy demanded as he ran to the car.

"I don't know," Murphy said. "We'll have to ask the first cops on the scene. You wait here and I'll check it out."

Murphy ambled toward the house and a group of uniformed police officers standing near the front door. He spoke with them for a few seconds, pointing back toward the police car, where Kennedy stood fuming. After some back and forth, he walked back over to the car.

"Two cops responded to a 911 call from a neighbor reporting the front door wide open; something that doesn't happen in this neighborhood. When they arrived, they bumped into Miss Chambers apparently fleeing the house. They stopped her and checked inside, where they found the occupant, one Dudley

Lakeworth, with his head caved in. They then took Miss Chambers into custody."

Kennedy made a growling sound. "You don't seriously think Alison killed anyone do you, Al? I mean, that's fucking crazy."

Murphy shrugged. "Doesn't matter what I think, Lee. The officers on the scene made a judgment call."

Ignoring the detective, Kennedy opened the squad car's rear door and slipped in beside Alison. He pulled her against him, hugging her tightly.

She burrowed her head into his shoulder, shaking. "Lee, why do they have me handcuffed like a prisoner? I've done nothing." Her voice was almost a whimper, and this made her angry. She'd never been one to cry. Not when she'd been a child, running through the pine forests set in the red clay hills near her home in Georgia, barefoot and chasing behind her dog, Big Boy, a mongrel that was part sheep dog, part basset. She hadn't even cried when a redneck driving a rusty pickup truck had run Big Boy down in the road near their house one day, breaking his back and leaving him sprawled there in the red dirt, his life slowly seeping away. She'd sat beside him in the ditch beside the road and watched him die, a slow painful death. But, Big Boy had never whimpered, had merely gazed up at her with a querying look in his big brown eyes until they glazed over and the heaving of his massive chest stopped. Her eyes burned, but she hadn't shed a tear, and afterwards, she'd dragged the body into a glade in the forest and dug a hole and put him in it. Her eyes remained dry as she scraped the red dirt over his broken body. The only emotion she'd felt was anger.

Now, seeing Lakeworth lying broken and battered on his living room floor, she felt empty. So, why did she feel like crying? She dug deep to rediscover the anger she remembered from her childhood. She'd dismayed her mother by not being as ladylike as a southern girl was expected to be. She needed that now if she was to maintain her sanity. The warmth of Lee's body against hers helped. The smell of his after shave tickling her nose comforted her.

Kennedy stroked her back, holding tight to her. "Don't worry, sweetheart," he said. "I'll get you out of this." He kissed her lightly on the forehead.

Releasing her, he backed out of the car and turned to face Murphy. "I want to see the crime scene."

"Look, Lee," the cop said. "You're personally involved in this. That might not be a good idea."

"You're damn right I'm personally involved. Alison didn't kill the guy; that I know. Now, if you're the friend I've always thought you to be, you'll let me see the scene."

Murphy shrugged. "Okay, let's go. I need to look at it myself anyway."

The two men walked slowly back into the house. The uniformed cops regarded Kennedy warily, but since he was with Murphy, they simply moved aside and let them proceed unmolested.

Inside the bedroom, the crime scene technicians were measuring, photographing, and bagging evidence. The body remained where Alison had seen it. The smell in the room was still almost overpowering. Everyone wore masks to try and minimize it as much as possible. Murphy put on a mask and handed one to Kennedy.

Slipping the mask over his face, Kennedy took in the whole room at a glance, and then looked down at the body. His brows furrowed as he took in the spatter of blood and bits of what had not too long before been a living breathing human being. He locked his gaze with Murphy. Both men nodded.

"I think you can see," he said. "There's no way Alison did this."

Chapter 39

Sunday – Monday, May 25-26, 1975, Dagastan

It had been nearly one in the morning on Sunday by the time Morgan, Jeffers, and Raine had returned Ellingsworth's body to the embassy. Morgan had roused Cornelius and his administrative section staff from their beds and brought them in to make arrangements to ship the dead man's body back to the U.S.

Working with Raine, Morgan had drafted an emergency cable to Washington, informing them of Ellingsworth's death. They'd decided that it wouldn't do to give the actual details, so had cooked up a story that the ambassador and Morgan, on the way to meet a government official, had been caught in a street fight between a group of peasants drunk from the spring festival celebrations. There had been gunfire, and stray rounds had struck the senior envoy, killing him on the spot. This was also the story Morgan had given Cornelius. He made an emergency phone call through the State Department's Operations Center to James Whitman, the country director, who was at home having Sunday dinner with his family.

Following protocol, Morgan assumed charge of the embassy, and instructed Jeffers to have the flags at the chancery and the ambassador's residence flown at half-staff until further notice.

The ambassador's body had been packed in dry ice and sealed in a plain wooden box, which was then placed in a hermetically sealed metal container from the embassy's supply of burial supplies kept in the basement of the building for use in case of emergencies involving American citizens. A few phone calls to the U.S. military command in Rhein-Main Air Base in Germany had secured a military plane, and calls to the Dagastani Foreign Ministry had obtained flight and landing clearances. The plane landed just after noon, and four members of the embassy's Marine Security Guard Detachment had acted as pall bearers and an honor guard to place the coffin on board. Morgan had assigned Cornelius the sad duty of escorting the remains back to the states.

They were back in the embassy at two, haggard and exhausted; Morgan, Jeffers, and Raine, sitting around the low table in the corner of Morgan's office.

"Well," Raine said. "What do we do now?"

"For starters, I think we need to know why we were ambushed," Jeffers said.

"Don't you want to know who ambushed you?"

Morgan and Jeffers looked at Raine. "Do you know?" Morgan asked.

Raine nodded. "I checked the bodies before I came out of the alley. I recognized two of them. They were close aides of Dragov."

"What? But, Ellingsworth was supposed to be meeting with Dragov," Morgan said. "Why would the man he was supposed to be meeting ambush him?"

"Ellingsworth wasn't the target. He must have been hit by stray rounds." Raine's face was creased with a look of concern. "I got there a bit ahead of you guys, to recon the site. One of those guys had been at the building with Ellingsworth just before your car arrived. I saw them talking, and then he went into the alley where the others were waiting. That ambush was for the two of you, and I think Ellingsworth set it up."

"Holy shit," Jeffers said. "Why would the ambassador want to have us killed? That doesn't make any sense."

"Well, unfortunately, we can't ask him now. You're right, though. It doesn't make any sense, unless you two were close to something Ellingsworth didn't want you to find."

An image of the scene just before the

shooting started drifted across Morgan's mind. "You know, the ambassador did look over toward that alley just before the first shots were fired. I just find it hard to believe that he'd resort to such drastic measures."

Raine looked into Morgan's eyes. His own eyes narrowed. "Dave, I'm going to tell you two something that has to stay in this room for now. My guys at Langley have stumbled onto some kind of deal that's been cooking in DC for a while. It involves a bunch of senior officials, and is somehow tied to Dagastan. Nothing's gone through official channels, and we've only been able to identify a few of those involved in Washington. We think they're planning something, but no one's been able to figure out just what it is."

"Does it have anything to do with this White Dragon that keeps cropping up?"

"Yeah, and we can't figure out what the hell White Dragon is. Every time someone gets close to it, they end up dead. You two almost joined that group."

Morgan shook his head. "If I'm close enough to it to be a threat, it must really be secret. I haven't a fucking clue."

"Well, we'd better figure out what it is, and soon," Raine said.

Just then, Lieutenant Duggan, the defense

attaché, and Dennis Larson, the political counselor, excited expressions on their faces, burst into Morgan's office.

"There's been a coup," Duggan said, his voice ragged with excitement. "Dragov's taken power from Kovasc during the early hours of the morning. They let our plane leave, but nothing else's allowed in or out for the duration."

"I called the Foreign Ministry," Larson said. "They gave me the runaround for over two hours. But, finally a low level official I know confirmed it. Kovasc has been placed under house arrest, and Dragov has convened the central committee and politburo to form a new government."

"Looks like the shit has hit the fan," Raine said. "I got a feeling we might be about to find out what's going on."

"They know you're in charge now, David," Larson said. "Dragov's asking for a meeting with you immediately. What do I tell the Foreign Ministry?"

CHARLES RAY

Chapter 40

In unfamiliar territory, Morgan had wrestled with the appropriate response to the summons to meet with Dragov. Finally, he decided that it would be best to take a firm line, so he had instructed Larson to inform the ministry that he would have to get instructions from Washington before any meeting.

It was three-thirty in the afternoon, so when the Operations Center staffer rang Whitman's phone at his home, it was three-thirty in the morning. Whitman's voice was dull with sleep when he answered, but when the caller identified himself and the purpose of the call, he brightened.

"David," he said, stifling a yawn. "Tell me that Ambassador's body got off okay."

Morgan took a deep breath. He didn't want to sound excited on his first call as charge d'affaires – he didn't count the call informing Washington of Ellingsworth's death – especially calling about the events that were unfolding. He wanted them to think that he was capably executing his duties.

"Yes, no problems there," he said. "But, that's not why I'm calling at this ungodly hour. There's been an unscheduled change in government here."

There was a pause. Morgan could hear the buzz of static on the line, probably from the local exchange.

"Dragov's taken over," Whitman said simply.

"You don't seem surprised. Were you expecting this?"

More pause. The static was a warbling sound now. Morgan began to feel a coldness at the nape of his neck. Finally, Whitman's voice came over the line.

"Well, Ambassador Ellingsworth did think it likely that Dragov would make a move on Kovasc sometime during the holiday."

Morgan's brown cheeks flamed with anger. Ellingsworth and Whitman had been sitting on information that impacted the security of every person in the embassy, and had kept him and everyone else in the dark.

"Dammit, Jim, why was I not told about this?"

"Obviously, the ambassador felt that you had no need to know."

"No need to know? You son of a bitch. The

two of you put every person in this embassy at risk, and I have no need to know?"

"There's no need to take that tone, Dave. You have to appreciate the bigger picture."

Morgan made a snorting sound. "Bigger picture? The ambassador's dead, and it's only luck that we don't have more people dead. And, now, we have a coup on our hands."

"Ah yes," Whitman said. "We want you to get to know Dragov better. See if there are ways we can work with his government."

"I'm not sure about that, Jim. Things are probably still unsettled here. My understanding is that it's been our policy to keep our distance when there's been an unconstitutional change in government unless there are critical U.S. national interests at play. Dagastan is of no strategic importance to us, so wouldn't it be sending a bad signal if we were seen to be getting in bed with a guy who just staged a coup?"

"Look, I don't expect you to fully understand this, Dave, but, Ambassador Ellingsworth has already laid the groundwork for this, and, there *is* a critical interest in Dagastan right now."

Morgan's bullshit meter pinged. He'd been in the country longer than Ellingsworth, and prided himself on knowing as much, if not more, about the country than his deceased boss. Dagastan wasn't of any importance to anyone; had never been. He found it straining credibility to believe that the pompous, self-important Ellingsworth had discovered something that people like Larson, Duggan, and even Carlton Raine, had missed. Furthermore, Whitman's condescending tone of voice was beginning to irritate him.

"Be that as it may," he said. "If I get written instructions, I'll do my best to carry them out. But, I want to be on record as expressing my serious concerns about any such move on our part before we have a better idea of what's going on here."

More silence. For a moment, he thought Whitman might have broken the connection.

"I appreciate your concerns," Whitman's voice came tinnily over the line. "But, I must insist that you do what I ask."

You can insist all you want, Morgan thought, but, I'm not putting this embassy on the line without some kind of official paper to cover our asses. "And, I must insist on getting those instructions in writing."

"Dammit, Dave, you're being difficult - -"

"No, Jim, I'm being prudent. You're asking me to do something that I know is not in line with normal policy. I'd be a fool to cozy up to a junta without some kind of assurance that it was approved policy. It's not that I don't trust you." But, the fact was, he didn't. "But, there needs to be a written record."

"Yeah, okay. But, it would be easier if we could show that the folks on the ground were already moving in that direction. You know how long it takes to get cables cleared in this building. This is an opportunity that is fleeting. If we don't move fast, we risk leaving the field to the opposition."

"The opposition? I wasn't aware that there was an opposing side in our relations with Dagastan."

"Don't be naïve, Dave. You know full well that we're in a head to head competition with the Soviets just about everywhere in the world. We lost out to them in Vietnam. We don't want to see a repeat of that in Dagastan."

Morgan knew that Whitman had never served in Vietnam; that he was just repeating the mantra of many about Vietnam being one of the dominos in a global game against World Communism, and that when it fell, the rest of Southeast Asia would fall with it. His own time there had shown him a different story. Yes, the Soviets had backed the North Vietnamese in their fight to take over the south, but the antipathy between the Vietnamese and their northern neighbor, China, was too deep to make a monolithic communist campaign a reality, and anyone who didn't have his head in rectal defilade knew that the Russians and the Chinese didn't get along. How Whitman could be comparing an insignificant, landlocked backwater like Dagastan to Vietnam struck Morgan as more than naiveté; it was just plain stupid.

"I'll say this again, Jim. There is nothing of strategic importance in this country to justify putting us out on a limb like this. Unless you give me something in writing, I plan to follow normal procedure. I'll maintain relations as normally as I can, but I don't think we should take any action that shows we approve of what's happening here."

"You're wrong about there being nothing of strategic importance."

"Then, tell me what it is."

"I'm sorry, but I can't do that right now. Trust me; you'll know what you need to know when the time is right. I might also remind you that your career is riding on how you handle this situation."

There it was, out in the open. He was being pushed into a corner. If he refused to comply with Whitman's instructions, as unorthodox as they were, the country director could – would – use his connections to sabotage Morgan's chances of future assignments. It was the situation he'd faced in his dealings with

Ellingsworth, and the man's death hadn't changed things. But, his own sense of honor also hadn't changed.

"I'll be waiting for your written instructions," he said, and broke the connection.

CHARLES RAY

Chapter 41

After ending his conversation with Whitman, Morgan called Larson and instructed him to contact the Foreign Ministry and confirm an appointment with Dragov. He also told him to tell them that he would be taking Larson and Raine with him to the meeting.

To his surprise, the request was immediately granted for the following morning at eight, and the ministry made no complaint at the makeup of his party.

Everyone rode in Morgan's car, Raine in the front with Achmed the driver, and Larson in the back with him. They'd all met up at Morgan's residence at six and breakfasted together. After eating in silence, for there was little any of them could think of to say, they piled in the car. Achmed remembered to set the American flag on the right front fender before starting out.

"I wonder why his nibs is requesting to see us." Larson asked as the car passed through the residence's front gate. "I asked the ministry if any of the other embassies had been called, and they said no."

Morgan had his suspicions, but wasn't sure he was ready to share them with his young political officer. He felt guilty at the thought. After the way Ellingsworth had kept information from him, it somehow seemed wrong. On the other hand, perhaps the less Larson knew, the safer he'd be in the end. His mind was a jumble of the craziest thoughts. He looked at Raine, sitting quietly in the front, his eyes on the terrain rolling past; knowing the intelligence officer was probably having some of the same thoughts.

"I guess we'll find out when we see him," he said simply.

Morgan cracked the window on his side a bit. The acrid smell of smoke from cooking fires quickly invaded the car's interior, but he didn't find it at all unpleasant. It was the view that depressed him; the view and the sounds. The buildings they passed stood like gray, somber stone monuments, leaning precariously as if at any moment they would crumble into fragments. Behind the closed and curtained doors, even over the hum of the engine and the crackle of the tires on the dusty pavement, he could hear the faint sound of weeping, the solemn chanting of black-robed priests, echoing across the deserted streets.

The crowds of the previous evening had vanished, as if into thin air, leaving the dusty streets empty except for an occasional scrap of trash fluttering in the afternoon breeze, and the soldiers, in groups of four, at every intersection; serious faced young men in gray-green combat gear, their almond eyes narrow slits over their high, sallow cheeks as they stood, staring at the vacant faces of the buildings, their shoulders tenses as expecting a sniper's bullet from a rooftop or window.

The mood of the city was as gray as the sky, which hung overhead like a burial shroud.

Kazbektun could never be called a lively city, not by any stretch of the imagination. But, now, it looked like a ghost town, the sentries at the intersections, standing still and alert, their only movement an occasional turn of their heads to peer nervously at the empty alleyways, looking like gray-green plinths standing at the entrance to a graveyard.

As they neared State House, there was some sign of life. Military trucks, medium-sized and large, loaded down with more combat-clad troops armed with automatic weapons held alertly across their chests, patrolled the streets around the compound.

Guards in the green dress uniform of the elite security service stood stiffly at the large wrought iron gates. As Achmed slowed and turned into the entrance drive, the soldiers snapped to attention and saluted. The gates swung ponderously inward, and an officer, distinguished by the red tabs on his collar, waved them in.

They drove slowly along the circular drive and under the portico at the entrance to the central building. More guards stood alert beside the great wooden doors. A short, rotund man, with a swarthy complexion and stringy black hair, dressed in a black suit that hung poorly on his portly frame, stood in front of the door wringing his hands nervously.

As they exited the vehicle, the man rushed to Morgan, bowing and extending his hand. "Mister Ambassador," he said. "Please to come with me. His Excellency is waiting."

Morgan recognized Karol Wochak, the Foreign Minister, having met him once with the previous ambassador. Despite the chill in the air, beads of sweat dotted the man's furrowed brow. His hand trembled as Morgan shook it.

The guards opened the door, and, with Wochak nearly prancing in the lead, and with Larson and Raine behind him, Morgan entered the building.

They passed through a great entrance hall, with pink marble floors and high walls upon which hung paintings of Dagastan's past heroes, gaudy oil paintings done in the Soviet style of overly muscled men sitting astride majestic looking black horses, their gazes on something in the far distance. Through an arched center door, they proceeded down a long hallway, also lined with paintings representing Dagastan's history, coming finally to a plain wooden door, before which stood two more guards, their expressions as fixed as bronze statues.

Wochak knocked lightly on the door. There were muffled words, and the door swung open.

Wochak stepped aside and motioned Morgan to enter. The room was long and narrow, only slightly wider than the hallway. A long, low wooden table ran down the center, flanked by high backed chairs with ornately embroidered cushions. Samovars and cups were spaced evenly on both sides of the table. At the far end was another wooden chair, but with a higher back, and cushions that looked like they were embroidered with gold threads on the back, seat and arms. A small table sat to the right of the chair. On it were a silver urn and a silver flagon.

Wochak motioned Morgan to the chair on the left nearest the end and moved around to take the chair facing him. Larson and Raine were left to find their own seats. They sat next to Morgan.

"His Excellency will be with us soon," Wochak said. His lips trembled and he kept looking around as if expecting someone or something to jump out of the walls.

While they waited, Morgan took the time to look around the room. The floor was covered with what looked to him like an expensive Persian carpet, and the walls were covered with similar material. They were otherwise bare, but large light rectangular areas indicated that at one time pictures had hung there.

Suddenly, Wochak jumped to his feet, turning toward the door, which was swinging open. "Gentlemen, His Excellency, Comrade Milosevic Dragov, First Secretary of the Communist Party of Dagastan, and Chairman of the Presidium." He bowed at the waist until his head was almost touching the edge of the table.

Morgan and the other two stood, facing the man who entered. Morgan kept his back straight and looked the man in the eye. It was important, he thought, to maintain the dignity expected of the senior American representative to the government, but he would not have bowed in any case. David Morgan bowed to no man. The other two followed his example.

Milosevic Dragov was tall for a Dagastani. Broad shoulders and narrow waist, but for the oriental cast of his eyes and his almost yellow complexion, he could have passed for a Russian. He had a square head, a wide forehead with prominent black brows, a razor-sharp nose over thin lips, and a prominent square jaw. He was dressed in a simple green tunic that stretched over his muscular chest, green pants that showed the bulge of well-developed thigh muscles, and black riding boots that were polished to a high gloss.

He walked down the left side of the room, stopping as he came abreast of Morgan.

"Ambassador Morgan," he said in a deep resonant voice. "Thank you for coming. Please to accept the condolences of my government for untimely death of Ambassador Ellingsworth."

When they shook hands, Morgan was impressed with the strength in the man's grip. The slitted eyes, like tiny obsidian marbles, regarded him without expression.

"My pleasure, sir," Morgan said. "Thank you for your concern. I must state for the record, though, I'm not an ambassador. Until a replacement for Ambassador Ellingsworth has been named, I am only the charge d'affaires."

Dragov laughed; a deep throaty sound. "Is only title. Is not important. To Dagastan, you are ambassador." He continued to the head chair and sat, leaning toward Morgan. "Please, gentlemen, to enjoy a cup of Dagastan tea."

Dragov lifted the silver urn and poured a dark beverage into the flagon. When he lifted the vessel to his lips, the others poured tea into the cups near them. Morgan noticed that Wochak's hands trembled as he poured.

He sipped the hot tea, regarding Dragov over the rim of the cup. The tea was pleasant, with a hint of jasmine. Morgan put his cup back on the table and sat back in his chair, gazing levelly at Dragov.

After a few more sips of tea, Dragov put the flagon back on the table and leaned forward, placing his large hands on his knees.

"You wonder why I ask to see you, no."

Morgan nodded. "I understand there has been a change in government. I assume you will brief us on the new organization, and tell us the condition of the previous leader."

"Is not for America to worry," Dragov said. He laughed again, and took another sip of tea. "Comrade Kovasc is not harmed. He will stay in residence until People's Tribunal makes decision."

"People's Tribunal?" Morgan noticed out of the corner of his eye that Larson was scribbling furiously on a small note pad he'd taken from his jacket pocket. Wochak, his coat now showing dark rings of sweat under both arms, eyed him nervously, but said nothing.

"Yes," Dragov said. "Is People's Tribunal must decide how Comrade Kovasc must pay for his crimes against Dagastan people. Is rule of law; is not right, Comrade Wochak?"

The foreign minister's head bobbed up and

down. "That is correct, Excellency."

Morgan knew that, Whitman's injunction to try and find a way to work with the new government notwithstanding, others in Washington would want as much detail as possible. What he really wanted was to get as far away from Dragov as possible. The man radiated menace, from his stony expression, dominated by soulless eyes that seemed to bore down to the center of your soul, to the casual way he sat as those around him bowed and scraped, and quaked in fear. Here, Morgan thought, was a man you didn't want as an enemy.

"What crimes are former First Secretary Kovasc charged with?" Morgan asked.

"Crimes too many to tell all," Dragov said. "Comrade Kovasc lived like king while people of Dagastan starve." Not exactly true, Morgan thought; there had been no reports of starvation, despite dips in food production. Kovasc had lived a sumptuous life, but, then, so did the rest of Dagastan's military and civilian elite – Dragov included, Morgan guessed. But he held his tongue. "He dishonored Dagastan tradition, did nothing to develop country. He make us slave to Russians. Dagastan is proud country, with rich history, but Comrade Kovasc make us like poor province of Russia, like poor relative asking for handout at table of rich Russian relative."

Morgan heard nothing that constituted an act in violation of what he knew about Dagastan's criminal code. But, previous experience in other countries had taught him that military juntas had a way of redefining the statutes to justify their actions. He knew that Larson would draft a cable containing all that Dragov had said, and it would be up to him to provide explanatory comments for the benefit of those in Washington who were responsible for determining what the policy response would be.

"Well, Mr. First Secretary," he said. "I would appreciate if we could be kept informed of what's happening."

Dragov nodded. "Is not problem. Dagastan wishes to be friends with America. Is hoping that America will understand and support new Dagastan government."

This was the crucial point, Morgan knew. What he said next had to be carefully phrased; on the one hand not to make commitments to Dragov that Washington might disavow, on the other, not to burn bridges with the man that he might have to later cross. His words, or interpretations of his words, would be examined in minute detail at some future date by people who, though, having no direct knowledge of Dagastan or events unfolding in Dagastan, would sit in judgment on his actions.

"Mr. First Secretary," he said, measuring his

words carefully. "It is up to those in my government far senior to me to determine the relationship between our two countries. They must, before making a determination, consider the way the current change in administration has taken place. Our job in the embassy is merely to carry out the policies decided by our leadership." He took a deep breath. He reached down, lifted his cup, and took a sip of the tea. When his breathing calmed, he continued. "We will, of course, report what you have said to Washington, and we will inform you of their decision as quickly as possible."

Dragov looked from Morgan to Wochak, his eyes narrowed to the point that they looked like dark lines to either side of his nose. Then, he looked back at Morgan and nodded.

"Is understood. Please, to tell Washington one more thing. Engineers have discovered in mountains to west very big deposit of uranium. Ambassador Ellingsworth believe that Comrade Kovasc would allow Russians to take uranium and people of Dagastan get no benefit. He say, America would not like new source of uranium to be controlled by Russia. If America support my government, I think can be good for both countries."

Morgan nodded, trying to keep his face from showing emotion. So, that was what Ellingsworth had been up to. It made no sense, though. Russia had its own sources of uranium, and any additional supply of the mineral that would come from Dagastan was unlikely to make a significant difference in the strategic situation between the U.S. and the USSR in regards to nuclear capacity. Both countries already possessed enough nuclear missiles between them to turn the globe into a sterile, lifeless, glowing ball of rock. It was highly unlikely that the administration, still smarting from the ignominious retreat from Vietnam the previous month, would risk another confrontation in a remote location unknown to the average American.

"I will report all of this to my government, sir," he said.

Chapter 42

Friday-Monday, May 23 – 26, 1975, Washington, DC

"You're right," Murphy said. "Miss Chambers couldn't have done it. Based on how the blood has thickened, I'd say he was killed before midnight, and we know she was with you then. The ME will have to determine as best he can time and cause of death, but from the looks of it, someone with a large amount of upper body strength, bashed his skull in with some heavy object."

"Yeah, and the way the room's splattered, there's no way Alison could have done it and not gotten blood and gunk on her clothing. You saw her, her dress is completely clean."

Murphy nodded. "Okay, Lee. I'll get her statement and you can take her home."

By the time the two men got back to the car, and Murphy removed the handcuffs, Alison had regained most of her composure. When she'd finished telling the detective her story, she was her old self again. Kennedy stayed at her side, silent, but with his hand around her waist. His nearness helped her immensely.

"You want to go home?" he asked her when they were sitting in his car, down the block from the crime scene.

"No, I think I want to go to the office. With Dudley dead, I think it changes my status. I need to get caught up on what's going on."

"You and me both," he said.

They rode the elevator together from the basement. Kennedy passed his floor, escorting Alison to her office. "Is that really necessary now?" she asked. "I mean, the guy who was trying to kill me is dead."

"We still don't know who's behind him. Besides, I kind of like walking with you. You don't mind, do you?"

"Not at all." She took his arm and leaned her head against his shoulder.

Inside her office, the secretary, Earline, met them, a look of concern on her face.

"Is it true? Did they find Dudley Lakeworth killed in his house?"

Alison and Kennedy nodded. "Someone murdered him," Alison said.

Earline made the sign of the cross. "What is this world coming to when a person's not safe in his own house?"

"Look, Earline; I don't want to seem uncaring, but I need you to find out if this changes my status. Dudley put me on administrative leave, but - -"

"Oh, that," Earline said, a slight smile creasing her face. "I hadn't quite got around to forwarding the paperwork on that." She reached into her desk and withdrew two neatly typed sheets. "He didn't get a chance to sign it, so I reckon there's no action."

Alison hugged the older woman, and then turned to Kennedy. "Well, I guess I can get back to work. Meet you at your office at five?"

Kennedy nodded, and kissed her on the cheek. After he'd gone, the secretary chuckled. "Looks like this has gone beyond him just being a bodyguard, huh?"

Alison blushed. She whirled and fled toward her office.

"You go, girl," Earline said to her retreating back.

In her office, Alison took the notebook from her purse and began listing every fact she could think of about the case, writing names in one column and incidents in another. She then drew lines from incident to name, trying to cross reference to determine who or what was involved in each.

Certain names, like Dudley Lakeworth and Lesley Carter, she ran a line through and noted that they were deceased. She put a star next to Lakeworth's name. She also noted that both these individuals were connected to events in DC and in Dagastan.

At the bottom of the page, she wrote 'White Dragon,' followed by a string of question marks. She was convinced that this mysterious phrase held the key to everything.

Kennedy arrived at his office to find Broadbent waiting for him. The man's face was flushed.

"Is it true? Did someone kill Dudley Lakeworth?"

"Yes," Kennedy said. "Someone cracked his head open like a ripe melon."

Broadbent put his hand to his mouth, his eyes wide in shock. "My God, what is this city coming to? A man isn't safe in his own house. Did someone break in?"

"There were no signs of forced entry, and nothing seemed to be missing. No, whoever did this had one objective, and one objective only – to kill him."

The color left Broadbent's face. He seemed to be looking inward. "Uh, how can you be sure of that? Surely you must be mistaken. Why would anyone want to kill Dudley?"

"Why would someone want to kill Lesley Carter? And, why would that same man try to kill Alison Chambers? Good questions, Melvin. You met the man, although you claim not to know who he was. Maybe this has to do with the fact that they were all too close to these mysterious White Dragons. Have you ever thought of that?"

Broadbent's mouth opened and closed. His eyes refocused on Kennedy who stood in front of him, his hands on his hips, his gaze boring into him. He shook his head. "I-I don't . . . know . . . what . . . you . . . mean. I don't know anything about any White Dragons." His eyes darted from side to side.

Kennedy knew then that he was lying. He knew something. And, whatever it was, it scared him silly.

"Then, maybe you're safe. Seems like anyone who gets too close to whatever it, or they, happens to be ends up dead."

The man's Adam's apple bobbed up and down. Sweat beaded on his upper lip. "T-that goes for you as well, don't you t-think? You and this Alison woman keep poking your noses into this thing. Aren't you afraid you might also be in danger?"

Fear wasn't exactly the right description of what Kennedy felt. Concern, yes, but mostly anger. He didn't like not knowing what was going on. Some of his anger was directed at the man standing before him. Broadbent was in this up to his scrawny neck. But, he was holding out. But, he also seemed not to be completely in the loop either. His expression was that of someone who has suddenly discovered that he's bitten off more than he can chew. Well, Kennedy thought, let him stew in it. His only concern was to make sure nothing happened to Alison. Of course, that meant, he had to make sure he stayed alive along enough to do it.

The day dragged on interminably. Kennedy, like Alison, had gone to his office and, taking a steno pad from his desk, made notes. He wrote down everything he knew about the situation, which was precious little. Except for Broadbent, the senator, and the mysterious Niles Hitchcock, the only people who seemed close to what was happening were him and Alison, and neither of them had a clue to what was going on.

Just before leaving the office to meet Alison, he called Pete Jeffers, waking the man from a sound sleep, to fill him in on what had happened in Washington and get an update on events in Dagastan. Jeffers informed him of Ellingsworth's death, and Morgan's plans to meet the new leader of Dagastan, and promised to fill him in on that meeting as soon as he could. After breaking the connection, Kennedy made some more notes on his pad.

Closing the pad, he tucked it into his belt and left to pick Alison up.

They spent the evening comparing notes, between conversations with Rachel about a school trip planned for a visit to the National Zoo on Saturday morning. After Rachel had gone to sleep, they sat shoulder to shoulder on the sofa, silently enjoying each other's company.

Around midnight, having mutually agreed that Rachel wouldn't be traumatized by them sharing a bed, they prepared to turn in. Just as Kennedy reached for the light switch, the phone rang.

"Yeah," he said.

"Mr. Kennedy?" A voice came over the line. "My pardon for such a late call but I think we need to talk."

"Who is this?"

"We've never met, Mr. Kennedy, but I think we have mutual interests. I'm Jonathan Appleby." Kennedy recognized the name. A moderate senator from North Dakota, and a member of the Senate Foreign Relations Committee, Appleby seldom appeared in public. Unlike many of his fellow legislators, he labored quietly behind the scenes to provide oversight of the country's foreign affairs. "Can you meet me tomorrow?"

"Of course, senator, but, can you tell me what this is about?"

"I'd rather not say on an open line, Mr. Kennedy. Meet me tomorrow morning at ten in front of the Lincoln Memorial. And, please bring Miss Chambers with you."

Kennedy's curiosity was aroused. Alison, hearing only his end of the conversation, was also interested. She stood near him, her brows raised.

"And, one other thing, Mr. Kennedy," Appleby said. "It would be prudent of you to make sure you're not followed."

The connection was broken. Kennedy looked puzzled as he put the handset back on its cradle.

"What was that all about?" Alison asked.

"I guess we'll find out tomorrow," Kennedy said, shrugging his shoulder. "This is getting stranger by the minute."

Chapter 43

Kennedy and Alison woke early on Saturday morning. After breakfast, they took Rachel to school where she joined her class for the trip to the zoo, and then returned home.

They set out for the District just before nine, arriving at Twenty-Third Street, near the Department of State, some fifteen minutes later. Kennedy found an empty parking space adjacent to the Naval Medical Center which is across the street from the State Department building. He and Alison walked back down Twenty-Third and across Constitution Avenue to the Lincoln Memorial.

By the time they arrived at the circular drive at the marble steps of the memorial, it was fifteen minutes before ten, and crowds of tourists had already started to gather; lines of foreigners with guides speaking their native languages, pointing and taking pictures, groups of teenagers, ignoring the entreaties of their teachers to stay together, jostling each other as they ran to and fro over the drive, and up and down the steps.

They found a place at the south side of the steps and stood looking out toward the Reflecting Pool, and the phallic-shaped Washington Monument in the distance beyond. Standing thus, they failed to see the distinguished looking man who approached them from the top of the steps.

He was tall and angular, shoulders not too broad but held squarely as he walked erect down the steps. He wore brown corduroy pants, a green shirt, and a light tan jacket. His pants broke sharply over dark brown cowboy boots that were scuffed from much use. He had a sharp nose over thin lips that looked like they would turn up in a smile at any excuse, and he looked down at them through bright blue eyes under craggy brown brows with a dusting of white hairs scattered amidst the brown. His dusty brown hair, also flecked with gray, was combed back along his skull. He had the look of a cowboy, in town to see the sights. That, in fact, was what he'd been before being elected to the senate from his home state of North Dakota eighteen years earlier.

The click of Jonathan Appleby's cowboy boots on the marble steps alerted Kennedy and Alison to his presence when he was but two steps above them. They both turned, looking up.

"Mr. Kennedy, Miss Chambers," he said, his voice deep with a hint of a nasal twang. "Thank you for agreeing to meet with me."

He walked forward, thrusting out a sun browned hand, shaking first with Kennedy, and then lingering a bit as he grasped Alison's hand. His hands were rough, but not unpleasantly so, reminding Alison of her father's work worn hands.

"It's our pleasure, senator," she said. "I'm just a bit confused, though, about why you wanted to speak with us."

Appleby's eyes twinkled, and the lips turned up in that smile that had been waiting for an excuse. "I like that. A woman who gets right to the point." He stepped down the last step. "Why don't we walk along the Reflecting Pool? Our conversation can be more private there. With so many people around here, no one can focus easily on any one group talking."

Kennedy was curious. He wondered why a United States senator would worry about his conversation being overheard. But, he agreed that, if someone *was* trying to eavesdrop on them, their being in the middle of a warbling crowd of tourists and teenagers made it more difficult. Taking Alison's arm, he fell in beside the senator as they walked toward the long rectangular pool upon which a flock of ducks swam, occasionally ducking their heads to feed. The noise of many conversations around them was like a low hum.

"I too have been wondering why you wanted to talk to the two of us, sir," he said. "We're just low level employees of the State Department."

"You're a security officer, Mr. Kennedy, and you, Miss Chambers are an intelligence analyst. Both of you know full well that Washington is a town full of secrets, but that nothing here is ever *really* secret." He moved to put Alison between them and laid a hand on her arm. They looked like three tourists out for a Saturday morning stroll on the Mall. "As you know, I'm on the Foreign Relations Committee, so the activities of your department are of importance to me. It has come to my attention that you have encountered information of a disturbing nature, information regarding events in Dagastan – yes, I'm familiar with the country, with many obscure countries, in fact – and the possible involvement of senior American officials in the affairs of that country."

"Yes, sir," Alison said. "There seems to be something happening, but none of my analysis tells me what, and there have been efforts to stop me from looking into it."

"I take it, Mr. Kennedy, that you have experienced something similar."

It was a statement, not a question. The man, Kennedy was convinced, knew more about what was going on than they did.

"That's right, senator. Furthermore, two

people who were involved in this have been killed here in Washington, and an attempt was made on Alison, Miss Chambers' life."

"Yes, I was told. You killed the assailant. That was very brave of you."

Kennedy shrugged. "You're very well informed, sir."

"One of the perks of being a senator." Appleby smiled more broadly. "People tell you things. Now, tell me, what have you two discovered about the White Dragons?"

Alison's eyes grew round. Kennedy regarded the man through narrowed eyes.

"Nothing," Kennedy said. "Other than they seem to have the substance of fog, but are up to their asses in whatever's going on."

"Lee, you shouldn't use such language with a senator," Alison said.

"That's quite all right, Miss Chambers," Appleby said. "I appreciate a man who speaks his mind in plain language. And, he's right; the White Dragons are up to their asses in this."

"Who . . . er, what are the White Dragons?" she asked.

"That, unfortunately I cannot tell you. Let's just say they are a group of people who like to control events from behind the scenes.

Faceless, nameless men who have in this instance, I fear, overreached."

"But, Dagastan is a nothing place," she said. "It's of no importance to anyone."

"Ordinarily, that would be the case. But, recently, uranium deposits were discovered there. The ambassador - Ellingsworth wasn't it – was involved with the White Dragons in an effort to ensure that the Soviet Union didn't gain control over the disposition of that uranium. He was, I'm told, working with the deputy head of the security service, Milosevic Dragov, to ensure that. There has already been, or soon will be, a change of government in Dagastan; one the White Dragons will be more aligned with the U.S. than the Soviet Union."

"There has already been a coup," Kennedy said. "And, Dragov has taken power. Ambassador Ellingsworth, though, was killed in an accident recently, and the embassy is now under the command of the number two."

"That would be Mr. Morgan, right?"

Now, it was Kennedy's turn to stare wide-eyed. "Yes," he said.

"Oh, don't look so surprised," Appleby said. "Like I said, I take my duties on the committee seriously, and that means knowing the people involved in carrying out our foreign affairs. I understand that Morgan is not the usual officer who would be assigned to such a position?"

"That's right," Alison said. "First, he's not a political officer. That would normally be the person assigned as number two. Secondly, he's black, and we don't have many minorities in leadership positions outside a few of the smaller embassies in Africa."

"How well do you know him?"

"I don't know him, but I know his reputation," she said. "He's a very intelligent and dedicated man. He's also an army Special Forces veteran with war experience in Vietnam. Frankly, I can't think of anyone better to be in charge in Dagastan under the present circumstances."

"But," Kennedy said. "We can't be sure what kind of support he's getting from his country director."

Appleby rubbed his chin. "Of course. Isn't it always like that. A country that no one pays much attention to. Policy is often made at the lowest level, and it only rises to very senior attention when things go horribly wrong. I fear that our friends in the White Dragons have probably set things up to do just that."

"What can we do to help keep that from happening?" Alison asked.

"Right now, there's probably nothing else you can do. However, I'm not without some influence in this town. My advice to you two young people is to keep a very low profile for the next few days. Let me see what I can do. If I'm able to get to the right people, we might be able to keep this train from derailing."

Alison sighed. She felt as if a great weight had been lifted from her shoulders. For days now, she and Lee had been fighting a holding action against senior people determined to keep them from finding things out, and a cold-blooded killer who wanted to eliminate them. Now, they had the force of a United States senator behind them.

Kennedy continued to regard the senator warily. Maybe, he thought, it was just his cop's instinct not to trust anyone. It all seemed just too pat, the senator swooping in like the Lone Ranger, to save them at the last minute. But, the man was right. There wasn't much more he and Alison could do alone. Things couldn't get much worse. Finally, he nodded.

"Thank you, senator," he said. "Will you let us know when things are right again?"

"Keep your ears and eyes open," Appleby said. "You'll know."

Chapter 44

Tuesday, May 27, 1975, Dagastan

Immediately upon returning to the embassy, Morgan had had Larson draft a NIACT cable – a telegram of such priority that people would be called out of bed to read it – to Washington, reporting his meeting with Dragov. He'd added a comment recommending a cautious approach to the question of recognition of the new government until the embassy had more opportunity to assess its performance and the reaction of Dagastan's population to it. The signs had been disturbing, with the deserted streets and the overwhelming presence of armed military units throughout the city.

He knew it would take Washington time to digest the information and then undergo the time-consuming process of crafting a U.S. position, fully vetted through the Washington bureaucracy. He'd instructed Larson, Duggan and Raine to reach out to all their sources to try and gauge the mood of the place, but cautioned them to exercise extreme care in doing so.

He spent a sleepless night, tossing and turning until, at three in the morning, he'd given up and gone out to his patio to sit and gaze up at the stars.

At six, he gave up and called his driver to take him to the embassy.

The sun was casting a pink glow on the sky as he drove through the empty streets. Shops were shuttered, and there were no pedestrians, just the armed soldiers still standing alert sentinel at intersections who studiously ignored his car as it drove past.

Larson, Duggan, Raine, and Jeffers were waiting for him in the front office, standing near Mary Sung's desk when he walked in. Everyone had a somber look, even Mary as she handed him a mug of steaming coffee.

"Okay, guys," he said. "Let's go to my office and see where we are."

They filed in, taking seats around the table in the corner, leaving the corner chair for him. He took a sip from the mug and placed it on the table.

"Who wants to go first?"

Duggan, his eyes red from lack of sleep, and needing a shave, leaned forward. "The place's locked down tight, Dave. None of my military contacts will return my calls."

"I have one or two sources I was able to get to last night," Raine said. "They say the word's out to cool it with the Americans until we announce recognition of the new government. A lot of my best sources, though, have gone silent."

"Same here," Larson said. "My sources, including some I thought I had a good personal relationship with, won't talk to me. I went to one guy's house, and he wouldn't even open the door. He seemed scared to death that someone would see me there, and begged me to go away."

"Shit," Morgan said. "Sounds bad all around. We'll need to get this to Washington first thing. It'll impact on their final decision for sure. Pete, what have you seen?"

The young security officer had remained silent, with a brooding look on his face. He too looked as if he hadn't slept in days.

"For starters, some of our local employees are staying home. I've had three security guards resign, and the ones who've come to work are scared shitless. People are staying locked in their houses. But, there's one thing that really worries me."

"What is it, Pete?"

"You remember that guy that came to see you, Vechkov something or other?"

"Yeah, Anton Vechkov. He was part of some

pro-democracy outfit."

"Well, one of my guards who happens to live in his neighborhood, told me he was found this morning, lying in a ditch behind his house with a bullet in the back of his head."

Chapter 45

Wednesday, May 28, 1975, Washington, DC

It had been a tense three days for Alison Chambers and Lee Kennedy. They'd done as Appleby suggested and laid off looking into events in Dagastan. Nothing about the place appeared in the *Washington Post*, and no one in INR or DS mentioned it. Lakeworth still hadn't been replaced, so Alison went back to work on projects that had lain on her desk since the day she'd received the note from Lesley Carter that started her down the murky path she'd been on for what seemed like a lifetime. Broadbent avoided Kennedy, ducking back into his office whenever he spotted him in the reception area.

When Kennedy came to work on Wednesday morning, he noticed that Broadbent's office door was open and looked deserted. A new secretary, a young woman with red hair and freckles, sat at the receptionist's desk.

"Is Broadbent in?" he asked her.

"Oh, he's been reassigned," she said, looking up from her typewriter. "Got the word at close of business yesterday. He cleaned out his desk and left. He didn't say where he was going. I think his replacement is due in by the end of the month."

Kennedy shrugged. Good riddance, he thought. The man was a lousy security agent anyway. He went into his office and called Alison to tell her the news.

"That's funny," she said. "I got a call from the Dagastan desk this morning. Whitman was reassigned yesterday, and they have a new country director and desk officer. They told me they've instructed the embassy to maintain cordial but arms-length relations with the new government because of allegations of human rights violations. Dave Morgan's being left as charge d'affaires for the time being, and he's taking somewhat of a hard line with the government. They pulled out the few dependents who were at post and are buttoned down for the moment."

"I don't envy them," Kennedy said. "But, that won't hurt Morgan's career being the man in charge right now."

"That's for sure. The new country director told me they're looking at him for a possible chief of mission assignment when he transfers from Dagastan."

"Well, sounds like things just might be working out. Hey, how about lunch? I know a great little place up near K Street. An outdoor café; and the weather's perfect for that right now."

"You're on. Meet you in the E Street lobby at noon."

They walked, holding hands, up Twenty-First Street, through the George Washington University campus, to K Street and then right toward Nineteenth Street. Bistro Paree was the near the corner, a small restaurant frequented mainly by the lawyers and lobbyists who had their offices along the street.

They took a small table near the entrance, where the sound of music on a local station from the speaker above the bar came through clearly, and ordered light lunches.

Lunch, washed down with unsweetened tea, was pleasant. For a change, they didn't feel they had to look over their shoulders. Traffic along K Street was uncharacteristically light, and the music and hum of nearby conversations was comforting. They were enjoying each other's company. Both were thinking of the future – and seeing the other in that future.

At first, they almost missed the announcer's voice. " --- the program to bring you this special announcement. The U.S. Senate today announced the untimely death of Alabama

Senator Carlton Longroux. The senator, a member of the Foreign Relations Committee, reportedly fell from a ladder at his Georgetown residence, breaking his neck. He was pronounced dead at the scene by paramedics. The remains will lie in state in the Capitol Rotunda for three days before being flown to his home state for interment. Senator Jonathan Appleby, a colleague on the Foreign Relations Committee told this reporter that Senator Longroux will be missed and that he will forever be remembered for his contributions to America's national security and prestige in the world. We now return you to our regular program." The music, contemporary jazz, resumed.

Kennedy and Alison sat in stunned silence for a few moments, staring at each other across the white linen covered table, the remnants of their lunch forgotten.

Finally, Kennedy shook his head and broke the silence. "You don't think - -"

Alison raised her hand. "I'm not thinking anything. As far as I'm concerned, it's over and done with."

Epilogue

Thursday, May 29, 1975, Washington, DC

The house was a three-story red brick structure, built around the turn of the century, set back from the street and elevated above it, reached by a set of flagstone steps up from the warped and cracked sidewalk. It was surrounded by a high brick wall and in a compound with a four-car garage, a carriage house, and servant's quarters. There was no brass plate with name or number on the door, wall, or gate to the compound, and the yard had been paved over, with a few scraggly shoots of grass poking up through the graying concrete. Though the house had seen better days, it sat upon its little hill looking upon its neighbors with the disdain of a once-wealthy member of the gentry who has not come to terms with the decline in his fortune.

The street lamp at the corner cast long

shadows of the gnarled maple trees at the corner of the wall over the mold strewn brick walls. The house looked deserted, but upon close inspection, one could see that heavy drapes hung over all the windows. The solid oak entrance door had no window and was seated so securely in the frame, no light leaked out.

If one could have entered the dwelling, and that would have been impossible without an invitation, one would have noticed the dim entrance foyer, illuminated only by a single candle in a sconce canted from the wall. The carpeted floors would have creaked as one walked across them, through a large room with floor to ceiling book cases filled with rare and expensive first editions, leather bound and gold leafed, down a narrow hallway with gloomy looking oil paintings canted out from the walls and antique Chinese vases along the baseboard, to a dark wooden door.

Through this door, one would have entered another dimly lit room, like the hallway and entrance foyer, illuminated by large candles in sconces placed evenly around the walls, a perfect square, with a large circular wooden table in the center, with twelve chairs arranged around it. Eleven of the chairs were occupied.

Eleven elderly white men sat around the table, but one, sitting with his back to the heavily curtained window, his light tan jacket resting comfortably on broad shoulders, his brown hair, flecked with gray combed back along his skull, hard blue eyes gazing around the room from beneath gray speckled brown brows, was clearly in charge. His gaze now was on a slightly build man in a well-tailored blue suit who sat across from. He was sweating, large dark circles seen under his arms. Everyone avoided looking at the empty chair. When the man with the icy blue eyes opened his mouth to speak, all eyes turned in his direction.

"You and Carlton overreached on this one, Niles," Senator Jonathan Appleby said. There was steel in his voice, and even though he spoke softly, everyone else around the table sat with their shoulders tensed. "Ellingsworth made a mistake in keeping his deputy in the dark, and it cost him his life. In addition, the eliminations that occurred were not sanctioned by this group."

Niles Hitchcock wiped at his sweating brow with an expensive silk handkerchief.

"I-I know, Jonathan," he said. "I t-tried to tell Carlton that we should go slowly, but he just wouldn't listen."

"I know that he could be impulsive, but, you didn't come to me. You stood by as he risked compromising everything we've built over the years. That was most irresponsible of you."

Hitchcock looked around the table, his eyes

pleading desperately for support, but the others merely looked away.

"Tell me, Niles, what did the two of you hope to achieve from this senseless project?"

For a moment, just a brief moment, fire blazed in Hitchcock's eyes. But, under Appleby's withering glare, it sputtered and died. "We hoped to restore some of the honor lost through our ignominious retreat from Saigon. Like Carlton, the sight of Americans fleeing in panic as an army of brown peasants operating tanks given them by the Soviets swept in to take over disgusted me. Our prestige is at an all-time low, and something had to be done to restore the proper order."

Appleby shook his head. A sad expression clouded his face. "And, the two of you thought you could achieve this by embroiling us in the petty disputes of some second rate country in a part of the world that Americans not only know nothing about, but care even less about?"

"Uh, it was a target of opportunity. Bob Ellingsworth met this man Dragov and sensed what he was planning. He saw it as an excellent, low cost opportunity to give the Soviets a black eye."

"Yet, neither of you saw fit to consult with the rest of the group. And, I must say, of all the people you could have chosen to be the point man on this, Ellingsworth would have been my last choice. We discussed him in the past; he was arrogant and self-centered, and frankly, not too bright. You see how badly he mangled things. Were it not for the fact that his deputy is a very capable individual, we might just be facing a real tragedy in Dagastan right now. As for the actions here – my first instinct was to simply turn you over to the police. They were unforgiveable."

"B-but, Carlton felt that it was important that we protect the identity of the group."

"By killing our own people? While, at the same time, that fool Ellingsworth was tossing the name about in conversations with a foreigner, and a fucking commie at that? I never took you for a fool, Niles, but you surprise me. If you'd wanted to protect the group, you would have consulted before setting out on this crusade."

"I-I suppose you're right. What do we do now?"

Appleby placed his weathered hands flat on the table and looked around at each man. "Hopefully, our people in place will manage it. For now, I think it best that we pull back. The value of this committee and the White Dragons is that we 'silently serve our nation when it needs us.' That is something I don't think Carlton ever fully understood, nor did that idiot Ellingsworth. We're not in this for our personal gain." He raised his right hand, his index finger poised, pointing at Hitchcock. "We also need to rethink the composition of both the committee and the White Dragons."

A portly man to Appleby's right, his three chins quivering, leaned forward. "What do you mean by that?" he asked.

"Look around you, gentlemen," Appleby said. "Here we sit, the eleven of us – and, we'll need to recruit a replacement for our dear departed friend Carlton Longroux – deciding the fate or our country, and often the free world. We oversee the activities of the White Dragons, who manage our relations with the rest of the world. But, look at us. Do we really represent this country? We, gentlemen, are a bunch of, as my daughter would say, 'old white men.' I fear that sometimes we're out of touch with the rest of the country. That was shown in Vietnam when the bulk of the population ignored our efforts to convince them of the need for the war. I'm afraid it will only get worse."

"Are you suggesting that we admit minorities to our group?" the portly man asked. "Are there any coloreds we believe qualified?"

Appleby winced slightly. "Leland, you make my point," he said. "We're out of touch with the country and the world. Take this man, David Morgan, for instance. He's far more capable than Ellingsworth ever was, but because he's a

Negro, he's been basically passed over for responsible jobs. If it hadn't been for the fact that Ellingsworth's predecessor was a woman, he wouldn't be in the job he's in. And, that's another issue. We have no women in the White Dragons or on this committee. This country's population is over fifty percent female."

"But, everyone knows that women are far too emotional for such demanding positions," a thin, hawk faced man sitting next to Hitchcock said. "Besides, the demands of their families would interfere with their availability to serve effectively."

"That's total bullshit, Henry," Appleby said, shaking his head and looking disgusted. "It's just an excuse to avoid sharing the wealth. If we don't want to be rendered as obsolete and extinct as the dinosaur, we'll have to adapt to changing times. As to women being too emotional, I wish you gentlemen had had an opportunity to meet a young lady named Alison Chambers. She's hardly too emotional, and intellectually, she'd run rings around each one of us." He slammed a fist on the table. "That, though, is business for a future meeting. For now, our job is to decide what to do to survive this Dagastan debacle." He glared again at the hapless Hitchcock. "For starters, Niles, I think that you need to take a very long vacation; perhaps to Costa Rica. In a year or two, things will have been forgotten." Hitchcock ducked his head. There would be no vote, nor did he think anyone would speak in his defense. Appleby's word on the committee was tantamount to imperial decree. "The others who were involved in this have been transferred; though, not before being instructed never to talk of this with anyone."

"What about Kennedy and Chambers?" Hitchcock asked. "They came close to uncovering the White Dragons."

"I think we can rest easy on that," Appleby said. "Recent events should put their minds at ease. We might have to keep a close eye on Mr. Kennedy. He's a good cop, with a cop's instincts, so he won't be as easily persuaded." He glared at Hitchcock. "It didn't help sending that man Hart after Miss Chambers. That made it personal as well as professional for Kennedy."

Hitchcock shrank down inside his jacket, looking down at the table.

"Let's hope that with the passage of time, this episode will fade from their minds and Mr. Kennedy and Miss Chambers will be preoccupied with other things. Whatever happens, there will be no more free lancing by any member of this committee. Do I make myself clear?"

There were nods around the table. Appleby reached behind him, grasping a silk cord that hung from the ceiling, and gave it a yank. From somewhere deep within the bowels of the old house, the tinkling of bells could be heard.

A few minutes later, the door opened, and a servant, a white haired old black man wearing a black tail coat over a red vest, and an immaculately done bow tie entered, carrying a large silver tray upon which rested a large teardrop shaped bottle of Jensen's Arcana cognac, eleven large snifters, and a dark wood box containing 24 cohiba cigars, imported quite illegally from Cuba.

Silently, and with the efficiency attained through many years of such service, the old man placed a snifter and a cigar before each of the men around the table. He then poured exactly one finger of the dark amber liquor into each snifter. That task completed, he removed an ornate lighter and a silver device from the pocket of his tail coat and moved from man to man, starting with Appleby, expertly snipping off a tiny piece of the tapered end of the cigar, and, after the man had placed it in his mouth, flicking the lighter and applying the flame to the end until the brown cylinder was burning evenly.

Once his task was completed, and the eleven men were sitting back in their chairs, their heads wreathed in a light cloud of smoke, tendrils of smoke drifting above the table like tiny snakes being wafted by an unfelt breeze before dissipating in the darkness of the ceiling, the servant bowed slightly at the waist, and as silently as he'd arrived, disappeared.

ABOUT THE AUTHOR

Charles Ray has been writing fiction since his teens, winning a Sunday school magazine short story contest for his first publication. His first full-length work was a book on leadership, but with *Die Sinner,* the first in his Al Pennyback mystery series, he returned to his first love, fiction. He has worked as a journalist for newspapers and magazines in Asia and the U.S., and wrote essays, poetry, and editorials for media in Africa and Europe as well. In addition to writing, he is an accomplished photographer and artist. He was editorial cartoonist for the Spring Lake (NC) News during the 1970s and regularly published cartoons in a number of publications such as Ebony, Eagle and Swan, and Essence. A frequent contributor to Yahoo!, he also writes for a number of other online news sites.

He served in the U.S. Army for 20 years, retiring in 1982 and joining the U.S. Foreign Service, where he served for 30 years before retiring in 2012. He's worked and traveled throughout the world. A native of Texas, he now calls Maryland home, when he's not globetrotting looking for new mountains to climb or new adventures to document. Visit his web site at http://charlesaray.blogspot.com, his blog at http://charlieray45.wordpress.com , or his author's Facebook page at http://www.facebook.com/charlieray45.

Other books by this author

Buffalo Soldier history series
Buffalo Soldier: Trial by Fire
Buffalo Soldier: Homecoming
Buffalo Soldier: Incident at Cactus Junction
Buffalo Soldier: Peacekeepers

Al Pennyback mysteries
Color Me Dead
Memorial to the Dead
Deadline
Dead, White, and Blue
A Good Day to Die
The Day the Music Died
Die, Sinner
Deadly Intentions
Death by Design
Till Death Do Us Part
Deadly Dose
Dead Man's Cove
Dead Men Don't Answer
Death From Unnatural Causes

Other fiction
Angel on His Shoulder
She's No Angel
Child of the Flame
Pip's Revenge
Wallace in Underland
Further Adventures of Wallace in Underland: Wallace Saves the King
*Dead Letters and Other Tales (a collection of short stories)**

Nonfiction
Things I Learned from My Grandmother About Leadership and Life
Taking Charge: Effective Leadership for the Twenty-first Century
Grab the Brass Ring
African Places: A Photographic Journey Through Zimbabwe and southern Africa

*Available only as an e-Book for Nook at Barnes and Noble.com. Other books available at most retail book sites in paperback or on Amazon.com for Kindle.

CHARLES RAY

www.ingramcontent.com/pod-product-compliance
Lightning Source LLC
Chambersburg PA
CBHW070753280626
47162CB00016B/213